Aunt Dimity Goes West

ALSO BY NANCY ATHERTON

Aunt Dimity Goes West

NANCY ATHERTON

VIKING

VIKING
Published by the Penguin Group
Penguin Group (USA) Inc., 375 Hudson Street,
New York, New York 10014, U.S.A.
Penguin Group (Canada), 90 Eglinton Avenue East, Suite 700,
Toronto, Ontario, Canada M4P 2Y3
(a division of Pearson Penguin Canada Inc.)
Penguin Books Ltd, 80 Strand, London WC2R 0RL, England
Penguin Ireland, 25 St. Stephen's Green, Dublin 2, Ireland
(a division of Penguin Books Ltd)
Penguin Books Australia Ltd, 250 Camberwell Road, Camberwell,
Victoria 3124, Australia
(a division of Pearson Australia Group Pty Ltd)
Penguin Books India Pvt Ltd, 11 Community Centre, Panchsheel Park,
New Delhi – 110 017, India
Penguin Group (NZ), 67 Apollo Drive, Mairangi Bay,
Auckland 1311, New Zealand
(a division of Pearson New Zealand Ltd)
Penguin Books (South Africa) (Pty) Ltd, 24 Sturdee Avenue,
Rosebank, Johannesburg 2196, South Africa

Penguin Books Ltd, Registered Offices:
80 Strand, London WC2R 0RL, England

First published in 2007 by Viking Penguin,
a member of Penguin Group (USA) Inc.

10   9   8   7   6   5   4   3   2   1

For
my friends in the Colorado Mountain Club,
who've taken me to new heights

Aunt Dimity Goes West

One

*T*hunder rolled and lightning stabbed the sky. Savage waves battered the cliffs, and stinging rain lashed my face as I sprawled across the stoney ground, hurt and helpless. A figure loomed above me, a dark-haired man with eyes as black and fathomless as the pits of hell. He raised a pale hand, to point at me. There was a blinding flash, a deafening explosion—

—and I woke up, heart racing. My blankets were a tangled mess, my pillows damp with sweat. With a sobbing gasp, I sat up in bed and stared into the darkness.

The night was calm and peaceful. A summer breeze wafted through the bedroom's open windows, and an early bird chirped in the back garden, as if to announce to all and sundry that it had successfully gotten the worm. I heard no thunder, no crashing waves, and the brightest light in the sky was a faint smudge of gray heralding the dawn. I wasn't sprawled at the edge of a storm-battered cliff, at the mercy of a cold-blooded killer. I was safe at home.

My husband cleared his throat as he rolled over and propped himself up on an elbow.

"Again?" he said, caressing my back.

"Yeah," I managed shakily.

"I'll make a cup of tea for you." Bill fell back on his pillows and rubbed his tired eyes, then heaved himself out of bed and reached for his bathrobe.

"You don't have to," I said hastily. "I'm okay now, really."

"A nice cup of tea," Bill murmured sleepily. He stepped into his leather bedroom slippers and padded softly into the hallway.

Stanley, our black cat, took advantage of the open door by trotting into the bedroom and vaulting gracefully into my lap for a morning cuddle. He purred softly as I stroked the sweet spot between his ears. Calmed by his soothing rumble, I closed my eyes and released a tremulous sigh.

Six weeks had passed since an obsessed lunatic known as Abaddon had put a bullet just below my left collarbone at point-blank range, nicking an artery and shredding a ridiculous amount of muscle tissue. A host of excellent doctors had helped to heal the garish hole Abaddon had left in my body, but they'd so far failed to repair the damage he'd done to my peace of mind.

For the past month and a half, my moods had swung like a giddy pendulum, shifting from listless to restless, from cranky to weepy, without rhyme or reason, at least fifty times a day. Sleep brought no respite because with it came nightmares, except that in my case there was only *one* nightmare, the same vivid reliving of heart-chilling horror, night after night after night.

It was hardly surprising. For the past seven years, my husband and I had lived an idyllic life in a cozy, honey-colored cottage amidst the picturesque, patchwork fields of rural England. Although we were Americans, the nearby village of Finch had become our own. Our five-year-old twins had been dandled on every knee in Finch. Bill was an honored member of the darts team at the pub. I arranged flowers at the church, brought casseroles to elderly neighbors, and swapped gossip with the fluency of a native. We were a normal family engaged in commonplace activities, none of which had prepared us in the slightest for the terrifying events that had spawned my nightmare.

I'd never dreamed that an insane stalker would threaten to kill me and my family. I'd never dreamed that Bill would send me and the boys to a remote Scottish island for our own protection. I'd most assuredly never dreamed that Abaddon would find the island, kidnap the twins, and try to murder me in the midst of a Force 9 gale. It wasn't the sort of thing I could have dreamed, until it happened. But once it happened, I could dream of nothing else.

I was sick of it. Abaddon was dead and gone, killed by a providential lightning bolt that had jolted him into the roiling sea, but he lived on in my mind, a deranged squatter who ignored insistent demands for his departure. I was desperate to evict him because he was making a mess of the place and the mess was hurting everyone I loved.

My bouncing, effervescent boys had emerged unscathed from their encounter with Abaddon, but they'd taken to tiptoeing around the cottage and speaking in unnaturally hushed voices because "the bad man hurt Mummy." Annelise Sciaparelli, the boys' inestimable nanny, walked on eggshells in my presence because she never knew from one moment to the next whether I'd burst into tears, snap her head off, or lapse into a morose silence. My husband, a high-priced attorney with a well-heeled international clientele, had taken so much time off from work that half of his clients thought he'd retired or died. And I was so addled by sleep deprivation that I couldn't muster the energy to arrange flowers, visit my elderly neighbors, or contribute my fair share to the great chain of gossip that connected everyone in Finch. My world would never spin smoothly on its axis again until I rid myself of Abaddon once and for all, but I didn't know how to make him leave.

Stanley's breathy purr became a loud rumble as Bill reentered the bedroom, carrying a cup of tea on a silver salver. Stanley was, to all intents and purposes, Bill's cat. He liked it when Bill stayed at home to look after me. My ongoing incapacitation was, in many respects, the best thing that had ever happened to Stanley.

Bill placed the salver on the bedside table and rubbed his eyes again. I stared at the steaming teacup and felt guilt settle over me like a lead cape. My husband was in his midthirties, active, attractive, and extremely good at his job. He'd spent half the night in front of his computer, yet here he was, serving tea to me at dawn. It wasn't fair. He was supposed to be running the European branch of his family's venerable law firm, not playing nursemaid to an invalid wife.

"Mind if I catch another forty winks?" he asked, yawning.

"Live it up," I told him. "Catch eighty."

Bill crawled back into bed, and Stanley left my lap to curl contentedly behind Bill's knees. I drank my tea in silence, then made my way to the bathroom to prepare myself to face another day. It was bound to be a hectic one because of the parade.

The parade, as Bill called it, was the kind of thing that happened in a tight-knit community when one of its members suffered a mishap. Since my mishap had been more newsworthy than most, our parade had become a popular social event. No one wanted to be left out of a story that had made headlines in the *Times,* so once a week—on Sunday—a steady stream of neighbors appeared on our doorstep, bearing gifts and basking in reflected glory.

"And today is Sunday," I muttered, closing the bathroom door. "Bath, breakfast, church, and on with the show!"

By the time I had finished dressing, Will and Rob were up, and by the time Annelise and I had finished dressing them, Bill was up again, so we trooped down to the kitchen en masse for a hearty breakfast. We were clearing the table when the doorbell rang. Annelise quickly took the boys into the back garden—they tended to get overexcited on parade days—and Bill went to answer the front door.

"Who was it?" I asked, when he returned to the kitchen.

"Terry Edmonds," Bill replied.

I stopped loading the dishwasher and gave him a puzzled glance. Terry Edmonds wasn't a neighbor. He was a professional courier who picked up and delivered legal papers for Bill's firm.

"Since when does Terry work on Sunday?" I asked.

"Special delivery," said Bill. "I put it in the study."

"He brought it *here?*" I winced as another twinge of guilt assailed me. Bill had a high-tech office overlooking the village green in Finch, but he hadn't set foot in it since I'd been shot. "If you don't get back to work soon, Bill, you're going to have to change the address on your letterhead."

"All in good time, my love," he said.

I swung around to face him.

"Look," I said, flexing my arm gingerly. "I'm as good as new. You don't have to play Nurse Nancy anymore."

"If I didn't know better, I'd suspect that you were trying to get rid of me," Bill observed mildly.

"I *am* trying to get rid of you," I scolded. "You can't work all night and take care of me all day. You'll make yourself ill and *then* where will we be? It's mid-June already, Bill, time for you to resume a normal schedule. Annelise and I can look after the boys, and I can look after myself. I don't need a babysitter anymore. I'm perfectly capable of—"

"—being on time for church," Bill inserted, "which we won't be if we don't get a move on."

I smiled grudgingly, closed the dishwasher, and called Annelise and the boys in from the back garden.

The parade began within an hour of our return from church. The doorbell rang almost nonstop for the rest of the day.

Sally Pyne, the plump and pleasantly chatty owner of the tearoom, dropped off a basket filled with her delectable Crazy Quilt Cookies, which had everything in them except coconut because Sally knew I wasn't fond of coconut. The imperious Peggy Taxman, who ruled Finch with an iron hand and a voice that could penetrate granite, gave Will and Rob bags of candy from her general store, along with a stern lecture on dental hygiene. Miranda Morrow, Finch's red-haired professional witch, bestowed an unlabeled packet of healing herbs upon us, and Dick Peacock, the rotund and amiable publican, gave us three bottles of his homemade wine. Since Dick's wine was undrinkable and Miranda's herbs were quite possibly illegal, Bill flushed both down the toilet after everyone had left.

Ruth and Louise Pym, the ancient and utterly identical twin sisters who lived up the lane from us, delivered flowers and fresh vegetables from their gardens. Mr. Malvern, the dairy farmer next door, supplied us with milk, cream, butter, and cheese. Mr. Barlow, the local handyman, brought only his tools, but he used them to mend the sticky hinge on the back door. Lilian Bunting, the vicar's wife, filled my freezer with casseroles, stews, and soups, and the vicar brought an armload of books he found comforting in troubled times.

My favorite part of the parade occurred after the rush was over, when my best friend Emma Harris showed up to chat quietly over a cup of tea, but even she felt compelled to drop off a few jars of her homemade jams. No one ever left without leaving something. As a result I hadn't had to cook or bake or shop for groceries since we'd returned from Scotland.

"I'm going to bankrupt the villagers if I don't snap out of my funk," I said gloomily.

The parade was over, as was dinner. Annelise had taken the boys upstairs for their baths. I'd offered to lend a hand, but Bill had insisted that I rest after my action-packed day, so he, Stanley, and I had retreated to the sofa in the living room to munch on Crazy Quilt Cookies, put our feet—and paws—up, and watch the fire.

"It's not a funk," said Bill. "It's post-traumatic stress and it's not something you snap out of. It's something you recover from."

"But I'm *not* recovering," I moaned. "In the past month I've tried counselors, psychiatrists, the vicar, pills, meditation, hypnotherapy—"

"—aromatherapy, massage therapy, hydrotherapy, acupuncture," Bill put in.

"And nothing's worked," I concluded.

"If I were foolish enough to risk rousing your wrath," Bill said, after a pause, "I'd point out that you haven't done anything long enough to *know* whether it was working or not. But I'm not, so I won't."

I nodded ruefully, acknowledging the hit. "Patience was never my strong suit. I don't seem to *have* any strong suits at the moment. I don't know what to try next."

"That's okay," said Bill. "I do."

He smiled mysteriously, shifted Stanley from his lap to the floor, and left the living room. He returned a moment later with one hand tucked behind his back, sidestepped his way around the couch, to keep me from seeing his hidden hand, and perched on the edge of the coffee table, facing me. His expression reminded me of the twins' when they'd accomplished a particularly ingenious bit of mischief.

"What are you up to?" I asked, eyeing him warily.

"Remember the special delivery Terry Edmonds made this morning?" he asked. "It's for you. I ordered it last night."

"It's a brain," I said promptly. "You want me to try a brain transplant."

"Wrong," he said, his eyes dancing.

"Well?" I demanded. "What is it?"

Grinning from ear to ear, Bill brought his hand around to reveal his big surprise. It was a large, white, cowboy hat. He placed it on my head.

"Saddle up, little lady," he drawled. "The Wild West is a-callin'!"

Two

"*Y*ee-ha!" Bill cried, slapping his thigh.

Startled, Stanley bolted from the room, but I was too bewildered to move a muscle. My husband was the Harvard-educated scion of a Boston Brahmin family. He didn't drawl or slap his thigh, and the closest he'd ever come to the Wild West was a legal conference in Denver. I stared at him, dumbfounded, and wondered what on earth had come over him. Had the fumes from Dick Peacock's wine pickled his brain? Had he finally cracked under the strain of caretaking? Had I strayed into an alternate universe?

I touched the cowboy hat's crown, to make sure I wasn't hallucinating, then said, very carefully, "Bill? What are you talking about?"

"I'm talking about the one thing we haven't tried so far," he replied, beaming. "A complete change of scene, and I *do* mean complete." He swept an arm toward the cottage's bay window. "Go west, young woman! Seek your fortune in the glorious, untamed wilderness of the Colorado Rockies!"

"Are you saying that we should go to Colorado?" I asked, struggling to keep up. "As in . . . *Colorado?*"

"The one and only!" Bill exclaimed happily. "Finch isn't doing you any good. It's too familiar. You need to jump-start your batteries by plugging into a place that bears no resemblance to Finch whatsoever. And what could be more different from our too-tame English village than a log cabin in the glorious, untamed—"

"*Log cabin?*" I squeaked, alarmed.

"You remember Danny Auerbach, the real estate developer?" Bill registered my blank look and rushed on. "I've done a lot of work for Danny over the years. He built a cabin in the mountains a

couple of years ago, and he's offered it to me a thousand times. I finally decided to take him up on his offer."

"You've bought a *log cabin?*" I said, my head spinning. "In *Colorado?*"

"I'm just borrowing it," Bill explained. "Danny likes to have
friends stay there. It's near a small mountain town—"

"Aspen?" I said hopefully.

"No," said Bill, dashing my hopes. "Danny doesn't care for
Aspen—he says it's overbuilt and overpriced—so he built his place
near a mountain town called Bluebird, on a piece of land that's been
in his family for ages. With Bluebird nearby you won't feel cut off
from civilization, but you'll be far enough away from city lights to
enjoy a feeling of . . ." He stretched his arms wide and stuck out his
chest. *"Expansiveness."*

"Expansiveness," I echoed doubtfully.

"It's what you need, Lori," said Bill, "and it's exactly what you
won't find in our cozy corner of the world."

I could do nothing for a moment but gape at him. He'd evidently
forgotten how much I loved our cozy corner of the world. Finch was
a sleepy backwater that scarcely merited a dot on most maps, but it
pulsated with the seething passions of everyday life, and I was caught
up in those passions. Would the vicar defy tradition and invite a rock
band to perform at the church fête? Would Sally Pyne wear her luminous purple tracksuit to the flower show? Would the all-powerful
Peggy Taxman expand her empire to include the greengrocer's shop,
now that old Mr. Farnham had retired? The high drama never ceased,
and the thought of missing out on a single day's worth of juicy gossip was intolerable.

Gossip deprivation aside, it just seemed wrong to leave the cottage and flee to a log cabin half a world away from Finch. The cottage was our home. To abandon it, even temporarily, would be to
give in to the black-eyed demon who'd hijacked my dreams.

"I don't know, Bill," I said. "It seems like cowardice to me, like
we're letting Abaddon run us out of town."

"Nonsense." Bill tossed his head dismissively. "If you go to Colorado, you'll be declaring your *independence* from Abaddon. You'll be saying, 'I'm not going to curl up in a fetal position for the rest of my life because a nutcase got the better of me. I'm going to seize the day!'" He put a hand on my knee and added earnestly, "I've seen you disagree with Peggy Taxman—*out loud* and in front of *witnesses*. You're no coward, Lori."

"What about the boys?" I said worriedly. "We'll be uprooting them, won't we? Upsetting their routine?"

"Of course we'll be upsetting their routine," Bill retorted. "Do you honestly think they'll mind? It's mid-June, Lori, a wonderful time of year to visit the Rockies. The boys can go hiking and trout fishing and fossil hunting, and they can pan for gold in the river. If they're lucky, they'll catch their first glimpse of elk, buffalo, and bighorn sheep. There's even a ranch nearby, where they'll be able to ride with *real cowboys*." Bill bobbed his head enthusiastically. "They'll have a tale or two to tell their friends when they start school in the fall, that's for sure."

"I don't know if Annelise—" I began, but Bill rode right over me.

"It'll be the adventure of a lifetime for Annelise," he declared. "She's been to America before, with us, but she's never traveled outside of Boston. She'll jump at the chance to see the Rockies."

I sat back on the sofa, folded my arms, and regarded Bill narrowly. He was trying much too hard to persuade me that his scheme was flawless. Wifely instinct told me that he was withholding a vital piece of information.

"Okay," I said. "What's the catch?"

"Catch?" said Bill, with an air of injured innocence. "Why do you think there's a catch?"

"Because you're chirping like a deranged cheerleader, that's why." I made a beckoning motion with my hand. "Out with it, Bill. Spill the beans. What haven't you told me?"

"Well, yes, now that you mention it, there is one small catch." Bill cleared his throat, squared his shoulders, and said, "I can't go."

"You . . . *what?*" My jaw dropped. "Are you out of your mind? Do you seriously expect me to tackle the glorious, untamed wilderness *without* you?"

"I'm sorry, Lori, but I have no choice." His shoulders drooped and he hung his head, like a defeated Little Leaguer. "As you pointed out after breakfast, I have to get back to work. Things have piled up since I've been gone, things I can't pass on to the London office. I have to see to them personally or we'll lose at least seven of our best clients. You know I'd come with you if I could, but . . ."

His words trailed off on a crestfallen sigh that cut me to the quick. Bill had devoted himself to me, day and night, for weeks on end. He'd never run out of patience or good humor, and he'd never uttered one word of complaint. He'd conceived of a marvelous journey with nothing but my well-being in mind, and all I could do was whine about him staying behind. Shame flooded through me like molten lava.

"Is this"—I ran a finger along the cowboy hat's brim—"why you were up so late last night? Were you using your computer to plan the trip?"

"Yes," Bill answered, without looking at me.

"Well," I said softly, "I'll miss you like blazes, but apart from that, I think it's a brilliant plan."

Bill's head snapped up. "You do?"

"As you said, it's the only thing we haven't tried." I shrugged. "Who knows? It just might work."

"It will," said Bill, with great conviction. "I know it will."

I brushed a few stray cat hairs from the sofa. "I can't wait to tell Stanley. He'll be thrilled to have you all to himself. And you can fill me in on breaking news while I'm away."

"If Sally Pyne wears her hideous tracksuit to the flower show, you'll be the first to know," Bill said, with his hand on his heart.

He took the hat from my head and dropped it on the coffee table, then moved onto the couch and put his arms around me. I snuggled as close to him as my shoulder would allow.

"It's been a long time since I've taken a vacation in the States," I mused aloud.

"You won't have to lift a finger," Bill promised. "I've arranged everything, airline tickets, a rental car, a driver—"

"Why do we need a driver?" I asked, stiffening. It was a touchy subject. I didn't share my husband's low opinion of my driving skills.

"Your arm may feel better, but your range of motion is still limited," Bill explained gently. "You won't be able to handle mountain roads."

"Maybe not," I said, conceding the point, "but what about Annelise? She can drive."

"Annelise is English," he reminded me. "Do you really want her careering around hairpin bends on the wrong side of the road?" He shook his head. "I don't think so. I've hired the cabin's caretaker to look after you. His name is James Blackwell and he lives on the property, so he knows his way around. He'll pick you up at the airport, take you to the cabin, and act as your chauffeur while you're there. He'll be a great guide, Lori, and he'll see to it that the cabin is stocked with food, drink, and firewood."

"How long will we be away?" I asked.

"As long as you like," said Bill. "I booked open-ended airline tickets and I checked with Danny—he's not planning to use the cabin this summer and no one else has asked to borrow it."

I wondered briefly why the cabin was so unpopular, but decided not to question Bill about it. If the place turned out to be a one-room shack equipped with kerosene lanterns and an aromatic outhouse, I'd make the best of it. I'd do whatever I had to do to keep the smile on my husband's face.

"Wow," I said admiringly. "You really have thought of everything. What would you have done if I'd refused to go?"

"I would have canceled the trip and tried something else." Bill kissed the top of my head. "Like a brain transplant."

"I've always wanted to stay in a log cabin," I assured him hastily. "When do we leave?"

"The day after tomorrow," Bill replied.

I stifled an incredulous squawk and forced myself to comment benignly, "The sooner, the better. Bluebird, Colorado, here we come!"

I'd scarcely finished speaking when a chorus of earsplitting shouts came from the hallway.

"We're going!" bellowed Rob.

"We're going!" hollered Will.

Our pajama-clad sons galloped into the living room and pranced gleefully in front of the fireplace. Annelise followed at a more sedate pace, but her face was shining. I pursed my lips and looked at my husband, whose eyes were trained on the ceiling.

"You wouldn't have mentioned the trip to Will, Rob, and Annelise before telling *me* about it, would you?" I asked.

"I might have let a few details slip," Bill allowed. "Inadvertently."

I transferred my gaze to Annelise. "You and the boys wouldn't have eavesdropped on our conversation, would you?"

"We might have overheard a word or two," she admitted. "Purely by accident."

"We're going to Colorado!" Rob roared. "We're going to pan for gold!"

"We're going to ride with cowboys!" Will yelled. "We're going to see buffalo!"

It sounded as though Bill had let more than a few details slip, but I didn't mind. I couldn't remember the last time the twins had made so much noise. They were hopping up and down instead of tiptoeing, and their voices were anything but hushed. Annelise's eyes were bright with anticipation and Bill was beaming like Santa Claus on Christmas Eve. Their joy was so contagious that I felt as if my troubles were at an end.

I should have known better.

Three

We brought the evening's celebrations to a close with a marathon reading of the entire *Cowboy Sam* series, then put Rob and Will to bed. Annelise promptly retired to her room and Bill staggered into our bedroom, with Stanley at his heels, to catch up on the sleep he'd missed the night before.

I stayed with him until he nodded off, then slipped quietly out of the bedroom and went downstairs to the study. It would have been pointless for me to stay in bed. I wouldn't have been able to close my eyes if I'd missed my nightly private chat with Aunt Dimity.

A private chat was the only kind of chat I *could* have with Aunt Dimity. Don't get me wrong. I wasn't ashamed to be seen with her. She was the most intelligent, compassionate, and courageous woman I knew, but there was simply no getting around the fact that she wasn't, strictly speaking, alive.

To complicate matters further, Aunt Dimity wasn't my aunt. She was an Englishwoman named Dimity Westwood, and she'd been my late mother's closest friend. The two women had met in London while serving their respective countries during the Second World War. When the war ended and my mother returned to the States, they continued their friendship by sending hundreds of letters back and forth across the Atlantic.

Those letters meant the world to my mother. After my father's early death, she'd raised me on her own while working full time as a schoolteacher. She hadn't had an easy life, but the hard times had been softened by her correspondence with Dimity. The letters my mother sent and received became a refuge for her, a place where she could go when the twin burdens of widowhood and single motherhood became too heavy for her to bear.

My mother kept her refuge a closely held secret, even from her only child. She never whispered a word to me about her old friend or the letters that meant so much to her. As a child I knew Dimity Westwood only as Aunt Dimity, the redoubtable heroine of a series of bedtime stories invented by my mother.

I didn't learn the truth about Dimity Westwood until after she and my mother had died, when Dimity bequeathed to me a considerable fortune, the honey-colored cottage in which she'd grown up, the precious letters she and my mother had exchanged, and a curious blue leather–bound journal with blank pages. It was through the blue journal that I'd come to know Dimity not as a fictional heroine, but as a very real—some would say surreal—friend.

Whenever I opened the journal, Dimity's handwriting would appear, an old-fashioned copperplate taught in the village school at a time when little girls still dressed in pinafores. I'd nearly come unglued the first time Dimity greeted me from beyond the grave, but one mention of my mother's name had been enough to reassure me that her intentions toward me were kindly. I'd long since come to regard her as my most cherished confidante, and I hoped the day would never come when the pages of the journal remained blank.

The study was a bit messier than usual, strewn with papers that should have been filed at Bill's office. I tidied them into neat piles and placed them beside his laptop on the old oak desk beneath the ivy-covered window. Once the room was in order, I turned to say hello to a small, pink flannel rabbit named Reginald, who spent most of his time perched in a special niche on the study's bookshelves.

The sight of a grown woman conversing with a pink flannel rabbit might strike some people as odd, but to me it was as natural as breathing. Reginald had been at my side for as long as I could remember. I'd shared moments of triumph, woe, and everything in between with him for nearly forty years, and I wasn't about to stop now.

"Hey, Reg," I said, touching the faded grape-juice stain on his snout. "Ever picture yourself in a cowboy hat?"

Reginald's black button eyes glimmered in a way that seemed to say, if only to me, that he'd never in his life imagined himself wearing anything as silly as a cowboy hat, but that, if I insisted, he'd put up with it.

"Don't worry," I said. "I don't think they make them in your size."

Reginald glimmered his relief. I gave his long ears a friendly tweak, took the blue journal down from its place on the bookshelves, and curled comfortably in one of the pair of tall leather armchairs that sat before the hearth.

"Dimity?" I said, opening the journal. "Got a minute?"

I smiled as the familiar lines of elegant copperplate began to flow gracefully across the page.

I have all the minutes you need, my dear. How are you feeling today?

"Fine," I said. Then I recalled to whom I was speaking and instantly revised my answer. "Okay, so the nightmare woke me up again this morning, and I didn't have a moment's peace all day because of the parade, and my shoulder's a little achy, but other than that I'm doing pretty well." I glanced at the laptop and thought of Bill staying up half the night, planning every detail of the trip. "As a matter of fact, I'm feeling better than I have in a long time."

Splendid! To what do you owe your improvement? Acupuncture? Meditation? Hydrotherapy? Or have you decided to try something new?

"Something new," I replied. "How do you feel about log cabins, Dimity?"

I can't honestly say that I've ever felt anything about log cabins. Why? Are you planning to build one, as a form of work therapy? If so, I'd advise starting on something a bit smaller. A bird table, perhaps, or a simple bookshelf. One can never have too many bookshelves.

"I'm not going to *build* a log cabin," I said. "I'm going to *stay* in one. In Colorado."

You've decided to leave England for America? Good heavens. Have you told Bill?

"It was Bill's idea," I told her. "It's his surefire cure for what ails me. He's convinced that a radical change of scene will exorcise Abaddon, so he's sending me, Annelise, and the twins to stay in a log cabin in Colorado, while he stays here to catch up on work. Have you ever been to Colorado?"

Never. It's mountainous, I believe.

"So I've heard. I've never been there, either. The thing is," I added, voicing for the first time a concern that had been troubling me, "I was born and raised in Chicago, Dimity. I don't really see myself as a mountain woman."

I sincerely doubt that you'll have to chop wood, haul water from a creek, or kill wild animals in order to put food on the table, if that's what's worrying you. Bill wouldn't send you to a place that wasn't equipped with a full range of modern conveniences.

"Bill's never seen the cabin," I said. "It belongs to one of his clients, a guy named Danny Auerbach, who never stays there. Danny likes to lend the cabin to friends, but not one of his friends has asked to use it this summer—not one!" I frowned anxiously. "I have a horrible feeling that there's something wrong with the place, something that scares people off."

Pull yourself together, Lori. Bill's clients are uniformly wealthy, and the wealthy do not own shabby properties. I'm sure the cabin will be lovely.

"There must be a crazy neighbor then," I insisted. "An old guy with a shotgun and a grudge against city folk."

Have you discussed your misgivings with Bill?

"No, and I'm not going to," I said quickly. "This is just between you and me, Dimity. I don't care if the cabin has a dirt floor and a trigger-happy old coot living next door—I'm not going to say a word to Bill. He needs a vacation from his lunatic wife, and I'm going to give him one."

I'm quite sure Bill doesn't see it that way, Lori.

"*I* see it that way," I declared. "Bill's been at my beck and call ever since we got back from Scotland. It's my turn to make a sacrifice, and if that means roughing it in the back of beyond for a couple of weeks, so be it."

Forgive me, Lori, but I was under the impression that you were feeling better. Did I misunderstand you?

"I *do* feel better," I insisted. "Will and Rob are out of their minds with excitement, Annelise can't wait to leave, and Bill's been walking on air ever since I agreed to go. How could I not feel better when there's so much happiness swirling around me?" I wrinkled my nose. "I'm just a little worried, that's all."

You wouldn't be yourself if you weren't a little worried about something, dearest Lori. Nevertheless, I'm glad Bill hatched such a delightful scheme. The brisk alpine air will do you a world of good. Besides, I've never visited the Rocky Mountains, and I'd very much like to go.

"Good, because you're coming with me," I said. "So is Reginald. There are some sacrifices I'm not willing to make, and facing the vast, untamed wilderness without you and Reg is one of them."

I can't tell you how pleased I am to hear it. We will face the wilderness together, my dear, but in the meantime, the hour is growing late. Don't you think you should toddle off to bed? You'll have lots to do tomorrow.

When I thought of the work involved in packing everything the twins and I would need for an open-ended, outdoorsy sort of trip, I couldn't help but agree.

"You're right," I said. "It's toddling time. Thanks for listening, Dimity."

Thank you, Lori, for allowing me to listen. Sleep well.

"I'll try," I promised, without much hope.

When the curving lines of royal-blue ink had faded from the page, I closed the journal and looked up at Reginald.

"Well, cowpoke," I said, in my best western drawl, "I hope Buffalo Bill hasn't gotten us in over our heads. If I have to hunt for food, we're a-goin' to get *mighty* hungry."

I awoke with a gasp before dawn the next day, but I had too much on my mind to waste time shuddering, so I got up, dressed, and went downstairs to pull suitcases out of storage. I'd managed to dislodge exactly one duffel bag from its shelf in the utility room when Bill charged in after me, removed the duffel bag from my grasp, and shooed me into the kitchen to start breakfast.

It soon became apparent that Dimity and I had grossly overestimated the amount of energy I'd need to prepare for the trip. Bill had promised that I wouldn't have to lift a finger, and he saw to it that I didn't. He and Annelise allowed me to watch them pack, but if I dared to tuck so much as a sock into a suitcase, they ordered me out of the room.

Since the twins and I were clearly underfoot, I piled them into the Range Rover for a farewell tour of Finch. Our abrupt, unannounced flight to Scotland had started the rumor mills churning at breakneck speed among my neighbors, and I didn't want our Colorado trip to start another frenzy of speculation. I wanted everyone to know that the boys and I were setting out on a pleasant vacation this time, not being chased from our home by a homicidal maniac.

The villagers with whom I spoke were unanimously in favor of Bill's big idea, except when it came to his choice of destinations.

"Colorado?" said Sally Pyne, offering me a plate of fresh-baked scones. "It's a bit rough and tumble out there, isn't it? All prickly plants and vipers? Why don't you ask Bill to find you a nice B&B in Cornwall instead? The sea air would put you right in no time."

"The Rocky Mountains?" said Mr. Barlow, wiping axle grease from his hands. "I had a cousin who went there once. Collapsed on his first day. Altitude sickness. Had to be airlifted to a lower altitude. I'd book a hotel in Skegness if I were you. The sea air's like a tonic."

"America!" thundered Peggy Taxman, closing her cash register with a bang. "Wouldn't go there if my life depended on it. Loud voices, fast food, vulgarity and violence everywhere you turn. You'd be better off in Blackpool. The twins'd love the donkey rides, and you'd be blooming after a week or two of fresh sea air."

Shy, balding, soft-spoken George Wetherhead approved of Bill's plan unreservedly, but only because he was a train enthusiast.

"The Pikes Peak Cog Railway is the highest in the world!" he exclaimed. "The views from the Royal Gorge train are breathtaking! The Cripple Creek and Victor Narrow Gauge Railroad has an 0-4-0 locomotive! Oh, how I envy you."

I didn't have the heart to tell him that a tour of historic railways was not on the agenda. Nor did I have the courage to disagree with everyone else. My neighbors were, after all, merely expressing my own doubts and misgivings.

After we'd made the rounds in Finch, I took Will and Rob to Anscombe Manor to say good-bye to Emma Harris, who owned the manor, and to the boys' ponies, who were stabled there.

Will and Rob were identical twins who bore a strong resemblance to their father. They had Bill's dark-brown hair and velvety chocolate-brown eyes, and they were, as he had been, so tall for their age that strangers couldn't believe they were only five. Like Bill, they were bright, sweet-natured, and energetic. Unlike him—and most definitely unlike me—they were completely and utterly horse-crazy.

When my sons weren't galloping over hill and dale on their ponies, Thunder and Storm, they liked to draw horses, talk about horses, sing songs about horses, and pretend to be horses. They liked to play cricket, squelch through mud puddles, and pretend to be dinosaurs, too, but they were never happier than when they were with their ponies. They couldn't leave England without saying good-bye to Thunder and Storm, and I, shaken by my neighbors' observations, couldn't face my well-meaning husband again until I'd had a calm, sensible conversation with Emma.

I found her in the stables, cleaning stalls.

"I used to think the lady of the manor had a glamorous life," I said, stepping carefully across the straw-strewn floor. "Boy, was I wrong."

Emma gave me a jaundiced look, leaned her pitchfork against the wheelbarrow, and fetched apples from a nearby basket for the boys to give to their ponies.

"Very funny," she said, wiping the sweat from her brow as we walked into the fresh air. "Anyone who thinks living in a manor house is glamorous has never come face-to-face with an eighteenth-century drain."

"I may be able to match you on that score before the summer's out," I said, and told her about our impending journey.

"It sounds fantastic," she said, when I'd finished. "You'll have miles of trails to explore, and the mountains will be awash in wild-flowers. It's a beautiful time of year to be in the Rockies."

"I'm not so sure," I said doubtfully. "Peggy's got a point, you know. America *is* loud and vulgar and violent."

"*Some* of America is nasty," Emma temporized, "but *most* of it is nice. The same could be said of England or anywhere else in the world, for that matter. And what would Peggy know about it, any-way? She's never been to America."

"But what about Mr. Barlow's cousin?" I asked. "He didn't have such a great time in the Rockies."

"He's the exception that proves the rule," Emma said firmly. "Colorado wouldn't have much of a tourist industry if visitors were falling over every five minutes from altitude sickness. You and the boys will be fine."

"What about the cabin, then?" I said. "Don't you think there must be something wrong with it? Like bad drains?"

"The drains will be fine, Lori," said Emma. "Everything will be fine. You'll see. You'll come back from Colorado with roses in your cheeks. I wish I could come with you."

"You can!" I said, brightening.

"No, I can't," said Emma. "I've got to run the riding school and tend the garden and repair the drains and . . ." She took a deep breath, then said in a rush, "And Nell is coming home."

"*Nell's* coming home?" I cried. *"When?"*

"Tomorrow," Emma replied.

Nell was Nell Harris, Emma's eighteen-year-old stepdaughter, and the most exquisitely beautiful girl I'd ever seen or imagined. She'd been in Paris for the past year, studying at the Sorbonne.

"Does Kit know?" I asked.

"Not yet," said Emma. "I'm going to break it to him tonight, after dinner."

Kit was Kit Smith, Emma's stable master and the object of Nell's unwavering affection, an affection he tried hard not to return because he was twice Nell's age, and he thought the age difference mattered. No one else did. Nell was an extraordinarily mature eighteen-year-old.

"Good grief," I said faintly, then turned to grip Emma's wrist. "What if Kit changes his mind? What if he *proposes* to Nell? I absolutely *forbid* him to marry her until I'm back from Colorado!"

"I don't think you have much to worry about," Emma said dryly. "Kit's as stubborn as you are."

I looked toward the stables. "Lucky for Kit, so is Nell."

Once Emma had promised that she wouldn't let Kit marry anyone until I'd returned, and I had promised to bombard her with postcards, I rounded up the boys and left for home, feeling more despondent than ever.

I'd been eagerly awaiting Kit and Nell's reunion for over a year, and now it would take place without me. I didn't want to be thousands of miles away while the romance of the century was taking place. I wanted to be on hand, on the spot, if possible, when Kit's resistance melted and he gave in to the urgings of his heart. As we turned out of Anscombe Manor's curving drive, I composed a suitable message for Emma's first postcard.

"Killed bear last night," I muttered. "Skinned it this morning. If Kit and Nell elope while I'm away, I'll skin *you!*"

Four

Since Will, Rob, Annelise, and I were a seasoned team of travelers, our flight from London to Denver would have been pleasantly uneventful if only I'd been able to stay awake. Unfortunately, I dozed off somewhere over the Atlantic and nearly caused an international incident when I woke up screaming.

Annelise managed to convince the rattled cabin crew that I'd simply had a bad dream, but the other passengers watched me closely from then on, as if they were mapping out ways to subdue me if I suddenly went berserk and tried to break into the cockpit with my teeth. To avoid alarming them further—and because I don't like coffee—I kept myself awake by eating chocolate and drinking many cups of cola.

By the time we disembarked in Denver I was so hyped on sugar and caffeine I could easily have been mistaken for an amphetamine addict, so I put Annelise in charge of our passports. She got us through Customs without undue delay, and I collared a skycap to deal with our luggage. While he loaded our bags onto his cart, I put in a quick call to Bill to let him know that we'd arrived safely, carefully omitting any reference to screaming.

It wasn't hard to spot the driver Bill had hired. He was waiting for us at the end of the Arrivals barrier, holding a hand-lettered sign with my name on it; but it wasn't the sign that caught my attention, it was the man himself.

Because he wasn't a man. He was a boy: a tall, lean, broad-shouldered boy with long white-blond hair, big blue eyes, and the smooth, innocent face of a cherub. He wore a bright-red water-proof jacket, an unbuttoned flannel shirt over a T-shirt that read ROCKY MOUNTAIN HI!, and a pair of hiking trousers with zip-off legs and many, many pockets. His trousers were spattered with the same reddish mud that caked his hiking boots and stained the blue day pack that lay at his feet. He looked as though he'd hiked from Bluebird to Denver, and for a brief, hysterical moment I wondered if he expected us to hike back with him.

He'd evidently seen photographs of us because he stuffed the sign into his day pack and gave us a friendly wave as we approached. When we passed the barrier, he ushered us and the skycap out of the main stream of passenger traffic in order to greet us properly.

"Ms. Shepherd, Ms. Sciaparelli," he said, nodding to me and Annelise in turn. "Welcome to Colorado."

"James?" I said hesitantly.

"No," he replied. "Tobias. Toby. Toby Cooper. I'm James Blackwell's replacement."

"Replacement?" I said. "My husband didn't mention a replacement."

"He probably doesn't know about it yet," Toby said. "I only found out about it yesterday." He reached into an outside pocket of the day pack and produced a flimsy sheet of fax paper. "From Mr. Auerbach. It'll explain everything."

I took the fax from him and read:

> Dear Ms. Shepherd,
>
> Welcome to Colorado! Please accept my apologies for the last-minute change in personnel. James Blackwell left my employment yesterday, rather unexpectedly, and Toby Cooper generously agreed to take his place.
>
> Toby's father and I are old school friends. Toby's a fine young man and will do everything he can to make your stay in Colorado enjoyable. If you have any questions, please feel free to contact me.
>
> Sincerely,
>
> Danny Auerbach

I noted the phone number printed beneath Danny's name, then looked up to find Toby anxiously scanning my face.

"Why did James Blackwell quit?" I asked.

Toby shrugged. "I don't know. I don't know James, and Mr. Auerbach didn't give me any details when he asked me to fill in. Maybe James just decided it was time to move on."

"I see," I said. "Do you mind if I ask how old you are?"

"Twenty-one," Toby replied. "I go to college in Boulder, but I'm on summer break."

Annelise and I exchanged a glance that said, "Now we have *three* little boys to look after." Our expressions must have alarmed Toby because he began to speak at top speed.

"I know Bluebird like the back of my hand," he said. "My dad was born and raised there, and I spent every summer there with my grandparents when I was a kid. I know the hiking trails and the best fishing spots, and I can fix things, too, like a leaky pipe or a broken window— my granddad showed me how—so if anything goes wrong, I'll take care of it. I'm a good driver, too—no speeding tickets—and I've never been involved in an accident, not even a fender bender." A note of desperation entered his voice. "I had a summer job lined up in the administration office at school, but it fell through, so I . . . I was really glad when Mr. Auerbach offered me this one. I may be a little younger than James Blackwell, but I'm a hard worker, Ms. Shepherd, and I'm very dependable. You won't be disappointed."

The eager-puppy look in his eyes was irresistible. I stuffed the fax into my carry-on bag and decided to go with the flow.

"I'm sure I won't," I said reassuringly. "And, please, call me Lori."

"Annelise will do for me," Annelise put in. "Sciaparelli is a bit of a mouthful for everyday use."

Rob tugged on Toby's trouser leg, and Toby squatted down to look him in the eye.

"We know a pony named Toby," Rob informed him importantly. "Do you know any ponies?"

"Are you a cowboy?" Will asked, cutting to the chase. My sons were not known for their reticence.

"Not exactly," said Toby, "but your father told Mr. Auerbach that you like cowboys, so I've brought an essential piece of cowboy equipment for each of you." He reached into his day pack and brought forth a pair of bandanas, one red and one blue. "Which one of you is Will?"

"I am," said Will, stepping forward.

Toby promptly knotted the red bandana around Will's neck and the blue one around Rob's, thus effectively distinguishing one twin from the other. I gave him full marks for cleverness.

"Would you call a bandana equipment?" Annelise inquired.

"Absolutely," Toby replied, standing tall. "Pull a bandana over your nose and you'll breathe easier during a dust storm. Tie a damp bandana around your forehead on a hot day and you'll avoid sunstroke. If a rattlesnake strikes, a bandana makes a good tourniquet."

"Useful things, bandanas," Annelise agreed.

The boys were gazing up at Toby as if he held the keys to a kingdom of thrilling adventures, but I stared at him, aghast. What kind of vacation included dust storms, heat stroke, and deadly snakes in its itinerary? It sounded as though Bill had sent us on a survival course instead of a jolly family holiday.

"Are you all right, Lori?" Toby asked, noticing my expression.

I let out an embarrassingly high-pitched giggle, for which I immediately apologized.

"Sorry," I said. "Too much caffeine."

"You should avoid caffeine while you're here, for the first few days at least," Toby advised. He delved into the main compartment of his day pack and handed a bottle of water to each of us. "Water's your best bet. It'll help you adjust to the altitude as well as the dry air. There's lots more in the van, so drink up. And by the way," he added, straightening, "local time is seven forty-seven P.M., and yes, it's still Tuesday." The corners of his eyes crinkled charmingly as he grinned. "It's easy to lose track of time after crossing so many time zones."

"Your boots are all dirty," Will commented, peering interestedly at Toby's hiking boots.

"It's pretty muddy up in Bluebird," Toby explained. "It snowed two days ago, and we're still waiting for the last few drifts to finish melting."

"*Snow?*" I said, horrified. "In *June?*"

"We had snow in July a few years ago," Toby said cheerfully.

"But we're not dressed for snow," I protested. "And we didn't pack our winter coats."

"Yes, we did," said Annelise. "They're in the brown suitcase. Bill thought we might need them."

"Bill *knew* about the snow?" I exclaimed, rounding on her.

Toby quickly intervened. "I'm sure Mr. Auerbach told your husband to pack clothes for all seasons, Lori. Mountain weather is pretty changeable. It's best to be prepared for everything."

I silently added frostbite to my lengthening list of holiday hazards.

Toby hoisted the day pack to his shoulders and reached for my carry-on bag.

"I can manage, thanks," I said, backing away a step. Aunt Dimity's journal and Reginald were in my bag. I wouldn't let Annelise carry it, much less a total stranger.

"I guess we're all set, then." Toby looked down at the twins. "Are you buckaroos ready to head for the hills?"

Will and Rob nodded eagerly and took hold of Toby's outstretched hands, hoping, no doubt, that he'd take them straight to the nearest rattlesnakes. They seemed mildly disappointed when he informed them that we were going instead to the parking garage. I signaled for the skycap to follow, and we set off, with the three boys in the lead.

It felt good to stretch my legs after the ten-hour flight, but the parking garage was a long way away from the Arrivals barrier, and I was soon struggling to keep up with the trio ahead of me. The twins seemed fine, if a bit pinker than usual, but Annelise and I were red-faced and gasping before Toby noticed that we were lagging behind.

"Sorry," he said, slowing his pace. "It's the thin air. You'll get used to it."

I took a swig from my water bottle and plodded on, thinking darkly of Mr. Barlow's cousin and wondering how long it would take to be airlifted from Bluebird to Kansas.

We arrived, eventually, at a sleek, streamlined black van liberally spattered with reddish mud. It held three rows of comfortable seats, and it was equipped with four-wheel drive, heavy-duty suspension, a high clearance chassis, and many other features I associated with bad roads.

"Great," I muttered hoarsely to Annelise. "There may be no air to breathe, but at least there are plenty of potholes to look forward to."

Annelise simply nodded. She was probably conserving oxygen.

While Toby and the skycap piled our luggage into the van's rear compartment, Annelise and I strapped the twins firmly into the middle row's booster seats. Once we were satisfied that the boys wouldn't hit the roof if we encountered uneven pavement, Annelise climbed in to sit behind them, and I hoisted myself into the front passenger seat.

Toby finished loading the luggage and tipped the skycap, but instead of climbing into the driver's seat, he opened the van's side door and passed a wicker hamper to Annelise.

"Sandwiches," he explained. "In case you're hungry. We've got a two-hour drive ahead of us."

"Did you make the sandwiches?" Annelise asked, peering into the hamper.

"Nope," said Toby. "I picked them up in Bluebird this afternoon, from Caroline's Cafe. Carrie Vyne makes the best sandwiches in the world. She packed some of her chocolate chip cookies, too. She makes great cookies."

Toby closed the side door, circled the van, and slid behind the steering wheel. After a brief glance at the boys, he turned the key in the ignition and called out, "Wagons, ho!"

"Yee-ha!" they yodeled.

Their father would have been proud of them.

The interstate highway out of Denver was in reassuringly good condition, but the scenery left much to be desired. Although the mountains beckoned, our immediate surroundings consisted of great swathes of boring tract houses separated by forlorn-looking patches of prairie. Since there was nothing much to look at, we concentrated on the sandwiches and the cookies. They were delicious.

"Do you *know* any cowboys?" Will asked hopefully, when we'd emptied the hamper.

"I sure do," said Toby. "They live one valley over from Bluebird, at the Brockman Ranch. Mr. Auerbach's arranged for you two to ride there while you're here."

"Will there be cows?" asked Rob.

"Not as many as there were in the old days," Toby said, with a reminiscent sigh. "I remember when the boys drove fifty thousand head of cattle from South Dakota all the way to Texas. It was rough going in those days. Cowpokes had to face all sorts of obstacles: floods, grass fires, storms so vicious they'd snatch the teeth right out of your mouth—"

"Were there Indians?" Rob interrupted, enthralled.

"Whole tribes of them," Toby confirmed. "Most of them were friendly, but even the bad ones weren't as bad as the rustlers."

"There were rustlers?" Will asked, wide-eyed.

Toby snorted. "More than you could count, all armed to the teeth and meaner than a bear with a blistered paw. I remember one time . . ."

I gave Toby an amused, sidelong glance as he went on to describe a hair-raising battle with a gang of desperadoes. I was no expert on American history, but I was pretty sure that the great cattle drives had ended in the late nineteenth century, when ranchers began transporting livestock by rail. If Toby could remember those days, he was remarkably well preserved, but I suspected that he was simply introducing the boys to the fine western tradition of telling tall tales.

"How high is Bluebird?" I asked, when the twins had fallen into a bedazzled silence.

"About eight thousand feet," Toby replied.

"Eight thousand feet," I said weakly. The caffeine had definitely worn off. "How long will it take us to get used to living at eight thousand feet?"

"No more than a few days," he assured me. "It's normal to feel a little lightheaded at first, but if you feel a headache coming on—a serious headache, that is, as if someone were driving a chisel into your skull—let me know right away. It could be a sign of altitude sickness, and that's no laughing matter."

I closed my eyes and decided that it would be much better for my peace of mind if I refrained from asking any more questions. When I opened them again, I was swaying slightly from side to side and squinting in the glare of oncoming headlights.

The broad interstate and the wide open spaces had vanished, replaced by a two-lane highway that wound halfway up the wall of a twisting, serpentine canyon. In the dim light of the dying day, I could see a white-water stream foaming below us, while above us pine trees appeared to cling by their root tips to whatever soil they could find in the rocky terrain.

The road seemed to be made up entirely of blind curves bordered intermittently by bent and dented guardrails. As cars, campers, and trucks hurtled toward us out of nowhere, it became bloodcurdlingly clear to me that my husband had been both wise and farsighted to hire a local driver for us. Had I been foolish enough to take the wheel, I would have sent the van crashing into the canyon wall or plummeting into the rushing stream before we'd rounded the first bend.

I must have flinched, because Toby noticed that I was awake.

"Enjoy your nap?" he asked softly. He jutted his chin toward the backseats. "The others have dozed off, too."

"I wish I were still asleep," I confessed, tightening my seat belt. "I enjoyed the drive more when I was unconscious."

"It takes getting used to," Toby conceded, "but we're almost there, and you wouldn't want to miss this next part."

He'd barely finished speaking when the canyon opened out onto a scene of such startling beauty that I caught my breath. We'd entered a long valley surrounded by high mountain ranges. A black lake filled the valley floor, reflecting the handful of stars that had appeared in the darkening sky. The lights of a town twinkled at the lake's western tip, like birthday candles set in black velvet, surmounted by the serried silhouettes of peaks backlit by the setting sun.

"Welcome to the Vulgamore Valley," said Toby. "Bluebird's just ahead. Nice, isn't it?"

"It's gorgeous," I said softly. "Absolutely gorgeous. I didn't expect a lake."

"Technically, it's a reservoir," said Toby. "But we call it Lake Matula, in honor of Annabelle Matula, the first woman to settle in the Vulgamore Valley."

"Are there fish?" asked a sleepy voice behind us.

"Lots of them," Toby replied. "And you'll find fishing poles at the cabin."

"Good," murmured Will. "I like fishing."

"Me, too," Rob chimed in, though he sounded even more drowsy than his brother.

When I next looked over my shoulder, they were both nodding in their booster seats, fast asleep. It had been a long day for my little guys.

The two-lane highway followed Lake Matula's northern shore, but trees grew right down to the edge of its southern shore. Search as I might, I could discover no glimmer of light in the forest, no sign of habitation anywhere but in the cluster of buildings to the west. It looked as though every human being in the Vulgamore Valley lived in Bluebird. Where, I wondered, was the cabin?

The posted speed limit fell from fifty to twenty when we reached Bluebird, at the far end of Lake Matula. The town had looked tiny from a distance, but it was at least three times larger than Finch. I could tell at a glance that it differed from Finch in many other ways as well. The golden limestone used to build Finch's houses had come from one quarry, so the village possessed a pleasing homogeneity that attracted world-class artists to its cobbled streets.

The same could not be said of Bluebird, which seemed to pride itself on the helter-skelter individuality of its dwellings. We drove past tiny Victorian cottages, stark cinderblock huts, ramshackle wooden houses, and at least one geodesic dome. It was too dark to pass judgment on the church, and I had only the briefest glimpse of the business district, but the gas station was a brightly lit eyesore flanked by heaps of dirty snow.

Toby turned left at the gas station onto a side street that became a dirt road at the edge of town. The stars vanished from view as we entered the dense, pitch-black forest bordering Lake Matula's southern shore. Toby followed the dirt road for about fifty yards, then slowed the van to a crawl and turned onto an even narrower dirt road that zigged and zagged upward.

"Lots of deer in these woods," he explained. "I wouldn't want to hit one on your first night here."

"Or any other night," I said, and peered anxiously ahead, hoping that our bouncing, juddering headlights would discourage all woodland creatures from crossing the road.

After what seemed an eternity, we reached a level clearing in the forest. Toby promptly shut off the engine and doused the head-lights.

"Wait here," he said. "I'll be back in a minute."

I waited nervously while he disappeared into the gloom, wondering if bears knew how to open car doors; then I shrank back, blinking, as a blinding blaze of light drove away the darkness.

There, in the clearing, illuminated by a constellation of flood-lights, stood Danny Auerbach's log cabin.

It wasn't a shack.

Five

*D*anny's cabin was unlike any building I'd ever seen. It sprawled across the clearing and climbed up the hillside like the roots of a gigantic tree, bending itself around boulders, bridging small gulleys, and encircling saplings.

In some places the cabin was one story tall; in others it rose to three, but each level bristled with balconies, decks, and porches. There seemed to be hundreds of sparkling windows, and they came in all shapes and sizes: portholes, stars, octagons, massive sheets of plate glass, tiny panes of leaded glass. At least six stone chimneys, three weathervanes, and a flagless flagpole rose from the irregular roofline. The largest chimney belonged to the cabin's central feature: a soaring A-frame structure, with a front wall made almost entirely of glass, that extended into the clearing like the prow of a ship.

"Wow," I said faintly.

"Pretty cool, huh?" said Toby.

"It's . . . it's *wonderful,*" I managed, wishing I could think of a bigger word. "It's magical, incredible, better than I—" I broke off, pricked by a sudden suspicion, and turned toward Toby so quickly that the seat belt snapped taut across my chest. "Does a crazy neighbor live nearby? With a shotgun?"

Toby eyed me in puzzlement. "The Auerbachs have owned the south side of the valley for five generations, Lori. They've never allowed anyone else to build here. Our nearest neighbor is Dick Major, and he lives at the edge of town, where the dirt road begins." Toby pointed to the east end of the cabin. "My apartment's behind the garage, and I don't own a shotgun."

"Just checking," I said, and settled back, relieved to know that two of my biggest worries had failed to materialize. The cabin wasn't a dilapidated shanty, and I wouldn't have to deal with a crazy neighbor. So far, so good, I thought. Now we'll see about the drains.

Toby restarted the engine, drove past the central A-frame, and parked the van in front of a short, broad staircase that led to an imposing wooden door incised with images of soaring eagles.

"Welcome to the Aerie," he said. "I'll get the luggage while you and Annelise bring the boys in. We can take them straight to bed, if you like."

I turned to look at the twins, who were still fast asleep. "Bed is where they need to be, but I can't lift either one of them. I hurt my shoulder a few weeks ago and it's still a little weak, so would you mind . . . ?"

"No problem," Toby said and stepped out into the crisp night air.

An hour later, the boys were in bed, Annelise was enjoying a well-earned bubble bath in a bathroom fit for a queen, and Toby and I were sitting on a huge, soft leather sofa in the great room, sipping hot chocolate in front of a roaring fire.

"Are you *sure* we're supposed to use the family's bedrooms?" I asked for the third or fourth time.

Toby nodded. "James left a note instructing me to put you in the family rooms. He thought you'd like being on the same corridor, but if you want to move—"

"No, no," I said hastily. "I don't want to change a thing."

Will and Rob would have disowned me if I'd moved them from the room James Blackwell had assigned to them. The boys' bedroom was a *boy's* bedroom. The furniture was child-sized and made from rough-hewn logs. The chest of drawers had horseshoe handles, the twin beds had cartwheel headboards, and the metal bases of the bedside lamps were shaped like bucking broncos. The wide-planked floor was covered with Navajo-style rugs, the beds with

Navajo-style blankets, and colorful paintings of hardworking cowboys hung on the walls.

The pièce de résistance was the open archway in the rear wall that led to an enormous playroom. The playroom's cupboards were filled with toys and board games, and a freestanding tent stood in the back corner, but the main attraction was the log fort with its rope ladder, slide, and tower. Annelise and I agreed that the fort would be a godsend if summer blizzards kept the twins cooped up indoors. The playroom also had a large picture window, but, thankfully, no porch, deck, or balcony from which my adventurous offspring could tumble.

Annelise, too, would have objected to any suggestion that she move from the room James Blackwell had selected for her, for practical as well as aesthetic reasons. Her bedroom was conveniently located directly across the hall from the twins' and next door to a splendid family bathroom, but it was also charmingly furnished and had its own little balcony.

The master suite, at the end of the same corridor, was sparely but beautifully furnished with simple pine furniture. White curtains hung at the windows, fluffy white rugs covered the polished plank floor, and the king-sized bed was draped with a crocheted white coverlet over a white duvet. A pair of white-upholstered armchairs sat before a corner fireplace made of smooth river stones, and the bathroom was a spacious oasis of comfort, with a cedar-clad Jacuzzi tub, a glass-walled shower stall, and double sinks set into an antique sideboard. A set of French doors in the bedroom led to a deck that overlooked the clearing in front of the Aerie. I had no desire whatsoever to exchange the master suite for another room.

"It's just a bit strange," I said, turning to Toby. "I mean, there are clothes hanging in the closets. I feel as if we're intruding."

"You're not," he assured me. "James Blackwell was supposed to ship the Auerbachs' stuff to them, but I guess he never got around to it. I'll take care of it tomorrow. But if you want to move to one of the guest suites—"

"No, thanks," I said firmly. "James Blackwell made the right call. I like being near my sons and Annelise. How many children does Danny Auerbach have?"

"Three," he replied. "Two young sons and a teenaged daughter."

I looked around the great room and sighed. "They must be the happiest kids on earth."

The great room was the A-frame structure at the center of the Aerie, a vast open space divided by furniture into three distinct zones. The ultramodern kitchen and the dining area took up the back half of the room, separated by a granite-topped breakfast bar, and the living room filled the front half—and I do mean *filled*.

The living room was jammed with leather sofas and chairs, wooden benches, pine tables, Indian rugs, carved chests, and a gaily painted upright piano that looked as though it had once seen action in a bordello. Rustic, glass-fronted cabinets held family photographs, rocks, feathers, bones, old spoons, antlers, and interesting bits of wood. Indian baskets, kerosene lamps, old cowboy hats, and tin plates filled shelves that had been mounted at various heights on the log walls, and quilts lay across the backs of chairs and on ottomans, as if to provide an extra source of warmth on chilly evenings. Some of the furniture was clustered before the enormous plate-glass windows, and some sat before the magnificent stone hearth, but none of it was formally arranged, and all of it looked well used.

The great room was cluttered beyond belief, and I fell in love with it at first sight. The Aerie wasn't a model home decorated by a fashionable designer. It was a real home where real people really lived, exuberant people who found the world fascinating and surrounded themselves with its colors and textures and their happy memories.

"It's wonderful," I murmured. "Just wonderful."

"I think so, too," Toby said agreeably. "Were you able to reach your husband?"

"Yes," I said. "He wanted me to use a laptop to do videoconferencing while we're here, but I'm not very good with computers. Fortunately, my mobile, er, my cell phone is working just fine. I know how to use a telephone."

"What time was it in England when you spoke with him?" asked Toby.

"Half past five in the morning," I said with a guilty wince. "Bill was pretty groggy, so we didn't have a long conversation."

"I'm surprised *you* aren't groggy," Toby commented.

"I will be, but I need to wind down a bit first." I raised my mug to salute him. "Hot chocolate always does the trick. Thanks for making it." I took a sip, then asked, "Do your grandparents still live in Bluebird?"

"No, but they're buried in the cemetery," said Toby, and when I looked distressed, he continued, "It's what they always wanted. They loved Bluebird. Granddad was the town doctor. He hoped Dad would take up the practice after him, but Dad went to school back east and decided to stay there. I grew up in Connecticut, but I came back here every summer. I love it here. I don't ever want to leave."

The double doors to the foyer opened, and we both looked over the back of the sofa as Annelise appeared, dressed in her robe and nightgown, with her luxuriant auburn hair streaming down her back.

"Lori?" she said. "May I have a word?"

"I'll refill your mug," Toby offered, and busied himself in the kitchen while I crossed to speak with Annelise.

"How's your shoulder?" she asked quietly.

I glanced toward the kitchen, to make sure Toby wasn't listening. My gunshot wound was a private matter. I didn't want him or anyone else I met on holiday to know about it.

"My shoulder's stiff," I said, lowering my voice, "but so's the rest of me. I feel as though we crossed the plains in a covered wagon instead of a wide-bodied jet."

"I recommend a hot bath." She stepped closer to me and went on very softly, "If you have any . . . bad dreams . . . you know where to find me."

I bristled slightly, but kept my voice low. "Did Bill ask you to look after me as well as the boys while we're here? He shouldn't have. I'll be fine."

"You weren't fine on the plane," she reminded me.

"But I *was* fine in the van," I countered. "I napped and I woke up, just like a normal person. I intend to do the same from now on."

"Of course you do," said Annelise, "but if you have any trouble—"

"Thanks, but I won't," I snapped, straightening. "Good night, Annelise."

"Good night, Lori." She called good night to Toby, closed the double doors, and went to her room.

As I returned to the sofa I made a mental note to tell Bill that I was in no more need of a nanny than I was of a babysitter.

"Do your parents fuss over you?" I asked Toby as he returned from the kitchen.

"Sure." He handed the refilled mug to me and resumed his place on the sofa. "It's what parents do. That's why I loved staying with Granddad. He always treated me as if I were a grown-up. I used to chop firewood when I was eight or nine, with a real axe." Toby's blue eyes twinkled delightfully as the old memories came back to him. "Granddad would have been charged with child neglect back east, but no one in Bluebird even noticed. It was the best place imaginable to be a kid."

"I wish I could have met your grandfather." I turned to stare sullenly into the fire. "It would be nice to be treated like a grown-up."

"It was great," said Toby. "I had the run of the valley. The only place I couldn't go was up here."

"Why?" I asked.

"The Aerie was built on the site of the old Lord Stuart Mine," he explained. "Until two years ago, the clearing was filled with half-ruined buildings and rusty machinery. Mr. Auerbach used some of the timber from the old mine buildings when he built the Aerie, but when I was a kid, the place was a death trap. Granddad made it clear that if he ever caught me up here, I wouldn't be allowed to visit him again. He was afraid I'd fall down a mine shaft."

"Mine shaft?" I echoed hollowly. "Are there mine shafts up here?"

"Hundreds of them," said Toby, "but most of them are fenced off, and when Mr. Auerbach built the Aerie, he had a whole team of engineers seal the entrance to the Lord Stuart Mine. It's tight as a drum, Lori, so you don't have to worry about Will or Rob getting into it. Mr. Auerbach has children, too," he reminded me gently.

Chastened, I took a calming swig of hot chocolate. "How often do the Auerbachs use the Aerie?"

"They haven't been here since Christmas," Toby replied. "Mr. Auerbach is a busy man."

"If he's too busy to use the cabin," I said, "why did he build it in the first place?"

Toby grinned. "He told Granddad that his parents wouldn't allow him to have a tree house when he was a child. The cabin's his tree house."

"Some tree house," I said admiringly. I pointed to a door beside the hearth. "What's through there?"

"The library," said Toby.

"There's a *library*?" I heard the squeak of disbelief in my voice and smiled wryly at my own foolishness. "To be perfectly honest, Toby, I thought the cabin would be sort of . . . primitive. I wasn't sure it would have indoor plumbing, let alone a library."

Toby rolled his eyes. "You wouldn't catch Mrs. Auerbach using an outhouse. She likes her comfort. She added the outdoor spa and the home theater to Mr. Auerbach's building plans, and the library was her idea, too. She collects books. Would you like to take a tour?"

"Let's save it for tomorrow," I suggested, and we lapsed into a comfortable silence.

Several moments passed before I realized that I was staring fixedly at a lock of Toby's pale blond hair gleaming in the firelight and decided that it was time to go to bed. I quickly drained my mug, but before I could carry it into the kitchen, Toby took it from my hand.

"I'll do the dishes," he said. "You've had a tough day. Don't worry about the lights, either. I'll turn them off after you've gone."

"Do we have plans for tomorrow?" I asked, getting to my feet.

"If I were you, I'd take it easy for a few days," he advised, rising. "Let yourself adjust to the altitude before you attempt anything strenuous. Slow and steady wins the race."

"Slow and steady it is, then," I said. "Why don't you join us for breakfast? We should be up by eight," I added, though I knew I'd be up much earlier, "and we'll have breakfast on the table by nine. You can give us a tour of the Aerie afterward."

"Sounds good to me." Toby took a ring of keys from his pocket and handed them to me, saying, "They open every door in the Aerie. I have a duplicate set, so don't worry about losing them. My apartment's through there." He pointed to a passageway at the end of the kitchen. "If you need anything, come and get me." His eyes crinkled adorably as he smiled down at me. "I'm glad you're here, Lori. The Aerie's too big for just one person. I'll see you in the morning."

"Good night," I said. "And thanks, Toby. I've never met James Blackwell, but he couldn't be better than you."

"Aw, shucks, ma'am." Toby let his silky blond hair fall forward to hide his face. "You're making me blush."

I peered at him suspiciously. "Have you ever said 'Aw, shucks' before in your life?"

"Never," he said, raising his head and grinning playfully, "but it seemed appropriate."

I smiled, punched him lightly in the shoulder, and headed for the master suite. It was very late, so I settled for a hot shower instead of a bath, pulled on a flannel nightie, lit a fire in the corner fireplace, and sat in the armchair before the hearth, with Reginald in the crook of my arm and the blue journal in my lap. Aunt Dimity's old-fashioned copperplate began to spin across the page as soon as I opened the journal.

Is there a dirt floor? Does the roof leak? Is the loo out of doors?

"No, no, and definitely not," I replied. "It's wonderful, Dimity. The valley is wonderful, the cabin is wonderful, our rooms are wonderful, and Toby is wonderful. Everything is absolutely wonderful."

You seem giddy, my dear. Have you been drinking?

"Yes, but only hot chocolate," I told her. "I'm not drunk, Dimity. I'm ecstatic, euphoric, incredibly relieved that the cabin is so wonderful. . . ." I paused to get a grip on myself, then added, "Or maybe it's the altitude."

Rapture of the heights? Perhaps. Who, may I ask, is Toby?

"Toby Cooper," I replied. "He's the last-minute replacement for the original caretaker."

And he's wonderful, is he? Am I to assume that he's also good looking?

I shifted uncomfortably in the armchair. Aunt Dimity knew all too well that my track record with attractive men who were not my husband wasn't as spotless as it should have been. I'd never actually forgotten my wedding vows, but my memory had grown hazy from time to time. If I told Dimity that Toby Cooper was as cute as a cocker spaniel—a tall, broad-shouldered, manly cocker spaniel—she would get the wrong impression, so I elected to downplay his good looks.

"He's a child, Dimity," I said airily. "A nice kid. He's twenty-one years old and still in college."

Good. You've never shown much interest in younger men. What happened to the original caretaker?

"James Blackwell?" I said. "He quit two days ago. I don't know why. According to Danny Auerbach, he left unexpectedly."

Perhaps he grew tired of dealing with the crackpot neighbor.

"There isn't one," I said happily. "We have the whole mountainside to ourselves."

Perhaps Mr. Blackwell was overworked.

"Are you kidding?" I said. "No one's been here since Christmas."

He might have been lonely.

"The cabin's awfully big for just one person," I agreed, recalling Toby's words. "But it's splendid, Dimity. It has every luxury, but it still feels like a family home. I don't know why the Auerbachs don't use it more often. They left so much stuff behind that they wouldn't have to pack much more than an overnight bag."

What did the Auerbachs leave behind?

"This and that," I said. "A blouse and two pairs of trousers in my closet, a few T-shirts and a pair of sneakers in the boys' room."

It sounds like an abandoned ship. Why didn't the family take their clothes with them after their Christmas visit?

"They're rich," I said. "They probably have multiple wardrobes for multiple residences."

Did they leave entire wardrobes behind?

"No," I said. "Just odds and ends."

They left odds and ends, here and there. It suggests to me that they packed hastily. How very interesting.

"Is it?" I said vaguely. It was past midnight and the long day was catching up with me. I was suddenly too tired to follow Aunt Dimity's train of thought.

It's extremely interesting. If the Auerbachs packed in a rush, then we're dealing with two abrupt departures—the family's and James Blackwell's. If the cabin is as wonderful as you claim, why did they leave it in such a hurry?

"Don't know," I said.

You might ask Bill to look into it. He might know of some family emergency the Auerbachs experienced at Christmastime. And Mr. Auerbach may have told him why James Blackwell quit.

"I will," I said, suppressing a yawn. "I'll ask Bill tomorrow. Or today. I can't keep track anymore."

Of course you can't. Forgive me for prattling on, my dear. You must be exhausted. We'll continue our discussion after you've had a good rest. But don't forget to speak to Bill about it. I don't like abrupt departures, especially when they're unexplained.

"I'll remember, Dimity," I promised.

Sleep well, my dear.

"I think I might manage it tonight," I said to Reginald as the lines of royal-blue ink slowly faded from the page.

I placed the journal on the bedside table and brought Reginald to bed with me, to ward off my recurring nightmare. I lay awake for a short time, watching the firelight dance on the beamed ceiling and wondering why anyone would abandon such a lovely ship, but Toby's image kept swimming through my mind, distracting me.

"Like a cocker spaniel," I murmured, and smiling drowsily, I drifted into sleep.

Six

F awoke from a confused dream involving heroic dogs and sinking ships to find bright sunlight streaming through the French doors and the windows. A glance at the bedside clock told me that it was half past eight. I pushed the duvet aside, rolled out of bed with Reginald in my arms, and walked slowly toward the French doors, unable to believe my eyes. I hadn't slept past sunrise since I'd been shot.

Cold air rushed in as I threw open the doors, but the view made me forget that I was barefoot and wearing only a nightgown. My deck was no more than two feet off the ground, but I could see the entire valley from it: the glittering lake, the deep green forest, the snow-streaked peaks against a sky so dazzlingly blue that I couldn't look at it without squinting. The landscape was grandiose, extreme, almost frightening in its immensity. Nothing was tame or understated.

"Reginald," I said, under my breath, "I don't think we're in Finch anymore."

I shivered and wrapped my arms more tightly around myself and my pink rabbit, then realized with a start what the bedside clock had been trying to tell me.

"Eight-thirty!" I yelped. "Toby'll be here at nine!"

I hightailed it back into the suite, sped through my morning routine, and pulled on jeans, a T-shirt, a warm woolen sweater, and sneakers. I tried to run to the great room, but gave up halfway down the corridor. Once I'd stopped seeing pinpoints of light dance before my eyes, I continued at a more sedate pace and opened the double doors to the mouthwatering scent of frying bacon. The twins were perched on stools at the breakfast bar, Annelise hovered over several frying pans on the stove, and Toby stood across the granite-topped bar from the twins, filling their glasses with orange juice. I'd arrived just in time to hear him laying down the law to Will and Rob.

"First rule of the Aerie," Toby was saying. "Don't leave food lying around outside—not a peanut, not a hot dog, not a potato chip, *nothing.*"

I paused with my hands on the doorknobs and held my breath. If Toby explained that human food attracted wild animals, the boys would probably create a trail of leftovers to guide bears to the playroom window. But Toby didn't fail me.

"It's unhealthy for the squirrels," he went on. "If we feed the squirrels, they'll get fat and fall out of their trees, *splat.*" He smacked his hand on the breakfast bar, making the boys jump.

"We won't leave food out," Will promised, round eyed.

"We *like* squirrels," Rob said earnestly.

"Second rule of the Aerie," Toby went on. "No playing with matches. Forest fires are a very real danger in the high country. One careless match and"—Toby snapped his fingers—"no home for the squirrels."

"We *never* play with matches," Rob declared.

"*Never,*" Will asserted.

"Then we'll get along fine," said Toby.

"Morning, all," I called, crossing to give my sons their morning hugs.

"Good morning, Lori." Annelise favored me with a penetrating glance. "How did you sleep?"

"I don't remember," I said triumphantly. "I was asleep."

"I'm making tomato and spinach omelets to go along with the bacon," said Annelise, turning back to the frying pans. "You'll never guess what Toby brought for breakfast."

"Rattlesnake steaks?" I ventured, climbing onto a stool.

"Not for *breakfast,*" Toby scoffed, and pushed a large plate across the breakfast bar toward me.

"Scones?" I said, staring incredulously at the pile heaped on the plate. "You brought *scones?*"

"He brought homemade strawberry jam as well," said Annelise, sliding omelets onto our plates.

I looked from her to Toby. "Where on earth . . . ?"

"Caroline's Cafe," Toby answered. "Carrie Vyne makes her own jams and jellies, and she makes scones from scratch every morning. I ran down there in the van and bought a batch fresh from the oven. I thought you'd enjoy a taste of home."

I beamed at him. "If anyone had told me that I'd spend my first morning in the Rocky Mountains feasting on homemade strawberry jam and made-from-scratch scones, I would have told them they were dreaming."

"That's my job." He spooned jam onto a scone and offered it to me. "Making dreams come true."

Our fingers brushed as I took the scone from him, and I felt a distinctive jolt that had nothing to do with the altitude, so I passed the scone quickly to Rob, cut Will's omelet into bite-sized pieces, and ordered myself sternly to act my age.

"When do we get to see the cowboys?" Rob asked, through a mouthful of scone.

"Not for a couple of days," I said. "We have to get used to the altitude before we go riding. But there are plenty of other things to do while we're here. Toby's going to give us a tour of the Aerie after breakfast."

Rob and Will were seriously underwhelmed by the prospect of traipsing through the Aerie, looking at rooms—the playroom was the only room that interested them, and they'd already seen *that*—so I suggested that Toby take them on a short hike after breakfast while Annelise and I poked around the Aerie on our own.

"Great idea," said Toby. "We'll go up to see the eagle's nest."

The boys brightened visibly, gobbled their breakfast, and ran off to fetch their hiking boots. I would have bundled them up in their warmest winter jackets as well if Toby hadn't stopped me.

"Light windbreakers over their sweatshirts will do," he said. "Hiking's hot work."

"But there's snow on the ground," I protested.

"It'll be gone by noon," he said, laughing. "We have four seasons every day in Colorado. Granddad used to say it should be the state motto. You'll see."

Annelise and I spent an hour exploring the Aerie before we were spent. After meandering through three guest suites, the laundry room, the arcade game room, the billiards room, the home theater, the library, the outdoor spa—which included a sauna and a massage cubicle as well as a beautifully landscaped hot tub—and myriad decks, balconies, and porches, we staggered back to the great room for a gulp of water and a well-deserved rest.

"Too many stairs," said Annelise, her chest heaving. "It's like climbing Mount Everest."

"Without oxygen tanks." I peeled off my sweater and sprawled on the sofa. I'd just put my feet up when my cell phone rang.

"Lori?" Bill sounded far more alert than he had when I'd called him in the middle of his night. "Why are you out of breath? You're not overdoing things, are you? You've only just arrived."

"You'll be happy to know that I'm reclining on a couch as we speak," I said. "Will and Rob are out hiking with Toby, but Annelise and I are taking it easy."

"Then why are you out of breath?" Bill pressed.

"Annelise and I have been hiking through the cabin," I said. "It's like Versailles. Glorious, but *big*."

"I knew you'd like it," said Bill. "Danny never does anything halfway. About Toby Cooper—I didn't know the other caretaker had quit until I read Danny's e-mail last night. Is Toby okay?"

"He's great. The boys are crazy about him." So are you, muttered my conscience. I told it to shut up and hurriedly changed the subject. "It's strange about James Blackwell, though. Did Danny tell you why he quit?"

"Danny doesn't have a clue," said Bill. "Blackwell had worked as his caretaker since just before Christmas. The pay was good and the job was relatively undemanding, so Danny can't understand why he took off the way he did, without giving notice. Danny's pretty upset about it, but he assured me that Toby Cooper would take good care of you."

"He brought us fresh-baked scones this morning," I said.

"Say no more," said Bill, sounding relieved. "I'll tell Danny you're happy with him."

I sat up on the couch and looked toward Annelise, who was standing at the window wall, dutifully drinking water while surveying the stunning scenery. Since she wasn't privy to the secret of the blue journal, I couldn't mention Aunt Dimity while she was within earshot, so I acted as if the next question were my own.

"Bill," I said, "did Danny have a family emergency last Christmas?"

"I don't know," Bill replied. "I wasn't in regular contact with him back then. Why do you ask?"

"He and his family spent Christmas at the cabin," I explained, "and they left some of their clothes behind. It looks as though they packed without double-checking the drawers and closets. I was wondering if something happened to make them leave in a panic."

"They're probably just absentminded." Bill's voice was edged with concern. "What's all this about a panic? You're not getting spooked are you, Lori? How did you sleep last night?"

"Like a log," I said flatly. "Until half past eight."

"No nightmare?" Bill asked incredulously.

"Abaddon took the night off," I told him. "I'm not spooked, Bill. I'm curious. Would you ask Danny if anything happened at Christmas?"

"I will." Bill paused. "You really slept through the night?"

"I really slept through the night, undisturbed by my creepy nighttime companion," I told him. "You're a genius. The mountain air is like a tonic."

"Yay," he cheered softly, and went on to bring me up to date on affairs in Finch.

Nell Harris had returned from France but wedding bells hadn't yet chimed for her and Kit Smith, Peggy Taxman had made a ludicrously low offer for the greengrocer's shop, and the weather had been drizzly. I tried to describe the Aerie and the view from my deck, but failed so miserably that I gave up in the end, and told Bill he'd simply have to fly over and see it for himself.

"I wish I could," said Bill. "I know you had doubts about the trip, Lori—"

"And I was a fool to have them," I interrupted. "Your brilliant idea was truly brilliant, Bill. The only thing missing is you."

After promising to pay closer attention to the time difference when calling him, I rang off.

"The snow's all but gone," Annelise observed, turning away from the window wall. "And there's hardly a puddle to be seen. There's something to be said for dry air." She strolled toward the sofa. "All's well at home?"

"I'll fill you in while we fix lunch," I said, getting to my feet. "The boys will be famished when they get back."

"I'm a bit peckish myself," said Annelise. "And I intend to take a nap after lunch."

"We'll *all* take naps after lunch," I said determinedly. "Slow and steady wins the race."

We stayed in or near the Aerie for three full days, but no one was bored. We took long hikes after breakfast, naps after lunch, and slightly shorter hikes before dinner. While we napped, Toby packed the Auerbachs' possessions and took the boxes to the Bluebird post office for shipping. He came back from town each day with something new to round out our wardrobes: wide-brimmed hats with ventilated crowns, shock-absorbing hiking poles, and lightweight headlamps for night hiking. Since my injured shoulder made wearing a day pack uncomfortable, I asked Toby to buy a waist pack for me; it came with pouches for two water bottles and a zippered compartment for small essentials.

Toby joined us for every meal and spent the evenings with us around the fire pit near the outdoor spa, singing songs, telling stories, and making beautifully gooey s'mores. It seemed a shame not to take advantage of the arcade games and the home theater, but no one wanted to stay indoors when the outdoors was so enticing.

When I finally took the time to explore Mrs. Auerbach's library, I found that it contained books on Colorado flora, fauna, geology, art, architecture, folklore, photography, and history, as well as biographies of prominent Coloradans. I selected a volume on Colorado pottery to read in bed, but I never made it beyond the first paragraph of the introduction because I couldn't keep my eyes open long enough to read further. The thin air was like a narcotic.

The trails around the Aerie were narrow, rock-strewn, and crisscrossed with tree roots, which made them far more challenging than the smooth, well-trodden paths surrounding Finch. Since I'd been all but bedridden for six weeks, I had trouble keeping up with the others, but Toby was never in a hurry and he always found clever ways to keep the twins occupied while I plodded slowly uphill, wishing I had an ice pack for my throbbing shoulder.

Toby was the ideal guide, extending our hikes gradually each day as our stamina increased. He pointed out famous landmarks and repeated their names until we knew them by heart: Ruley's Peak,

Mount Schroeder, Chaney Canyon, the Bartos Range. We waded in Willie Brown Creek, picnicked in Getty's Gulch, and snapped photographs of mule deer grazing near the defunct Luddington Mine.

Toby had us stand stock-still and listen as the leaves chattered in stands of white-barked aspens. He drew us close to ponderosa pines, to smell the vanilla fragrance in the deeply creviced bark. He spotted a pair of luminous Mountain Bluebirds perched atop an old fence post at the edge of a meadow, and told us that an early prospector had named the town after a pair that had guided him to his first gold strike.

Toby also taught us to wear gallons of sunblock, to *stay with the group,* and to bring extra water on every hike. Thanks to his sage advice, and good fortune with the weather, we managed to avoid dust storms, sunstroke, rattlesnake bites, hypothermia, altitude sickness, and a host of other woes that awaited unwary travelers in the mountains.

Rob and Will were so carried away by their high altitude adventure that they insisted on "camping out" in the playroom every night. They got a huge kick out of crawling into the sleeping bags in the freestanding tent and furtively switching on their headlamps after I'd called for lights out. I didn't mind. I liked knowing that the only bears in their wilderness were plush and toothless.

Bill called after breakfast every morning, but he was unable to answer Dimity's most pressing question. Danny Auerbach had switched his e-mail to auto-reply while he negotiated a new deal somewhere in Alaska, and Bill had been unable to reach him by telephone, so we still didn't know whether or not a family emergency had cropped up for the Auerbachs around Christmastime. Dimity found Danny's sudden inaccessibility deeply suspicious. I thought the altitude was making her daffy.

At our campfire on Friday, Toby made the momentous announcement that the boys were fit enough to ride the next day.

"I called ahead to the Brockman Ranch, so they'll be expecting us," he informed us. "They're providing two English-trained ponies, according to the instructions your husband gave them."

"Do they have English-trained ponies?" Annelise asked, surprised.

"Sure," Toby replied. "The Brockman used to be a working ranch, but beef isn't as profitable as it once was, so Deke and Sarah Brockman run it as a dude ranch now. They cater to riders from all over the world."

Will and Rob didn't like being thought of as dudes—once we'd explained to them what a dude was—but they were so anxious to climb into the saddle again that they *asked* to go to bed early. I left them zipped into their sleeping bags in their tent, to dream about horses, and shortly thereafter went to my bed, to dream about sweet-natured, blue-eyed cocker spaniels. Abaddon couldn't compete.

Seven

oby did a double take on Saturday morning when Will and Rob paraded before him, nattily attired in tailored black riding coats, white turtlenecks, fawn-colored breeches, and tall black boots, with sturdy black riding helmets in their hands.

"You were expecting blue jeans and cowboy hats?" I said, raising an eyebrow at him.

"It's what most people wear at the Brockman Ranch," said Toby, "wherever they come from."

"Well, my boys learned to ride in England, and they're accustomed to English riding clothes." I folded the twins' distinguishing bandanas and tucked them into their breast pockets, so that only the tips protruded. "I may pick up some western gear for them to wear after they get used to their new ponies, but for now I'd like everything to be as familiar as possible. But I'm bringing clothes for them to change into when they've finished riding."

"Can they ride?" Toby asked, eyeing the boys' formal outfits doubtfully.

"Like the wind," I said proudly. "Don't worry. No one who sees my sons on horseback will make fun of the way they're dressed."

Since it was our first nonhiking day, Annelise had donned a pretty sun dress, a pale blue cardigan, and a pair of canvas slip-ons that were entirely unsuited for the trail. I'd dressed in shorts, a T-shirt, and sneakers, with a zippered sweatshirt on top to ward off the morning chill, and Toby was clad in his usual ensemble: T-shirt, flannel shirt, multipocketed trousers, and hiking boots. We all wore our wide-brimmed hats and copious sunblock, and carried our trusty water bottles in our packs.

The morning was a carbon copy of the three that had preceded it. The sun shone like a blowtorch, the sky was preposterously blue, and the air was so crisp it almost twinkled. Bill called after breakfast with nothing to report but the vicar's decision to leave rock and roll alone and ask the old reliable brass band to play their usual selection of familiar tunes at the village fête, a decision which had met with the villagers' heartfelt—and loudly expressed—approval. After the boys had taken turns telling their father about their plans for the day— "We're going to ride with cowboys!"—we all piled into the van.

Toby took the two-lane highway west out of Bluebird, over a mountain pass and down into a rolling valley dotted with stands of aspen and bisected by a willow-lined creek. As we came down from the pass, we could see the Brockman Ranch laid out before us.

A dirt road led from the highway to a sprawling log house with a deep porch, three stone chimneys, and a huge rack of elk antlers nailed over the front door. Spread out behind the house were a large barn, a spacious riding ring, and assorted holding pens, paddocks, outbuildings, and sheds. A row of rustic-looking cabins sat among the willows along the creek, with cars and campers parked beside those that were, presumably, occupied by dudes. Rob and Will nearly popped out of their booster seats when they saw a herd of buffalo grazing in the distance and a string of horses munching hay in one of the paddocks.

"The Brockmans had to go to Denver today," Toby informed me, as he parked the van in front of the ranch house, "but I spoke with the head wrangler, Brett Whitcombe, and he said he'd look after Will and Rob personally. Ah, here he is now."

A tall, slender man with short-cropped gray hair had emerged from the house. He was dressed predictably, in faded jeans, a red-checked shirt, a tooled leather belt with a big silver-and-turquoise buckle, and pointy-toed boots. He carried a battered straw cowboy hat in one hand, but he put it on as he strode across the porch and came down the steps to greet us.

"Welcome to the Brockman," he said as he opened the passenger door for me. He looked as though he might be in his midthirties—too young to have gray hair, in my opinion—and his voice was gravelly but gentle. "I expect you'll be Ms. Shepherd."

"Lori," I said, staring up at him as I stepped out of the van. "Please, call me Lori." I pointed haphazardly over my shoulder. "Annelise, the boys' nanny, and Will and Rob, my sons."

"How do you do?" he said, tipping his hat in their general direction. "I'm Brett Whitcombe, head wrangler at the Brockman. Everyone calls me Brett. Good to see you, Tobe," he called as Toby came around the back of the van.

Toby nodded amiably, acknowledging the nickname. "Likewise, Brett."

While Annelise and Toby helped the twins out of the van, I stood frozen in place, unable to tear my gaze from Brett Whitcombe. The straw hat threw a shadow across his face, so I leaned in for a closer look.

"What color are your eyes?" I asked.

"My eyes?" Brett seemed surprised by the question, but he replied, "My wife tells me they're violet, but I've always thought of them as blue."

"No," I said, shaking my head decisively. "They're violet. It's an unusual shade. I've seen it only once before, back in England. My sons' riding instructor." I stepped back to survey the head wrangler's long lean body, short gray hair, and extraordinary eyes. "You're not related to an Englishman named Kit Smith, are you? His full name is Christopher Anscombe-Smith."

Brett threw a mystified glance in Toby's direction, then said politely, "I guess it's possible, but I couldn't say for sure. I've never taken much of an interest in genealogy."

"You could be Kit's brother," I marveled. "His *twin* brother. The resemblance is uncanny. Do you see it, Annelise?"

"Do I see what?" she asked, herding Will and Rob along until we formed a half circle in front of Brett.

"Doesn't Brett look like Kit?" I asked.

Annelise shrugged. "I suppose he does, a bit."

"A *bit*?" I pointed at Brett's face. "He's got *violet eyes*!"

"They're blue," said Annelise, elbowing me in the ribs. "You'll have to forgive Lori, Brett. She's still recovering from jet lag."

"It's a long flight from England," Brett said sympathetically. "Will you need a horse today, Annelise?"

"Not today, thank you," said Annelise. "Lori won't be riding, either."

"Mummy's afraid of horses," Will piped up.

"I'm *not* afraid of horses," I protested.

"Yes, you are," said Rob. "You're afraid to give Toby carrots, and he doesn't hardly have any teeth."

"He doesn't?" said Brett, with a bewildered glance at Toby.

"Toby's a pony," Annelise explained quickly. "An elderly pony. Back in England."

"We learned to ride on Toby," Rob informed the head wrangler.

"But we have our own ponies now," Will added. "They're faster than Toby."

"And they have more teeth," Rob continued. "They're called Thunder and Storm."

"We have a cat, too," said Will. "His name is Stanley. Do you have a cat?"

"Do you know Cowboy Sam?" Rob inquired.

Brett looked from one identical chattering boy to the other, grimaced slightly, and rubbed the back of his neck. "My wife has quite a few cats. I've known two or three cowboys named Sam, but they don't work at the Brockman. The ponies I rounded up for you are out back, in the riding ring. Want to meet them?"

"Yes, please," the boys chorused.

"Let's go," said Brett.

He and Toby strode off with the twins, but Annelise gripped my arm firmly and held me back until they'd disappeared around the side of the house.

"Honestly, Lori," she scolded. "You embarrassed that poor man to death, pointing at him like that."

"But—" I began.

"No *buts*," Annelise interrupted sternly. "And no more staring. And no more talk about Kit Smith. The poor man doesn't know Kit from a hole in the ground, so there's no use going on about it. He'll think you've lost your mind."

She released my arm and marched off to join the boys.

I replayed the scene in my head, realized that Annelise had been quite right to take me to task for my rude behavior, and trailed slowly after her, feeling as though I'd embarrassed myself far more than I'd embarrassed Brett Whitcombe. Kit Smith, whose manners were impeccable, would have been ashamed of me. I resolved to say nothing more about him to Brett.

A five-bar wooden fence encircled the riding ring. Brett and the twins stood inside the ring, near the swinging metal gate, where a pair of ponies were tethered. Annelise and Toby had taken seats on a set of wooden bleachers on the far side of the ring, in the shade of some cottonwood trees. A half dozen teen-aged boys in scruffy cowboys hats had gathered on the near side of the fence to watch the proceedings, attracted no doubt by the novelty of my sons' riding apparel. I edged my way past them until I was within a few yards of Brett, the twins, and the ponies.

Brett had rounded up a pair of palomino ponies for Will and Rob. They were called Nip and Tuck, and they didn't seem too ferocious. While Brett explained the rules of the riding ring, the twins ran knowing eyes over their prospective mounts.

"We'll take it one at a time, to begin with," Brett concluded. "And I don't want you to move till I say so."

He tightened Nip's girth, gave Rob a leg up into the saddle, and adjusted the stirrups, but when he took hold of the lead rope, to guide Nip into the ring, Rob objected.

"I know what to do," he said impatiently.

Brett gave me an inquiring glance, I answered it with a nod, and he released the lead rope. Rob walked Nip sedately once around the ring, then put him through his paces, going from a walk to a trot to a canter, bringing him smoothly back to a walk, and halting him smartly beside Tuck. Will gave Brett an arms-folded, I-told-you-so look, and the head wrangler gave him a leg up onto Tuck without further delay.

"Your boys have been well taught," Brett commented, as he climbed out of the ring to stand beside me. "My long-lost twin must be a fine instructor."

I felt myself blush a stunning shade of raspberry.

"You got a twin, Brett?" said one of the spectators.

"So I'm told." Brett grinned at me, then gestured to the knot of young men. "Let me introduce the crew. Lori Shepherd, this is Dusty, Lefty, Happy, Sneezy, Dopey, and Doc."

I was on the verge of saying good morning when it dawned on me that Brett was joking. I ducked my head sheepishly and joined in the general laughter that ensued. When the ranch hands had finished guffawing, they introduced themselves to me properly, welcomed me to the Brockman, and drifted off toward Annelise. I wondered if they were going to try the same gag on her.

Annelise had the video camera, and I was in charge of the digital camera. While she filmed the action, I snapped still shots of the twins, then settled down next to Brett to watch them enjoy their favorite pastime.

"How're you liking it up at the Aerie?" Brett rested his folded arms on the top bar of the fence. "Toby working out all right?"

"Toby's great," I said. "Very eager to please. If I didn't stop him, he'd cook our meals and do our laundry along with everything else he does. And I absolutely love the Aerie. If it were mine, and if I didn't have to fly so far to get here, I'd use it every weekend. I can't believe the Auerbachs haven't used it since Christmas."

"Me, neither." Brett shook his head. "Mrs. Auerbach and the kids used to spend every school holiday up there, and most weekends, too, but we haven't seen hide nor hair of them for six months now. In fact, no one's been there since the Auerbachs left, no one but the caretaker."

"Really?" I said. "I was under the impression that the Auerbachs let friends use the Aerie."

"They haven't had any takers lately," said Brett. "I reckon Bluebird isn't fashionable enough for the kind of people the Auerbachs know. They get bored looking at the lake, want fancy shops and restaurants. Caroline's Cafe serves up some mighty tasty grub, but I wouldn't call it fancy."

I watched Will and Rob steer their steeds through a series of figure eights, then asked, "If the Aerie's been empty since Christmas, why did the Auerbachs hire a live-in caretaker?"

"The caretaker's main job is just to be there," Brett explained. "You can't leave a place like that sitting empty. You never know what'll happen to it—frozen pipes, wind damage. Someone has to be on the spot to fix things when they break, and James could turn his hand to anything."

My ears pricked up. "Did you know James Blackwell?"

"I wouldn't say I knew him," Brett temporized. "James used to drop in on us now and again. He took an interest in local history. Asked all sorts of questions. Wanted to know what Bluebird was like in the olden days."

I recalled the books on Colorado history in the Aerie's library and asked, "Was James an amateur historian?"

"I suppose he may have been," said Brett, "but I'm not. I told him if he wanted to know about Bluebird, he should go to Bluebird. That's when he told me about Dick Major." Brett tilted his head toward me. "You met Dick yet?"

"No," I said. "I haven't been to town."

Brett's eyes narrowed. "Dick Major is a loudmouthed pain in the neck. Wish he'd go back where he came from, but it looks like he's dug in, in Bluebird. From what James said, he couldn't have a beer in the bar or a cup of coffee in the cafe without Dick's turning up. Parked himself at James's table without an invitation; told James he was a lazy good-for-nothing, a slacker who was taking money from the Auerbachs for doing nothing. Kept telling James to get a real job and stop sponging off his rich employers. Called him a worthless bum, right there, where everyone could hear him."

"Why did Dick Major pick on James?" I asked.

"Because he could," Brett said simply. "James wasn't from here, so he didn't have family to back him up. Didn't have any friends, either—"

"Why not?" I asked. "Why didn't he have any friends?"

"He was kind of shy," said Brett. "A nice enough guy, but quiet, studious—a prime target for a meathead like Dick."

"I *hate* bullies," I said vehemently.

"So do I." Brett shook his head. "If I'd seen Dick picking on James, I'd've put a stop to it, but Dick's sneaky. He never put a foot wrong in front of me. So after a while, James avoided Bluebird. He just stayed at the Aerie or came out here. I reckon he spent too much time on his own. Got to believing the stories he heard."

"What stories?" I asked.

"Tomfool stories," said Brett, snorting derisively. "He was always trying to find out if they were true. Then he up and left without saying a word to anyone. It's lucky Toby was free to take his place. Toby's a good kid. Known him since he was younger than your sons." Brett rested his chin on his folded arms, then gave me a sidelong glance. "Is it true that you're afraid of horses?"

"Uh, yes," I said, caught off guard by the abrupt change of subject. "My sons never lie, even when I wish they would."

"And this is your first time in the Rockies?" Brett went on.

"Yes," I said.

"Well, then," he said, turning to face me, "I have a suggestion to make. Why don't you leave Will and Rob here for the day? Annelise is welcome to stay with them. They can eat lunch with the rest of the guests and come along on the group trail ride this afternoon. In the meantime, you can take off with Toby, let him show you around. He knows every sight worth seeing in these parts. I'll have the twins back to the Aerie in plenty of time for dinner."

"Is your vehicle equipped with booster seats?" I asked.

"It can be," said Brett. "We have them on hand for people like you: overseas guests with young children. It won't take me but a minute to rustle up a pair for your boys. They work just fine in the family cab of my pickup."

"Sounds good to me," I said, "but I'll have to discuss it with Annelise. She's still getting used to the altitude. She may need a nap later on."

"She can use one of the guest cabins," said Brett. "My wife will make sure she's comfortable, and I'll look out for Will and Rob."

"You're very kind," I said, "but Annelise may not want to stay."

"On the other hand," said Brett, turning to look across the riding ring, "she may not want to leave."

I followed his gaze and saw that at least a dozen men had gathered around Annelise. Some were ranch hands, while others appeared to be dudes, but they'd all doffed their cowboy hats and they seemed to be vying with each other for her attention.

"Your sons' nanny has a fan club," Brett observed mildly. "Must be that pretty dress she's wearing. Most of the gals here wear jeans."

"She's engaged," I told him. "And she's extremely levelheaded."

"It does a young woman good to know she's admired," said Brett. "Even a levelheaded young woman who's engaged."

Brett evidently knew a lot about women, because Annelise was perfectly willing to remain at the ranch until the twins were ready to leave. Toby was equally willing to escort me wherever I wished to go. And I was more than willing to let the twins ride to their hearts' content while I went back to the Aerie. I had a lot to tell Aunt Dimity.

Will and Rob were eventually persuaded to dismount long enough for me to kiss them good-bye. Annelise fetched their extra clothes from the van, and Toby and I drove off, leaving Brett to field a multitude of questions from the twins about the upcoming trail ride.

Toby and I were halfway down the dirt road when a girl came toward us, riding an Appaloosa mare. The girl was in her late teens, long legged and slender, with a flawless oval face framed by a mane of golden curls that gleamed like corn silk in the sun. She reined in as we approached and regarded us with eyes that shone like dark sapphires.

"Howdy, Belle!" Toby shouted as we drove past.

"Belle?" I said faintly. "Who is Belle?"

"She's Deke and Sarah Brockman's daughter," said Toby. "She and Brett Whitcombe got married last fall. It took Belle two years to get him to the altar. Brett just couldn't believe that a lovely young thing like her could care for an old crock like him. Not that Brett's old, but he thought he was too old for Belle. Belle got through to him in the end, though. As they say, true love conquers all." Toby glanced at me. "What's wrong, Lori? You look as though you've seen a ghost. You don't disapprove of Belle and Brett, do you?"

"Me? Disapprove of true love? Not in a million years," I said, and let the subject drop. If I told Toby that Belle Whitcombe was the spitting image of Nell Harris, a teenager bent on marrying a man with violet eyes who was twice her age, he'd airlift me to the nearest lunatic asylum. But I was certainly going to tell Aunt Dimity. "I know we're supposed to be sightseeing, Toby, but do you mind if we go back to the Aerie instead? I'm a little tired."

"Has your shoulder stiffened up?" he asked.

My head snapped in his direction. "What do you know about my shoulder?"

"You told me you injured it a few weeks ago," he said. "And you rub it whenever you get tired. If it's bothering you, I'd recommend a long soak in the hot tub."

The thought of inviting Toby Cooper to join me in the hot tub was appallingly appealing, but I couldn't risk it. If Toby saw my scar, he'd inevitably ask questions I had no intention of answering. My brain had been blissfully Abaddon-free for four nights in a row and I wanted it to stay that way. To rehash the shooting would be to risk luring my black-eyed demon back again.

Apart from that, I felt an urgent need to tell Aunt Dimity everything I'd seen and heard at the Brockman Ranch, and I couldn't take the blue journal with me to the hot tub. I wasn't sure if Dimity's particular brand of ink would run when wet, but I didn't want to chance it.

"My shoulder's fine," I said brusquely. "I just need a nap. Let's go back to the Aerie."

"Your wish is my command," said Toby, and turned the van toward Bluebird.

Eight

When we reached the Aerie, Toby stayed outside to prune underbrush and chop down a small stand of saplings that had sprung up too near the fire pit, as if to illustrate Brett Whitcombe's observation that a place like the Aerie couldn't be left unattended for too long. The Aerie, Toby informed me, as he doffed his T-shirt and hefted his axe, needed constant attention to keep it from being overrun by the surrounding forest.

A weaker woman might have stuck around to watch him work up a sweat, but contrary to Aunt Dimity's belief, I was capable of exercising self-discipline. I excused myself and went to the master suite. The morning was so beautiful that I would have opened the French doors if I hadn't been worried about Toby passing beneath my deck and accidentally overhearing a lively conversation between me and thin air.

"I couldn't explain Aunt Dimity to him even if I wanted to," I said to Reginald as I retrieved the blue journal from the bedside table. "So we'll leave the French doors closed for now." I tweaked my pink bunny's ears, sat in the white armchair near the fireplace, opened the blue journal, and said excitedly, "Dimity? Are you there? I have so much to tell you!"

The curving lines of royal-blue ink zoomed across the page.

Have we heard from Danny Auerbach at last? Do we know why he and his family left the Aerie?

"I'll get to Danny in a minute. First, I have to tell you about"— I paused for dramatic effect—"*doppelgangers.*"

I know what a doppelganger is, my dear. Why do you feel the need to tell me about them?

"Because I saw *two* doppelgangers this morning, at the Brock-man Ranch." I launched into a detailed description of my encoun-ters with Belle and Brett Whitcombe, then awaited Dimity's reaction. It wasn't everything I'd hoped it would be.

They sound very much like Nell Harris and Kit Smith.

"They're *exactly* like Nell Harris and Kit Smith," I said. "Isn't it incredible?"

It's said that everyone has a double, Lori.

"But they don't just *look* alike," I persisted. "Belle's father owns the Brockman Ranch, where Brett's the head wrangler. Nell's father owns Anscombe Manor, where Kit's the stable master. Even their names are similar: Belle and Nell, Brett and Kit. And Brett didn't want to marry Belle because he thought he was too old for her—just like Kit! It's amazing, isn't it?"

Coincidences do happen, Lori. I wouldn't read too much into them.

"I'd read a lot into *these* coincidences," I retorted. "Don't you see, Dimity? It's an omen, a *good* omen. Everything worked out for Belle and Brett, so everything will work out for Nell and Kit." I cocked my head to one side and went on thoughtfully, "Maybe I should ask Belle how she persuaded Brett to marry her. Nell might appreciate a few tips."

You must promise me that you will do no such thing. Honestly, Lori, you can't pry into a stranger's intimate affairs simply because she reminds you of someone you know.

"I suppose not," I conceded reluctantly. "But if I get to know her better . . ."

You would have to know her well for several years before you could ask such a question. Are you planning to extend your stay at the Aerie until Will and Rob have outgrown their ponies?

"No," I said, laughing. "Okay, Dimity, I'll let it rest. And if I see anyone else who reminds me of home, I'll keep my mouth shut. I don't want Annelise to yell at me again. She made me feel as if I'd been caught red-handed scrawling graffiti on the vicarage."

Thank heavens for Annelise's good sense, as well as her good manners. Take it from me, Lori, no one wishes to be told that he or she is exactly like someone else. We all like to believe that we are unique. In nine cases out of ten it isn't true, but it's what we like to believe. Do your encounters with doppelgangers form the sum total of your news?

"I'm just getting started," I told her, and settled back in the chair. "Do you remember asking me to find out why James Blackwell and the Auerbachs left the Aerie so abruptly?"

I do.

"Well," I said, "I think I have the answer. Or part of the answer. Or something that might be the answer after I've investigated it more thoroughly."

You shouldn't be investigating anything, Lori! You're on holiday. You're supposed to be relaxing. I wish I'd never mentioned my misgivings.

"But you did mention them," I pointed out, "and there's no use telling me to forget about them, because I won't."

Of course you won't. You're like a dog with a bone when it comes to rooting out mysteries, but you're also like a kangaroo when it comes to jumping to conclusions. We've been here before, Lori.

"I know," I said, "but this time I'm sure I'm onto something. Well, I'm almost sure."

All right, then, let me hear your theory, or what might pass for a theory after you've investigated it more thoroughly.

I grinned at the page and continued confidently. "I found out some very interesting things while I was at the ranch. Brett Whitcombe told me that a bigmouthed blowhard named Dick Major used to make life miserable for James Blackwell whenever James went into town. Dick Major used to taunt James in public. He called James lazy and worthless and told him he should get a real job instead of taking money from his employers for doing nothing. I think Dick Major drove James away from the Aerie."

Are you suggesting that James Blackwell quit a comfortable and no doubt lucrative position because a local bully taunted him?

"Yes," I said. "Brett Whitcombe told me that James was quiet and shy, just the sort of meek little mouse who'd be cowed by a loudmouthed bully."

But James Blackwell held the position of caretaker for six months before he quit. If he was so meek and mild, why did it take so long for Dick Major to shame him into leaving?

I regarded the question uncertainly, then shrugged. "Everyone has a breaking point, Dimity. Maybe it took James Blackwell six months to reach his. Or maybe . . ." I nodded as a new and better explanation occurred to me. "Maybe James heard stories about Dick Major that frightened him. Brett Whitcombe told me that James wanted to know if some stories he'd heard were true."

Did the stories concern Dick Major?

"I don't know," I replied. "Brett didn't repeat them to me. Maybe he didn't want to make me nervous about staying at the Aerie. But what if James Blackwell left the Aerie because he'd heard rumors about Dick becoming violent? What if James was afraid Dick's taunts would turn into punches?"

I applaud your creativity, Lori, but I can't help wondering if your own recent experiences might be coloring your interpretation of events. It wasn't so long ago that you were forced to run for your life after being threatened by a homicidal maniac.

"Coincidences happen," I reminded her airily. "If Kit and Nell aren't the only Kit and Nell in the world, then Abaddon can't be the only murderous madman."

Your in kangaroo mode, my dear. With one fearless leap of the imagination you've transformed Dick Major from a loudmouthed bully into a murderous madman.

"But what if he *is* a murderous madman?" I asked. "It might explain why the Auerbachs left in such a hurry. They might have been afraid of him, too."

But why would Danny Auerbach leave his caretaker in the clutches of a murderous madman? Why would he allow you, Annelise, two small children, and young Toby Cooper to come to the Aerie if he was convinced that a murderous madman lived nearby? And why on earth would Danny run away from a murderous madman in the first place? Danny's a wealthy, high-powered businessman. If he thought his family was in danger, he wouldn't pack his bags in a hurry and flee. He'd contact his lawyers and go straight to the police. He's undoubtedly on good terms with the more influential members of the law enforcement community. I wouldn't be at all surprised to learn that they play golf together.

"I take your point," I said philosophically. "I'm rather fond of my theory, but I suppose it does have a few holes in it."

Your theory has more holes than a colander. I suggest you plug them before you leap to any more conclusions.

"No problem," I said. "I'll ask Toby if he's heard any scary stories about Dick Major. If he hasn't, I'll head into Bluebird and hook up to the local grapevine. One of the townspeople will be able to fill me in. Nothing goes unnoticed in a small community."

An excellent idea. I'd wish you luck, but I doubt you'll need it. You've become quite adept at monitoring grapevines since you moved to Finch. You'll bring Toby with you when you go to Bluebird, won't you?

"Of course," I said. "I'll need him to introduce me to the locals. Why?"

I'd rather you didn't run into Dick Major on your own. I don't want an obnoxious bully to spoil your holiday.

I smiled as Aunt Dimity's elegant script faded from the page, then I returned the journal to the bedside table and rubbed my palms together energetically. I hadn't swapped gossip since I'd been shot. I was looking forward to getting back in practice.

It was nearly two o'clock by the time I returned to the great room. Toby was in the kitchen, preparing a late lunch. He'd already set two places at the teak table on the breakfast deck, so we went out there to enjoy the sunshine and the scenery as well as our meal. I waited until we'd finished the fruit salad and started in on the rosemary chicken–stuffed croissants to ask if he'd heard any stories about the infamous Dick Major.

"Stories about Dick?" Toby gave a low whistle and rolled his eyes. "I've heard too many to count. I've never actually met the man, but he's made a real name for himself since he moved to Bluebird—several names, in fact, none of which should be repeated in polite company."

"Not Mr. Popular, huh?" I said.

"He's about as popular as a swarm of mosquitoes." Toby speared a piece of chilled asparagus. "Where did you hear about Dick Major?"

"Brett Whitcombe," I replied. "When we were at the ranch this morning, Brett told me that Dick used to bully James Blackwell."

"I'm not surprised," said Toby. "From what I hear, Dick's the kind of guy who gets his kicks out of intimidating people."

"Is he dangerous?" I asked.

"Dick's a pest, not a mobster," Toby said dismissively. "He started so many arguments with his next-door neighbor that the guy finally moved to a house on the other side of town, just to have a little peace and quiet. But word gets around; the house next to Dick's is *still* empty."

"When did he move to Bluebird?" I asked, wondering if Dick's arrival had coincided with the Auerbach's sudden departure.

"A year ago, I think," said Toby.

"A year ago?" I echoed disappointedly. "Not just before Christmas?"

"I'm pretty sure he was here way before Christmas," said Toby. "Why are you so interested in him?"

"I've been wondering why James Blackwell quit his job," I said. "I think maybe he got sick of being bullied by Dick."

"You could be right, though I'd hate to think I owe my job to someone like Dick Major." Toby grimaced adorably and went on eating.

"How have you avoided meeting Dick?" I asked.

"Just lucky, I guess." Toby pointed his fork at my plate. "How's the chicken?"

"It's delicious," I said. "Everything's delicious, but you shouldn't have gone to so much trouble."

"I didn't," said Toby, grinning. "I picked it up at the cafe."

As I took another bite of croissant, it occurred to me that if Caroline's Cafe was anything like Sally Pyne's tearoom in Finch, it would be the epicenter of gossip in Bluebird—a perfect starting point for my tour of the local rumor mill. Before I could suggest a quick run into town, however, my cell phone rang. I apologized to Toby and went into the great room to answer it.

"Lori?" Bill's voice came through as clearly as if he were standing beside me. "I finally managed to get ahold of Danny."

"Did you find out what happened at Christmas?" I asked eagerly.

"Not exactly," Bill answered. "Apparently *Florence* insisted on leaving."

"Who's Florence?" I asked.

"Danny's wife," said Bill. "She refused to explain why she wanted to leave, and she isn't the sort of woman you cross-examine, so Danny doesn't know what happened. Whatever it was, Florence has taken such a dislike to the Aerie that she refuses to go back there. In fact, Danny's put the place on the market."

"The Aerie's for *sale*?" I felt as if the wind had been knocked out of me. "I don't believe it."

"It's what property developers do, Lori," said Bill. "Build and sell."

I looked around the great room and shook my head. Feathers, bones, and interesting bits of wood, the harvest of many family hikes, had been lovingly arranged in the rustic cabinets. Rambunctious children had left their marks on the comfy furniture. Family meals had been prepared in the kitchen and eaten around the large dining table. It took no imagination whatsoever to picture Danny, his wife, sons, and daughter gathered around the fireplace, singing Christmas carols, roasting marshmallows, and sipping hot apple cider.

"Not the Aerie," I said firmly. "He didn't build the Aerie to sell. It's Danny's tree house, Bill."

"His what?" said Bill.

"His pride and joy," I clarified. "If you ask me, the Aerie's as important to him as the cottage is to us. I can't believe he's selling it. When did it go on the market?"

"Just after Christmas," said Bill.

"What are we supposed to do if prospective buyers show up?" I asked. "Hide in the woods until they leave?"

"Danny's put everything on hold while you're there," said Bill. "To tell you the truth, he's having a hard time attracting buyers. He's lowered the price twice in the past six months, but no one's made him an offer. I think he's beginning to regret his decision to build in such an out-of-the-way place."

"It's a *beautiful* place," I insisted.

"But it's not Aspen," said Bill.

"It's *better* than Aspen. It would break Danny's heart to sell the Aerie," I said sadly, and at that moment my own heart hardened. I didn't know what had happened to spoil the Aerie for Florence Auerbach, but I was determined to find out. If Dick Major was to blame, I'd find a way to make him mind his manners. I knew what it was like to be forced to leave a place I loved. I didn't want the same thing to happen to Danny and his family.

"Danny told me about the sale in confidence," Bill was saying, "so don't mention it to anyone, all right?"

"Does Toby know?" I asked.

"Toby Cooper?" said Bill. "I doubt it."

"But Toby was planning to spend the whole summer here," I said. "If Danny sells the Aerie after we leave, Toby will be out of a job."

"Danny hasn't had a nibble in six months," Bill said patiently.

"Unless a miracle happens, Toby will be able to keep his job until it's time for him to go back to school."

"I hope so," I said worriedly.

"We'll just have to wait and see," said Bill. "It's an unfortunate situation, but try not to dwell on it, Lori. You're there to enjoy yourself. I don't want you to get your knickers in a twist about something that's beyond your control."

My knickers were already in a twist, and I was far from convinced that the situation was beyond my control, but I knew better than to say as much to Bill. He'd only feel guilty for upsetting me.

"Are you at the ranch?" he asked.

"No," I replied, "but you won't believe who I saw there. . . ."

Bill's reaction to my descriptions of Belle and Brett Whitcombe was even more infuriatingly blasé than Aunt Dimity's had been. He seemed to think I'd perceived a strong resemblance between them and Kit and Nell simply because I was homesick. I was so incensed by his patronizing tone that I vowed to take photographs of Belle and Brett the next time I went to the ranch in order to document my claims.

"Don't let Annelise catch you at it," Bill advised. "She'll confiscate your camera and make you sit in the corner until you promise to behave yourself. I'll speak with you again tomorrow, love."

I could have sworn I heard him chuckle as he ended the call.

I was in a somewhat grumpy mood when I returned to the breakfast deck, but Toby restored my cheerfulness by asking if I planned to attend church in Bluebird the following day. I told him that I could think of no better way to spend my first Sunday morning in Colorado.

A church lawn after Sunday services was, in my experience, a splendid spot to fish for local gossip. Although Toby had dealt my pet theory a blow by placing Dick Major in Bluebird well before Christmas, I remained certain that the town bully had had something to do with James Blackwell's departure as well as the Auerbachs'. I was determined to get the dirt on him before the week was out.

My fishing expedition was, alas, delayed by one day because Will and Rob insisted on attending the cowboy church at the Brockman Ranch, which turned out to be an all-day affair. After the guitar-twanging, yodel-filled service came the huge picnic lunch, then a rodeo in which my sons demonstrated trick riding skills I didn't know they possessed and wished I'd never seen. I managed to keep smiling during their bravura performance, but I gripped the bleacher seat so hard I lost all feeling in my fingers.

The rodeo went on until the evening barbecue, which was followed by a bonfire, the singing of many cowboy songs, and the dramatic recitation of cowboy poetry. As we were getting ready to leave, Brett Whitcombe offered to pick up the boys and Annelise the next morning and bring them to the ranch for another day of riding.

After conferring with Annelise, I accepted the offer gratefully. I knew that the twins would be perfectly content to spend the rest of their vacation in the saddle. I'd also noted that Annelise, level-headed though she was, was thoroughly enjoying her first taste of cowboy charm.

It was approaching midnight when we returned to the Aerie with a pair of sleepy-headed but happy little cowpokes as well as a dozen covertly taken photographs of Brett and Belle. If I'd known how to use a laptop computer to transmit images, I would have e-mailed them directly to Bill.

Nine

*O*ur late-night festivities had not the slightest impact on Will or Rob. They crawled out of their tent bright and early on Monday morning, pulled on their freshly laundered riding clothes, and chattered like magpies with their father when he called at nine o'clock. After a quick breakfast, they stood by the window wall to keep watch for Brett Whitcombe's truck. He showed up at nine forty-five and took off with Annelise and the twins, leaving me and Toby to our own devices.

"Would it be okay if we went into Bluebird today?" I asked Toby as we loaded the dishwasher. "I'd like to explore the town."

"Sounds good to me." He closed the dishwasher and leaned back against it, with his arms folded across his chest and a challenging gleam in his eyes. "Walk or drive?"

"Walk," I said bravely. "Unless you think it's too far."

"It's not too far," he said. "If we go by the easiest trail, it'll take us twenty minutes to get there, tops. You won't even break a sweat."

"Only because we'll be going downhill," I pointed out.

"You can handle it, Lori," Toby said bracingly. "Grab your hat and pull on your hiking boots. It's another beautiful day in Colorado."

As far as I could tell, every day was beautiful in Colorado. I hadn't seen a cloud in the sky since we'd arrived, and the snow that had filled me with dread at the airport had disappeared from all but the shadiest nooks in the forest. Even though it was barely ten o'clock in the morning, it was already warm enough for me to dress in shorts and a T-shirt, but I took the precaution of adding a rain jacket to Toby's day pack before we took off, bearing in mind his oft-repeated, though still unproven, warning that mountain weather was nothing if not changeable.

The trail to town started at the western edge of the Aerie's clearing. It was wide and smooth and carpeted with pine needles that smelled like incense in the splashes of hot sunlight falling through the sheltering trees.

"We're on the Lord Stuart Trail," Toby informed me. "There used to be a narrow gauge rail line running along here, linking the mine head to the processing mill in Bluebird."

"Was the Lord Stuart Mine a big operation?" I asked.

"Biggest in the valley," said Toby. "Granddad told me that it employed a couple hundred men, all told. They used to walk along the sides of the track on their way to the mine from their lodgings in Bluebird. The Lord Stuart Trail was a major thoroughfare in its day."

"No wonder it's so easy," I said. "I *like* major thoroughfares."

"I knew you would," said Toby, with a satisfied nod.

A profusion of wildflowers bloomed in unkempt tangles along the well-trodden path. I tried to memorize the flowers' colorful names as Toby pointed them out—Orange Sneezeweed, Witches Thimble, Shooting Star, Fairy Trumpet—but when he reached Rosy Pussytoes, I burst out laughing.

"Rosy Pussytoes?" I exclaimed. "You've got to be kidding."

"That's what it's called," Toby insisted. "There are Alpine Pussytoes as well. In fact, if you stick *alpine* in front of any plant's name, you won't go far wrong. Alpine sunflower, alpine lily, alpine clover—"

"Alpine magnolia," I put in, "alpine eucalyptus—"

"—alpine palm tree, alpine rutabaga," he continued.

By the time we reached alpine bougainvillea, we were giggling so hard that we had to stop walking. While I leaned against a fir tree to catch my breath, it occurred to me that I hadn't had a good giggle since I'd been shot. Bill had been as caring as any human being could be, and my best friend Emma had been wonderfully sympathetic, but Toby, who knew nothing of my harrowing brush with death, was giving me something I hadn't realized I needed: a healthy dose of silliness. I felt a rush of gratitude toward him as we continued downhill.

The Lord Stuart Trail was so pretty and we were having such a good time that it came as something as a letdown when we finally reached the edge of town and the paved surface of Lake Street. The first house we saw would have had a lovely view of Lake Matula if it hadn't been surrounded by piles of highly unattractive junk. I stared in dismay at rusty bedsprings, an assortment of old washing machines, several rotting mattresses, a couch covered in split vinyl, a car radiator, and a myriad of other items that would no doubt fascinate some future archaeologist but which filled me with revulsion.

"Don't judge Bluebird by Dick Major's house," Toby advised.

"Dick Major lives here?" I stopped dead in my tracks and swung around for a closer look at the house. The roof seemed to be intact, but the paint on the walls was peeling badly and most of the windows were boarded up. "What a slob."

Toby hushed me and tugged gently on my elbow. "Keep your voice down and keep moving, please, Lori. I haven't had a run-in with Dick yet, and I don't want to push my luck."

"Sorry," I said, but as we walked away, I kept looking over my shoulder. It was hard to believe that anyone would willingly live in the midst of such a mess. "What does he do for a living? Collect garbage?"

"No idea," Toby replied.

"If you ask me, his next-door neighbor moved just to get away from the smell of moldy mattress," I commented.

"Could be," said Toby and increased our pace.

The houses became progressively tidier as we walked on. None reached the level of tidiness routinely maintained in Finch, but there was a certain careworn charm to most of them. I was particularly fond of a tiny Victorian cottage that had been painted lavender with bright purple trim. Its picket-fenced front garden was overflowing with a shaggy collection of lupines, columbines, and fluttering poppies as well as an assortment of vivid "alpine" flowers.

Most of Bluebird's businesses were located on Stafford Avenue, one block over from the highway that split the town in two. The buildings were made of wood or brick, in a Victorian style that suggested they'd been built before the turn of the last century. Whatever their original purposes, the buildings now housed a mixture of useful shops and places favored by travelers.

The hardware store stood beside Eric's Mountain Bikes, the grocery beside the Mother Lode Antique Mall, the post office beside an art gallery featuring watercolors by local artist Claudia Lechat. Sweet Jenny's Ice Cream Emporium specialized in Olde Tyme Fudge and Crazy Chris's Camping Supplies offered special deals on bait to those who fished Lake Matula or the trout streams that ran through the Vulgamore Valley.

Toby and I stopped at Dandy Don's Discount Pharmacy & Gifts, where I bought a handful of postcards depicting mountain scenes similar to those we'd seen during our hikes. Since I was a great believer in supporting local businesses, I didn't even try to resist padding my order with a packet of columbine seeds for Emma, a pair of gilded aspen-leaf earrings for Annelise, a pair of suede moccasins for me, and two adorable stuffed animals—buffalo—to remind Rob and Will of their first visit to the Wild West.

Tourists weren't exactly thronging the sidewalks on Stafford Avenue, but a fair number of them were moseying in and out of the shops, slurping ice-cream cones, studying maps, or snapping photographs of one another behind the hitching post in front of Altman's Saloon, HOME OF THE WORLD-FAMOUS ALTMAN'S BURGER. As I watched a family group posing for the camera, I thought of what a shame it would be if a bigmouthed bonehead like Dick Major spoiled their fun with rude remarks or crude gestures.

I was pleased to see that a real effort had been made to dress up the main drag. Baskets filled with multicolored pansies hung from the old-fashioned, cast-iron street lamps, and wooden benches with fancy scrollwork arms and legs sat next to many of the store entrances. A large banner strung across the street proclaimed BLUEBIRD

GOLD RUSH DAYS JULY 8-9-10 in bold print, but I had eyes only for a modest wooden sign hanging above a storefront on our right.

"Caroline's Cafe," I said, pointing to the sign. "Let's go in. I could do with a cold drink, and you can introduce me to Carrie Vyne. I'd like to tell her how much we've enjoyed everything we've tried from her cafe."

"After you," said Toby.

Tinkling bells jingled as he pulled the lace-curtained door open for me. I stepped inside, stopped short, and peered around the room in wonder. Caroline's Cafe reminded me so poignantly of the tearoom back in Finch, with its charmingly mismatched china, chairs, and tables, that a wave of homesickness threatened to overwhelm me.

"Where's Carrie Vyne?" I whispered to Toby.

"Behind the bakery counter," he whispered back. "What's wrong?"

"Nothing," I said, and breathed a sigh of relief as we made our way to an unoccupied table.

If Carrie Vyne had looked like Sally Pyne, the proprietress of Finch's one and only tearoom, I would have fainted dead away right then and there. Fortunately, she didn't. Both women were middle aged, but while Sally was short and round, Carrie was tall and stately. Sally's garish tracksuits were a favorite topic of caustic conversation in Finch, but Carrie would have aroused no comment at all, being tastefully dressed in blue jeans, sneakers, and a pale-pink, short-sleeved cotton blouse. And Sally wore her iron-gray hair clipped quite short while Carrie wore her white hair in soft waves that framed a lined but very kindly face.

"Back again, Toby?" she said, coming to our table to fill our water glasses. Her voice was light and musical, quite unlike Sally Pyne's staccato bark.

"Where else would I go for my midmorning munchies?" Toby responded, with a grin. He drew a hand through the air between

Carrie Vyne and me. "Carrie, this is Lori Shepherd. Lori, this is Carrie. Lori's the woman I told you about, Carrie. The one who's staying at the Aerie."

"Pleased to meet you, Lori," she said.

"Likewise," I said. "*Very* pleased. We've loved everything Toby's brought up from the cafe—the scones, the jams, the croissant sandwiches. You're a brilliant baker and a wonderful cook."

"Why, thank you," said Carrie, blushing rosily. "Are you enjoying your stay at the Aerie?"

"I am," I said. "I wish my sons were here so that I could introduce them to you, but they're spending the day at the Brockman Ranch."

"I've heard they're good little riders," said Carrie.

I almost said, "Of course you have," but caught myself just in time. I was delighted to know that Carrie Vyne had her ear to the rail, but I didn't want to risk insulting her by implying that she was a gossip.

"They do okay," I acknowledged.

"Better than okay, I'd say," said Carrie. "From what I've heard, they'll be roping calves before the week's out."

"Oh, Lord, I hope not," I said weakly.

"Brett'll watch over them," Carrie said reassuringly. She finished filling our glasses and left the water pitcher on the table for us to use. "What can I get for you, Lori? I already know what I'm going to bring Toby, but what kind of snack would you like?"

"I'll have whatever Toby's having," I said.

"Won't take but a minute."

Carrie returned to the bakery counter and came back five minutes later with two tall glasses of ice-cold lemonade, two small, mismatched plates, and a larger plate filled with cookies that looked disturbingly familiar.

"Calico Cookies!" Toby exclaimed. "My favorites! Thank you, Carrie. What's in them today?"

"You tell me," she said with a wink and went to serve another customer.

Toby seized a cookie, took a large bite, and chewed slowly, with a look of deep concentration on his face.

"Chocolate chips," he murmured, "dried cranberries, and . . . sliced almonds?" He came out of his trance and gestured for me to sample a cookie, explaining, "Carrie adds different goodies to the basic recipe every time, so you never know what you'll find. But she always leaves out the coconut when I'm in town. She knows I can't stand coconut."

I stared at the cookies as though they were hand grenades. If Toby was telling the truth—and I had no reason to think he wasn't—then Carrie Vyne's Calico Cookies could quite easily be mistaken for Sally Pyne's Crazy Quilt Cookies, right down to the absence of coconut. I raised a cookie slowly to my lips, bit into it, tasted the familiar blend of sweet, tangy, and faintly spicy flavors, and lowered it gingerly to my plate.

"Do you know where she got the recipe?" I asked, my voice trembling slightly.

"I think she made it up," said Toby. "Aren't they great?"

"They're great," I said, and turned to look over my shoulder as the front door's bells jingled and a large woman with a weathered face and rhinestone-studded glasses barreled into the cafe.

Toby followed my gaze, heaved a small sigh, and muttered, "Buckle your seat belt. Maggie Flaxton has arrived."

"Carrie!" bellowed Maggie Flaxton. "Why don't you have a sign in your window for Gold Rush Days? How are we going to draw a crowd if we don't advertise?"

"The banner is working fine," Carrie answered mildly. "All of my customers ask about the festival."

The large woman sniffed doubtfully and rounded on me. "What about you? Did *you* ask about the festival?"

"I only just got here," I said, fighting the urge to snap to attention. "I was *going* to ask—"

"You're up at the Auerbach place, aren't you?" Maggie Flaxton interrupted.

"Y-yes," I managed, cowed by her commanding voice.

"I don't suppose you'll stay long," she roared. "None of them do, and who can blame them? I wouldn't spend five minutes there if I could help it. But if you're still around in July, we could use your help. It's all hands on deck during Gold Rush Days. Toby's running the wood-splitting contest." She turned back to Carrie Vyne. "I want to see a sign in your window before the day is out, Carrie."

"It'll be there," Carrie promised resignedly.

"It had better be," shouted Maggie. "I can't do everything my-self, you know." Frowning fiercely, she spun on her heel and stomped out of the cafe.

"Whew," said Toby, leaning his head on his hand. "She could rule the world if she put her mind to it, Maggie could."

"Does she run the grocery?" I asked.

"Yes," said Toby, "and everything else in town. How did you know?"

"Lucky guess," I replied.

I popped the rest of the cookie into my mouth and told myself sternly *not* to tell Toby that Bluebird's Maggie Flaxton was very like Finch's Peggy Taxman. I'd promised Aunt Dimity that I wouldn't mention doppelgangers to anyone, and I intended to keep my promise, but apart from that, I didn't want Toby to think that the sun had fried my brains.

"I wonder why she wouldn't spend five minutes at the Aerie?" I said.

"I don't," said Toby, with a wry smile. "The Aerie's too far away from town for her liking. Maggie prefers to crack her whip at close range."

A moment later the bells jingled again and a small balding man put his head cautiously into the cafe.

"It's all right, Greg," Carrie called to him. "Maggie's gone."

"Greg Wilstead," Toby murmured, for my benefit. "The shyest man in Bluebird."

"Lori," Carrie said brightly, looking in my direction, "if your boys are interested in trains, you should bring them to visit Greg. You've got an amazing set of tracks laid out in your garage, haven't you Greg?"

The little man ducked his head, mumbled something incoherent, and refused to meet my eyes.

"Thanks, Carrie, I'll keep it in mind," I said dazedly, envisioning the shy and balding George Wetherhead, Finch's local expert on railroads.

"Lori's staying up at the Auerbach place," Carrie added.

Greg Wilstead's head came up and he peered at me, his eyes wide with something that closely resembled horror.

"Oh, my God," he whispered, and left the cafe without buying so much as a bread roll.

"What was *that* about?" I said, looking after him.

"Don't know," said Toby. "Drink your lemonade, Lori. It's squeezed fresh every morning."

I'd taken only a sip of the lemonade, which was splendidly refreshing, when the jingling bells announced the arrival of a middle-aged, deeply tanned, and extremely overweight couple dressed in brightly colored T-shirts and baggy shorts. They went straight to the bakery counter and ordered a dozen doughnuts, a dozen elephant ears, and a dozen blackberry tarts to go. While they waited for Carrie to put their order together, they turned to survey the cafe. Their faces lit up when they saw Toby.

"Howdy, Tobe," called the woman.

"How the heck are you, Tobe?" said the man.

"Just fine. Pull up some chairs while you're waiting." Toby turned to me as the couple joined us at our table. "Nick and Arlene Altman run Bluebird's most popular watering hole, Lori."

"Altman's Saloon?" I guessed. "Home of the world-famous Altman's burger?"

"That's right," said Nick proudly. "Arlene makes the biggest, juiciest burgers in the Rockies."

"We run a family-friendly bar, Lori," Arlene informed me. "Feel free to bring your little ones with you any time."

"And their good-looking nanny," Nick put in. "Heard all about her from the boys at the Brockman."

"Men," said Arlene, clucking her tongue.

"I'm sure Tobe's told you that I make my own beer," Nick said, ignoring his wife and turning toward me. "Are you a beer drinker, Lori?"

Behind him, Toby and Arlene were shaking their heads frantically.

"Uh, no," I said, reading the signal. "In fact, I don't drink much at all."

"You may start if you stay at the Aerie too long," said Nick, chuckling.

"Our order's ready, Nick," said Arlene, and they heaved themselves to their feet.

"Nice to meet you, Lori," said Nick. "You be careful up there, you hear?"

"Hush, Nick," said Arlene. "Pay no attention to my husband, Lori. He's full of hot air."

"No, I'm not." Nick patted his ample stomach. "I'm full of your big, juicy burgers."

He chuckled merrily as he and Arlene paid for their order and left.

Once they'd gone, Toby leaned in close to me.

"Do not *ever* try Nick Altman's beer," he said. "I had to drink a whole bottle of it on my eighteenth birthday, just to be polite. My head nearly fell off the next day. The stuff is *deadly.*"

I steadfastly refused to dwell on the startling similarities between the rotund Nick Altman and the equally plump Dick Peacock, who ran Peacock's Pub in Finch and made wine that could be used to strip paint, and focused instead on Nick's somewhat alarming comment concerning the Aerie.

"Why did Nick tell me to be careful up at the Aerie?" I asked.

"He's probably afraid you'll overexert yourself," said Toby. "He and Arlene don't believe in exercise."

"Really?" I said, in mock astonishment.

Toby began to laugh, but when the bells jingled again, he stopped abruptly.

"Oh no," he said under his breath. "My luck's run out."

"You're in early today, Dick," Carrie called. "What can I get for you?"

I took a surreptitious look over my shoulder and caught my first glimpse of the infamous Dick Major.

Ten

ick Major didn't look like a murderous lunatic *or* a garbage collector. He looked like a jolly grandfather, and to my intense relief, he didn't remind me of anyone in Finch.

His face was round and pink, silver-rimmed glasses framed his pale blue eyes, and he wore his grizzled gray hair in a precisely clipped crew cut. He was neatly dressed in a short-sleeved yellow shirt, lightweight tan trousers, and a well-worn pair of brown suede shoes. He wasn't a tall man, but he was imposing, thanks to broad shoulders and a barrel chest that strained the buttons of his shirt. His voice, when he replied to Carrie Vyne's question, was higher pitched than I would have expected from a man with his burly build, and it held an unexpected undertone of general bonhomie.

"The usual?" said Carrie.

"You bet," he said. "Black coffee and a couple of jelly doughnuts to go. You got elephant ears today?"

"I sure do," Carrie said.

"Throw in a couple of elephant ears, too," said Dick. "And make it a *large* black coffee."

"Coffee'll take a few minutes," Carrie warned. "I'm making a fresh pot."

"That's okay. I'll wait." Dick Major turned away from the bakery counter to cast a seemingly benevolent gaze on the cafe's customers. His pale blue eyes lit up when he spotted Toby and me, and a wide grin spread across his face. As he approached our table, I felt a flutter of unease. There was something strange about his eyes. He opened them too widely, and he seemed to wait too long between blinks. I wondered if he was on some sort of medication.

"Dick Major," he said, extending a large, thick-fingered hand to me. "You the little lady staying up at the Auerbach place?"

"Yes." I took his meaty hand with some trepidation, but his grip turned out to be pleasantly firm rather than crushing. "Danny Auerbach is an old friend of my husband's."

"But your husband ain't there," Dick observed, still grinning. "Just you and those little tykes of yours and that . . . What do you call her? A nanny? Must be nice to be able to afford a nanny."

I didn't know how to respond, but Toby saved me the trouble.

"They're not alone at the Aerie," he said staunchly. "I'm staying there, too."

"So I hear." Dick's upper lip curled disdainfully as he looked Toby up and down, but his manic grin flicked back into place when he returned his attention to me. "Having a fine time, are you? Enjoying yourself? Seeing the sights? Planning to stay long?"

"We're having a wonderful time, thanks to Toby," I replied, carefully emphasizing Toby's name. "I don't know how long we'll stay. Maybe a couple of weeks, maybe a month, maybe the rest of the summer. We'll just have to see how it goes."

Dick leaned forward and planted his ham-sized fists on the table. "I wouldn't let my wife and kid stay up there with nothing but a little pip-squeak of a college boy to protect them. But maybe you're braver than I am."

Toby stirred, but I signaled for him to keep his seat. I didn't want him to tangle with Dick Major. It would be like a choirboy going head to head with a professional wrestler.

"I'm quite sure that Toby could protect us if the need arose," I said haughtily, "but why should it?"

"Ain't you heard?" Dick leaned closer, until his large, pink, grinning face was mere inches from mine. "The Auerbach place is *cursed.*"

I stared at him openmouthed for a moment, then broke into a peal of laughter. Dick Major couldn't possibly know that I had a foolproof curse-alert system sitting on my bedside table at the

Aerie. If Aunt Dimity had detected the slightest trace of evil in our holiday home, she would have sounded the alarm. Her silence turned Dick's dire pronouncement into a harmless joke.

My reaction seemed to unnerve him. He pulled back, his grin faltering, and looked down at me uncertainly.

"I guess I *am* braver than you," I said, when I could speak. "I don't believe the Aerie's cursed."

"Your order's ready, Dick," called Carrie Vyne.

"Be there in a minute," Dick called back to her. His grin returned full force as he chucked me gently under the chin, saying softly, "Beliefs change, little lady. You'll see."

He left the table, paid for his coffee and pastries at the counter, and gave me a jovial, finger-waggling wave as he left the cafe.

"Wow," said Toby, gazing at me in respectful disbelief. "You could give Maggie Flaxton a run for her money, Lori. I've never heard of *anyone* laughing in Dick Major's face."

"I *wanted* to break his wrist," I said heatedly, rubbing my chin.

"So did I," Toby assured me.

"What did he think I'd do?" I said indignantly. "Tremble in my boots? Did he expect me to pack up and head for the airport because *he* believes in some stupid superstition?"

"I think that's *exactly* what he expected you to do," said Toby. "He was trying to frighten you."

"Well, he failed." I gazed reflectively at the sunburned tourists strolling past the plate-glass window at the front of the cafe. "So the Aerie's cursed, is it? How ridiculous. I've never stayed in a place that's *less* cursed, except for my cottage back in England. The atmosphere up there is good and wholesome. I feel *safe* up there. I've been sleeping through the night for the first time since I was—" I broke off, caught Toby's curious glance, and went on. "I've been sleeping through the night for the first time since I hurt my shoulder."

"How *did* you hurt your shoulder?" he asked.

"I fell off a horse," I lied, avoiding his eyes.

"*Oh,*" Toby said, as if he'd had a sudden revelation. "So *that's* why you're afraid of horses. It must have been a bad fall."

"It was pretty bad, yes, but my *point* is that the Aerie has good vibes," I said.

"I agree," said Toby.

"Mind you," I continued, after a brief, thoughtful silence, "Dick Major's not the only one in town who thinks the Aerie's cursed. It seems to be a popular belief. It would explain why Maggie Flaxton wouldn't spend five minutes up there, and why Greg Wilstead gave me such a frightened-rabbit look when Carrie told him I was staying there."

"Greg *always* looks like a frightened rabbit," Toby put in.

"I'll bet Nick Altman believes in it, too," I went on, ignoring Toby's remark. "He thinks the curse will drive me to drink." I finished my first cookie and reached for a second one. "Why didn't you tell me about the curse, Toby? The kids in town must have clued you in during your summer vacations. Did you ask your grandfather about it?"

"Of course I did." Toby laid aside his fourth Calico Cookie and regarded me intently. "Granddad told me that no rational person would waste so much as a single brain cell thinking about it. He was a doctor, a man of science. He had no use for superstitions."

"What about you?" I pressed.

"I'd like to think I'm a rational person," Toby replied, "not someone who perpetuates idiotic beliefs by passing them on."

"So that's why you didn't mention it to me," I said, nodding.

"That's right," said Toby. "Ghost stories around the campfire are one thing, but curses can get inside people's heads. Granddad would be ashamed of me if I even *pretended* to believe in such tripe, and I'd be ashamed of myself for . . . for worrying you."

"I promise you, I'm not worried," I said. "I'd just like to know more about it. Even rational people take an interest in local legends." I smiled coaxingly. "Come on, Toby, tell me about the curse.

I'm not going to swoon. I'm the woman who laughed in Dick Major's face, remember?"

Toby heaved an exasperated sigh, but gave in, grudgingly. "According to Granddad, a fair number of accidents happened at the old Lord Stuart Mine over the years, a few of them fatal. So many kids and idiot adults got hurt messing around up there that some people—a handful of gullible, superstitious people—started to believe that the place was jinxed."

"How did the accidents happen?" I asked.

"How do you think?" Toby retorted. "When people climb on old mining equipment and goof around inside unstable old buildings, someone's bound to get hurt. It *was* dangerous. That's why Granddad wouldn't let me go up there when I was little. He didn't want me to spend the rest of the summer with a cast on my leg—or worse."

As Toby spoke, I recalled something Aunt Dimity had told me only a few weeks earlier, though it seemed a lifetime ago: *If you want to keep people from visiting a place, you scare them off. You tell them the place is haunted or cursed or unlucky.* It seemed to me that the curse had served a good purpose in the past—to scare children away from an extremely perilous playground—but it was also clear to me that although the curse had outlived its purpose, belief in it lingered on.

"It's not dangerous up there anymore," Toby went on, "not since Mr. Auerbach cleared the site and sealed the mine. And whatever anyone tells you—Maggie, Nick, Greg, Amanda, Dick—"

"Who's Amanda?" I interrupted.

"The local loony-tune," Toby answered shortly. "She has a lot of crack-brained beliefs. But I don't care what *anyone* says, the Aerie *isn't* cursed."

"I never thought it was." I stretched out a placatory hand to him. "Thanks for filling me in."

Carrie Vyne appeared suddenly at our table and seated herself in the chair Arlene Altman had vacated. Although business was picking up, she seemed content to let her two matronly assistants handle the influx of new customers.

"I hope Dick Major didn't say anything to upset you," she said, her kindly face filled with concern. "He doesn't usually show up until dinnertime. I would have chased him off, but——"

"But you've got a business to run," I interrupted, with an understanding nod. "You can't afford to chase off regular customers, even when they're as . . . unusual . . . as Dick."

"He's not from here," said Carrie, as though Dick's nonnative roots explained his uncouth behavior. "He moved to Bluebird two years ago with his wife and teenaged daughter. The daughter got away from him just as soon as she got her driver's license, and his wife took off a couple of weeks later. I reckon she just couldn't take it anymore."

"Take what?" I prompted.

"Living in that dump." Carrie jutted her chin in the general direction of Dick's house. "The whole town's embarrassed by it, but Dick won't lift a finger to clean it up. And he was always quarreling with his neighbors. I reckon his poor wife just got fed up with the whole thing and took off."

"Any self-respecting woman would," I said. "Do you know where he came from?"

"Some place back east," said Carrie. "Claims he moved to the mountains for his health. I wish he'd picked some other mountains." She smiled mischievously. "There's been talk on the town council about officially designating his part of town the Grumpy Old Man Zone."

I chuckled appreciatively, then asked, "What's wrong with his health?"

"He claims that he had some sort of work-related accident back east," Carrie told me. "He must have gotten a good settlement out of his employer because he's been living off of it ever since."

"Is he on medication?" I asked, recalling Dick's strange, unblinking gaze.

"If he is, he doesn't get it from Dandy Don's," said Carrie. "And I haven't heard of him getting any packets in the mail."

I was beginning to love this woman. She was better informed than an FBI agent.

"I wonder what happened to him?" I said. "He looked pretty fit to me, apart from the beer belly."

"Could be his back," Carrie reasoned, cocking her head to one side. "Back troubles are hard to see, but they can lay you out in no time flat. They can make you pretty grouchy, too. I had sciatica once, and I was a perfect misery to everyone in sight until it cleared up."

We discussed the agony of sciatica for a while, moved from there to arthritis and rheumatism, and wound our way through the perils of asthma, allergies, and migraines before I managed to steer the conversation back in the direction I wanted it to go.

"I've heard that Dick was pretty hard on James Blackwell, the guy who used to have Toby's job at the Aerie," I said.

"Oh, he was just terrible to James," Carrie acknowledged, nodding sadly.

"Did he get physical?" I asked.

"Do you mean, did he beat James up?" Carrie shook her head rapidly. "Oh no, Dick's not like that, not like that at all. He's never raised a hand to anyone. He just enjoys getting under people's skin." Carrie crossed her forearms on the table and leaned forward, the classic pose of the experienced rumormonger. "He used to pass remarks to James when James was in here. Arlene Altman said he used to do the same thing to him at the saloon. After a while, James just stopped coming to town. The next thing I knew, he was gone. It's a pity. He was a nice man."

I folded my own forearms on the table to signal that I, too, was ready to get down to some serious gossip-swapping. "Dick told *me* that the Aerie was cursed."

"Not *that* old thing again!" Carrie snorted impatiently. "No one hardly talked about it until the Auerbachs built their place, and then it all started up again, same as before. I tell you, some people will believe anything. I hope Dick didn't rattle you."

"He didn't," I said, "but maybe he rattled James. I heard that James was trying to find out if some stories he'd heard were true. Maybe the stories were the ones Dick told him about the curse. Maybe Dick got under his skin deeply enough to make him *believe* in the curse."

"I doubt it," said Carrie. "Only dimwits and children take things like that seriously, and James Blackwell wasn't a dimwit or a child. He had a good head on his shoulders. He was a well-educated, well-read man. Always had a book with him when he came to my cafe, and he was polite, well spoken. I miss him."

Her words tweaked a memory that had been lurking in the back of my mind, a memory I'd failed to mention to Aunt Dimity. It was something Brett Whitcombe had said while we watched the twins ride at the Brockman Ranch. *James used to drop in on us now and again. He took an interest in local history. Asked all sorts of questions. Wanted to know what Bluebird was like in the olden days.*

"An amateur historian," I murmured, half to myself.

"Pardon?" said Carrie.

I put even more weight on my forearms and peered intently at her. "I heard that James Blackwell was interested in local history. Maybe he learned something about Bluebird's past that made him believe in Dick's story about the curse."

"I can't imagine what it could be," said Carrie, "but if you want to know about local history, you should talk to Rose Blanding. She's Pastor Blanding's wife. She runs the Bluebird Historical Society in the old school building, where the tourist information office is, but only from nine to one, when Claudia Lechat takes over."

"The artist," I said, recalling the sign in the art gallery's window.

"Claudia does a little bit of everything." Carrie chuckled softly. "She even designed a road sign for the Grumpy Old Man Zone. But if you want to know about local history, talk to Rose Blanding. She's the expert. She and Pastor Blanding live right next door to Good Shepherd Lutheran, out along the lake. Toby can show you the way. She'll be home by one-fifteen."

"I wouldn't want to bother her at home," I protested.

"It's no bother," Carrie assured me, waving off my objection. "Rose is a pastor's wife. Her door's always open to everyone. You don't even have to be a Lutheran." She looked around at the rapidly filling tables and smiled apologetically. "Well, I could sit here and talk with you all day, Lori, but I guess I'd better get back to work. The lunch crowd's arriving."

"You can take our order before you go," Toby suggested. He looked at me and shrugged. "We may as well stay for lunch. We have an hour to kill before we visit Mrs. Blanding."

"I'll have whatever Toby's having," I said without hesitation. "I'd also like to bring a box of Calico Cookies back to the Aerie. My sons have noticed that the cookie jar up there is depressingly empty."

Carrie lowered her eyes modestly. "Do you think your little boys will like my cookies?"

"I know they will," I said with absolute conviction.

Mindful of my promise to Aunt Dimity, I didn't explain that Will and Rob had already fallen in love with Carrie Vyne's cookies, half a world away.

Eleven

*C*arrie Vyne presented Toby and me with the perfect meal to carry us through until dinnertime: a bowl of tasty cream of broccoli soup, a hunk of sourdough bread, a generous wedge of quiche lorraine, and a small bunch of sweet red grapes, all of it homemade, except for the grapes, but even they came from a Colorado vineyard. At one o'clock we gathered up our belongings, paid our bill, thanked Carrie for her hospitality, and departed.

Toby pointed out various landmarks and reminisced about his childhood as we strolled down Stafford Avenue toward the lake, but I was too preoccupied to give him my full attention. He carried the box of Calico Cookies, I had my bag of goodies from Dandy Don's, and we both wore wide-brimmed hats and dusty hiking boots. We would have looked like a pair of carefree tourists if I hadn't been so pensive and so silent.

The more I thought about it, the more certain I became that I'd been wrong to blame James Blackwell's abrupt abandonment of the Aerie on Dick Major's bullying. I was now convinced that James had fled the Aerie because of the celebrated curse. Danny Auerbach's former employee might have been the most sensible person in the world, but I knew better than most that the right set of circumstances could spook anyone.

If a man had ever been in the right place at the right time to be well and truly spooked, I told myself, it had been James. He'd lived alone at the Aerie for nearly six months. He'd been just far enough away from Bluebird to feel isolated, and since neither the Auerbachs nor any of their friends had come to stay at the Aerie during that time, he'd had nothing to keep him occupied but a few routine chores. He would have had plenty of free time to wonder if the rumors he'd heard were true. And he'd heard those rumors, as I had, not just from Dick Major, but from responsible adults all over town.

It seemed to me that if James Blackwell was as well educated as Carrie Vyne thought he was, his natural inclination would be to find out more about the rumors. He'd ask Brett Whitcombe questions, look through the books in the Aerie's library, perhaps bring one with him to read while he sipped coffee at the cafe. He might also pay a visit to the local historical society.

He'd be told by some that the curse was blatant nonsense, by others that it was God's own truth, but with a hungry mind and plenty of time on his hands, he'd go on searching until, somewhere, he'd find a clue that tipped the balance away from reason and toward superstition. It wasn't hard to imagine what could have happened next.

James would lie awake in the dead of night, turning the clue over in his mind, and odd noises that had never bothered him before would make him flinch. A simple stumble would remind him of the host of injuries—some of them fatal—that had inspired the local legend. He'd begin to sleep less, to stumble more, until fear finally overcame common sense.

As an educated, intelligent man, he'd be too embarrassed to explain his misgivings to his employer. In the end, he'd pack his bags and leave, without giving notice, without leaving a forwarding address—he'd leave as suddenly and inexplicably as the Auerbachs had left.

"I wonder if Florence Auerbach knows about the curse?" I mused aloud.

"I have no idea," said Toby testily. "And I don't know how you can fill your head with such drivel when you have"—he swept his arm through the air—"*this* to look at."

"Huh? What?" I snapped out of my reverie and realized with a start that Toby had led me away from Stafford Avenue to the gravelly west shore of Lake Matula and one of the prettiest sights I'd yet seen.

The long, narrow lake lay at our feet, a light breeze wrinkling its surface into a million fluid facets that sparkled like fool's gold in the sun. To our left and slightly above us stood a white-painted church, its spire gleaming against a backdrop of dark pines. Next to it stood a large Victorian house with a wraparound porch, a turret that rivaled the church's spire in height, and a veritable sampler of lacy gingerbread trim. The house was painted a demure shade of dove gray, but nothing could disguise its flamboyant architecture.

"It's fantastic," I said, laughing with delight. "Like something out of a fairy tale."

"I'm glad you noticed," Toby said sarcastically. "It's the parsonage, where Mr. and Mrs. Blanding live." He scuffed the toe of his hiking boot in the gravel. "I wish you'd never heard about the curse, Lori. If you're not careful, you'll become obsessed by it."

"If I show the slightest sign of obsession," I said lightly, "you have my permission to throw me in the lake."

"I'll do it," Toby warned, shaking an index finger at me.

"I know you will." I hooked my arm through his. "Come on. Let's see if Mrs. Blanding is at home."

It took us five minutes to walk the rest of the way to the parsonage. The front door was open, as Carrie Vyne had told us it would be, but the screen door was shut. As I raised my hand to ring the doorbell, we heard voices approaching from within. Toby recognized them at once.

"It's Rufe and Lou Zimmer," he said, his face brightening. "You'll like the Zimmer brothers, Lori. There's no one else like them on earth."

After my experiences at the Brockman Ranch and Caroline's Cafe, I was more than ready to challenge the veracity of his last statement, but I held my tongue, a feat that became increasingly difficult to do when the men in question finally tottered into view.

The Zimmer brothers were tiny, ancient, and utterly identical, from the tips of their brown wingtip shoes to the tops of their bald heads. They carried matching straw boaters in their identical right hands and wore matching gold cuff links in the cuffs of their starched white shirts. Their shirts were tucked into pleated cream-colored trousers held up by matching pairs of red suspenders. When they spoke, they sounded so much alike that I wouldn't have been able to tell them apart in the dark. The only reason I could tell them apart in daylight was that one of them held a brown briefcase in his left hand.

". . . mighty kind of you, Rose," said the one holding the briefcase. "We'll be sure . . ."

". . . to bring the maps back when we're done with them," continued the other. "Shouldn't take us too long . . ."

". . . to work out where the Escalante forge used to be," the first went on. "Old Lou thinks it was on First Street . . ."

". . . and old Rufe swears it was on Third," said Lou. "But we'll work it out. We surely do . . ."

". . . appreciate the loan," finished Rufe.

"Oh . . . my . . . Lord," I breathed.

Despite my previous encounters with Bluebird's army of doppelgangers, I was dizzied by déjà vu. Rufe and Lou Zimmer appeared to be the exact male equivalents of the ancient, identical Pym sisters, who lived up the road from me in Finch. They even talked in the same ping-ponging fashion. If I hadn't been clinging to Toby's arm, I would have keeled over from the shock.

Rufe and Lou were accompanied by a slender, middle-aged woman with salt-and-pepper hair and a sun-burnished face. She was dressed for the warm weather in a rose-colored linen skirt, a sleeveless white silk blouse, and extremely sensible shoes. Although she had the refined, slightly pedantic manner of an old-fashioned schoolmistress, I assumed that she was Rose Blanding, the minister's wife.

"Please, take your time," she urged the brothers. "There's no need to bring the maps back quickly. I know you'll take good care of them." She glanced up, saw me and Toby through the screen door, and smiled broadly. "Why, look, boys, I have more visitors."

"It's young Tobe!" Rufe exclaimed.

Identical smiles lit the Zimmer brothers' faces as Mrs. Blanding ushered them out onto the porch. They greeted Toby fondly, asked after his family, and told him he'd grown at least two inches since they'd last seen him. Toby then conducted a round of introductions that turned out to be for my benefit rather than theirs. The Zimmers and Mrs. Blanding already knew who I was, where I was staying, and with whom.

"Rufus and Louis are Bluebird's oldest citizens," Mrs. Blanding informed me, beaming at the two elderly men. "Though, technically, Rufe is older than Lou by two minutes. Their birth certificates are on display at the historical society."

Rufe nodded. "Some people think we founded the town . . ."

". . . but we're not *that* old," said Lou.

The brothers chuckled wheezily, then turned to Toby.

"So, tell us, Tobe," said Rufe, "have you had any trouble . . ."

". . . up at the Auerbach place?" Lou asked.

"None," Toby declared, with a touch of impatience. "Everyone's healthy, happy, and having a great time."

"Hope your luck holds." Rufe glanced down at the briefcase. "Well, we'll get out of your way. We got us some map-reading to do. Mighty pleased to meet you, Lori. Hope to meet your boys . . ."

". . . one of these days," said Lou. "*And* their pretty nanny."

The Zimmer brothers winked simultaneously, placed their boaters on their heads at identical angles, and tottered down the stairs. I shook my head to clear it, but it didn't help because Rose Blanding reminded me so forcibly of Lilian Bunting, who was married to the vicar of St. George's Church in Finch. In this instance, however, the resemblance made a certain sort of sense to me. The wives of vicars and ministers probably had a lot in common, I reasoned, no matter where they lived.

"Will they get home all right, Mrs. Blanding?" I asked, observing the brothers' unsteady progress along the lakeside path.

"They'll be fine," she assured me. "Rufe and Lou may look frail, but they're as tough as old axe handles."

"Of course they are," I murmured. "Just like the Pyms."

"If I'm to call you Lori," she went on, "you must call me Rose. Please, leave your things in the hall and come into the front parlor. Can I get you a bite to eat or a cold drink? It looks as though you hiked down from the Aerie."

We left our packs and packages on a table in the entrance hall and followed Rose into a high-ceilinged, spacious room overlooking Lake Matula. While Toby refused her offer of refreshments, explaining that we'd had lunch at the cafe, I took in the front parlor.

There was a lot to take in. The house's demurely painted exterior concealed an interior that paid unrestrained tribute to grand Victorian style. The tables were made of heavily carved walnut, the chairs and sofas were upholstered in lush fabrics, and the walls were covered in a flocked wallpaper that imitated silk brocade. Layers of drapes drawn back by tasseled cords hung at the tall windows, and a large rug with a swirling floral pattern covered the polished hardwood floor.

Dainty whatnot shelves displayed a splendid collection of Victoriana: beaded reticules, kid leather baby shoes, embroidered gloves, tiny spectacles, cobalt-blue medicine bottles, impossibly elaborate Valentine's Day cards, and feathered fans. A stereopticon sat on a small, marble-topped table near the love seat in the bay window and a voluminous silk paisley shawl had been draped over the baby grand piano. Toby and I sat on the fringed, bottle-green velvet sofa, and Rose sat opposite us on a button-backed easy chair with low arms and braided trimming.

"You have a lovely home," I said, as soon as we were seated.

"Do you like it?" Rose asked, as her gaze made a leisurely circuit around the room. "It was once a bordello."

"A . . . a *bordello*?" I gaped at her in astonishment. "Next door to a *church*?"

"Not originally, but the situation did occur." Rose leaned back in the easy chair and shrugged nonchalantly. "It could hardly be avoided. At one time houses of prostitution outnumbered schools and churches in Bluebird by a factor of twenty to one."

My eyebrows shot up. "That's a lot of . . . entertainment . . . for such a small community."

"Bluebird wasn't small back then," said Rose. "Nearly eleven thousand people lived in the valley in 1865, and the vast majority of them—" She stopped short and tilted her head toward Toby. "Forgive me, Toby, I cast no aspersions on your noble sex, but the truth remains that the vast majority of the early residents were men. I'm sure there were some who didn't require such *entertainment,* as you so delicately put it, Lori, but evidently many of them did."

"Evidently," I said, smiling wryly.

"So many of them were single, you see," Rose continued, "or acted as if they were. Gold fever struck office workers, salesmen, farmers, and factory workers not only because it offered them a chance to get rich quickly, but also because it offered them a chance to escape the restrictive lives they'd led back East—to throw off their traces and kick up their heels."

"Hence, the multitude of bordellos," I put in.

"And drinking establishments and gambling hells. But respectable women came to Bluebird, eventually, and tamed some of its wilder aspects." Rose paused, lowered her eyes, and smiled self-consciously. "Forgive me. I'm lecturing. It's an occupational hazard when one is both preacher's wife *and* president of a historical society."

"Don't stop," I said. "It's fascinating. I had no idea that Bluebird used to be a metropolis."

Rose seemed only too pleased to carry on. "From 1865 to 1870, Bluebird's population doubled. Butchers, barbers, bakers, blacksmiths—every type of tradesman was needed to serve the mines and the miners, and many of the tradesmen brought their families with them."

"Families that needed schools and churches," I said, nodding.

"And much more," said Rose. "In its heyday, Bluebird had an opera house, a theater, a newspaper, two hotels, five boarding houses, seven law offices, four debating societies, countless gambling hells, saloons, and brothels, and no fewer than seven churches. I'd have to consult a reference book to give you the exact number of shops that once lined Bluebird's streets, but you could find almost anything here that you could find in Denver. Passenger trains stopped here seven times a day."

I gazed at her incredulously. "What happened? Not that Bluebird isn't lovely as it is," I added hastily, "but it's not exactly *metropolitan*."

"Boom and bust," Rose replied succinctly. "The price of silver plummeted in 1893, when the country went on the gold standard. The silver claims dried up, the miners moved on to other jobs, and businesses failed. Bluebird shrank. By 1930, there were fewer than a thousand people living in the Vulgamore Valley. The state authorities selected the valley as a good place to build a reservoir partly because there were so few people left to displace."

"Hold on a minute," I said, glancing toward the bay window. "Are you telling me that the town of Bluebird used to be where Lake Matula is now?"

"Yes," Rose said brightly, "and I can prove it. Would you like to see a photograph of Bluebird at the height of its prosperity?"

"Very much," I said.

Rose left the front parlor and returned a moment later carrying a framed, oblong, sepia-toned photograph that was at least three feet in length. Toby and I made room for her to sit between us and she propped the photograph on her lap for us to see.

"It's a composite photograph," she explained, "a collage made in 1888 by a photographer named Mervyn Blount. Mr. Blount came to the valley in the early days to document the prospectors' lives, and stayed on to photograph the burgeoning town. He was quite the outdoorsman. He took these photos from a vantage point halfway up Ruley's Peak, and that's a difficult mountain to climb."

I peered curiously at the panoramic view Mervyn Blount had pieced together from separate photographs. The Vulgamore Valley was scarcely recognizable. Buildings of all shapes and sizes jostled for space along streets that ran parallel to a narrow stream—"Bluebird Creek," Rose informed me—at the very bottom of the valley. Railroad tracks emerged from the serpentine canyon we'd passed through on the way from Denver to Bluebird, and great swathes of forest were missing from the surrounding slopes.

"Where are the trees?" I asked in dismay.

"Propping up mine shafts, heating stoves, housing machinery and people," Rose replied matter-of-factly. "Mining was not kind to the environment in those days. It still isn't." She pointed to a blurred complex of wooden buildings halfway up the northern wall of the valley. "The Lord Stuart Mine stayed open a bit longer than the silver mines because it produced gold, but the gold vein played out, as gold veins always do, and it closed in 1896."

"And forty years later, they built the reservoir and drowned the town," I said sadly.

"There wasn't much of a town left by the time they flooded the valley." Rose's fingers drifted from left to right over the photograph. "Long before the reservoir was built, a series of flash floods had driven the remaining townspeople to higher ground at the valley's western end. They'd already salvaged what they could from the ruins of the old town."

"Danny Auerbach followed their example," I commented. "He reused timber from the old mine buildings when he built the Aerie."

"Waste not, want not." Rose pointed to the photograph. "The parsonage was built where it now stands, but Good Shepherd's loyal congregation dismantled the church in 1934, a year before construction began on the reservoir, and moved it to its present location."

"Next door to a bordello?" I said questioningly.

Rose laughed. "My house was used as a bordello for only a few years, after which it was occupied by a series of fine, upstanding families. Still, my husband and I had to do a great deal of restoration work on it when we came to Bluebird, thirty-five years ago. Fortunately, the town was in the midst of a resurgence then, thanks to the outdoor adventure trade. We mine tourists now, instead of gold and silver." She swiveled her head from side to side. "Iced tea, anyone? Please say yes. I've talked myself dry!"

"Iced tea sounds great," said Toby, "but let me carry the photograph for you."

After he and Rose had left the room, I walked over to the bay window to gaze at the reservoir. I tried to superimpose Mervyn Blount's sepia-toned image of the bustling town onto Lake Matula, but I couldn't manage it. It was almost impossible for me to imagine clouds of smoke fouling the crystalline sky, train whistles blotting out birdsong, a vigorous community filling the Vulgamore Valley from end to end.

Rose and Toby returned, with Toby balancing a cut-glass pitcher and three tall glasses on a rosewood tray. He placed the tray on a round table next to Rose's easy chair, and resumed his seat while she filled glasses and passed them to us. I hadn't realized how thirsty I was until I took my first sip of iced tea, and Rose appeared to enjoy hers thoroughly.

"Ah, that's better," she said, after she'd drained half her glass.

"You know," I mused aloud, "Danny Auerbach would never have been allowed to tear down and recycle the old mine buildings in England, where I live. There, they'd be praised for their historic value and preserved by the National Trust."

"The site of the Lord Stuart Mine was a hazardous eyesore," Rose stated firmly. "It's also private property, so Mr. Auerbach was well within his rights to do with it as he pleased. The Auerbachs have owned land up there since 1860, when they bought out the claims of a few hardscrabble prospectors. Fortunately, they invested the profits from the mine wisely, so even when it closed, they prospered. Unlike their workers," she added, a note of disapproval entering her voice, "most of whom lived a hand-to-mouth existence. But don't get me started on working conditions in the mines. I'd bore you to death."

"You haven't so far," I told her earnestly. "You've opened my eyes to a whole new world. I've enjoyed every minute."

"Thank you," said Rose. "I'm always glad to share my knowledge of Bluebird's past."

"What about its folk legends?" I asked.

Toby heaved a despondent sigh, as if he knew where my question would lead and wished I wouldn't go there. Ice clinked as Rose took another sip of iced tea before answering.

"It's said that on a still night church bells can be heard beneath the waters of Lake Matula," she said, her eyes dancing. "There's even talk of a ghost train running along the tracks at the bottom of the lake." She chuckled indulgently and shook her head. "Long winters make for tall tales."

"Have you heard the church bells?" I asked.

"Certainly not," Rose said good-humoredly, "and those who think they have, have spent far too much time in Altman's Saloon."

"So I suppose a sighting of the ghost train is out of the question," I said.

"You suppose correctly. Even if I believed in the legend, the water isn't clear enough for anyone to see all the way to the bottom of the lake." Rose's gray eyes narrowed shrewdly. "I think I can guess why you're interested in ghost trains and phantom church bells, Lori. You've heard about the curse, haven't you?"

I nodded. "I'd like to hear more."

"Why?" Rose asked sharply. "Do you believe in such things?"

"No," I said, "but I find them interesting. Why do so many people in town still believe in the curse when it no longer serves a useful purpose?"

Rose placed her glass on the tray, rested her elbows on the easy chair's arms, and tented her fingers. "What useful purpose did it serve?"

"If it scared children away from the site," I said, "it probably saved a few lives."

"I see." Rose frowned slightly. "Who told you about the curse?"

"The usual suspects," Toby interpolated, rolling his eyes, "but I plead guilty to giving Lori the gory details, after she badgered me for them."

"What details did you give her?" Rose inquired.

Toby shrugged. "I told her what my grandfather told me. Kids used to get hurt playing on the old mining equipment. So many children were injured that people began to believe the site was jinxed."

"If only it were so simple. . . ." Rose tapped the tips of her thumbs together, then stood. She crossed to a small secretaire in the corner and took a modern brass key from one of its drawers. She slipped the key into her skirt pocket before asking, "Are you up for a walk?"

"You bet," I said, getting to my feet. "Toby's whipped me into shape."

"I'm always up for a walk," Toby chimed in.

"Good." Rose turned toward the entrance hall and motioned for us to follow her. "If you want to hear the true story behind the Lord Stuart curse, come with me."

Twelve

*T*oby and I retrieved our hats and sunglasses as we passed through the entrance hall, and Rose donned a straw hat that could have served as a small parasol, tying its rose-colored ribbons firmly beneath her chin before we went outside. There was no need for her to change into hiking boots. Her chunky, thick-soled shoes looked sturdy enough to handle all but the roughest terrain.

Although she pulled the front door shut as we left the parsonage, she didn't lock it.

"Have you ever been burgled?" I asked, as Toby and I followed her down the stairs.

"Not once in thirty-five years." She pointed to the rows of houses that rose in terraced ranks along Bluebird's steeply inclined streets. "Burglars don't prosper in Bluebird. There are too many eyes watching from behind too many curtains. It's one of the great advantages of having nosey neighbors."

"True," I said, thinking nostalgically of Finch's ceaselessly twitching curtains. "Nothing goes unnoticed in a small town."

"Not for long, at any rate," Rose added wisely.

She led us through Bluebird's back lanes, pausing to greet everyone we met along the way, to St. Barbara's Catholic Church, which stood at the top of Garnet Street, on the north side of the valley. Behind the church a dirt road climbed up the mountainside and disappeared into the forest. When Rose turned toward the dirt road, Toby stopped abruptly.

"I know where we're going," he said, eyeing the road unhappily.

"I knew you would," said Rose, "but let's keep it as a surprise for Lori."

"Some surprise," Toby muttered, but he walked on.

The road was wide enough for the three of us to walk comfortably side by side and shady enough for me to wish I'd brought my sweatshirt. It was properly maintained, as well, and cut at a gentle grade that made walking uphill a breeze. We'd climbed for no more than fifteen minutes when a ten-foot-wide iron gate came into view. Patches of rust showed through the gate's flaking layers of white paint, and above it an archway of lacy ironwork contained the words: BLUEBIRD CEMETERY.

"We're going to a cemetery?" I exclaimed, clasping my hands to my breast. "I *love* cemeteries."

"You do?" Toby looked at me as though I'd slipped a cog.

"I *always* visit cemeteries when I travel," I told him. "They're quiet and serene and—"

"Filled with dead bodies," Toby inserted, wrinkling his nose in distaste.

"They're filled with the past as well," I said, bubbling over with enthusiasm. "You can learn a lot about a place by visiting its graveyards. Isn't that right, Rose?"

"I couldn't have put it better myself," she said. "Shall we proceed?"

The gate was chained and padlocked, but Rose opened the lock with the key she'd taken from the secretaire, slid the chain around the gate post, and left it dangling. When she'd finished, Toby pushed the gate aside, and I stepped into a glade so lovely it took my breath away.

It was like a small cathedral, with pillars of white-barked aspens and a roof of sun-drenched leaves that glowed as richly as stained glass. The dirt road served as the center aisle, with a web of sunken paths winding from it through a maze of headstones, crosses, markers, and monuments. Above us, choirs of birds twittered among the shivering aspen leaves, as if to emphasize the sylvan silence that descended when they stopped.

"It's beautiful," I said softly.

Rose nodded her agreement, but Toby was clearly unmoved by our surroundings.

"For heaven's sake, Lori," he said impatiently. "You don't have to whisper. You won't disturb anyone."

"It's a sacred place," I retorted.

"For worms, maybe," he countered.

"What kind of comment is *that?*" I said, frowning at him.

"An honest one." He frowned back at me, then hung his head and muttered angrily, "We buried my grandparents here last year. It's not my favorite place to be, okay?"

"Oh," I said, brought up short. "I didn't realize . . . I'm so sorry, Toby. Do you want to leave?"

"No, he doesn't." Rose placed a comforting hand on Toby's shoulder. "Try to think of this place as your grandfather thought of it, Toby—as a repository of history. He used to spend a lot of time up here."

Toby's head came up. "He did?"

"He found it fascinating. You will, too, if you give it a chance." Rose gave his shoulder an encouraging squeeze. "Are you staying?"

"Yeah." Toby took a deep breath and glanced at us apologetically. "I'm staying."

"Then come along," Rose said briskly.

Toby and I followed Rose along the dirt road and onto a sunken path that branched off from it, to our right. I suspected that she would have moved at a faster clip if I hadn't expressed a keen interest in graveyards. As it was, she walked slowly enough for me to read the headstones whose inscriptions hadn't been obliterated by the passage of time.

It was like reading a roll call of nineteenth-century immigrants: Evgeny Krasikov, Padraig Doherty, Helmut Grauberger, Esteban Fernandez, Miroslav Simzisko, Leslinka Turek, and Alexis Laytonikis were just a few of the resoundingly ethnic names that caught my eye.

"It's like the United Nations up here," I marveled.

"It is," Rose agreed. "People from all over the world came to the Rocky Mountains to seek their fortunes. Bluebird even had a small Chinese community as well as a handful of Sikhs from northern India. Imagine the journeys they made to get here."

"In England," I said, as we continued down the path, "the old graveyards are near churches. Why is Bluebird's so far away from town?"

"Economics, for one thing," Rose replied. "At the time the cemetery was created, town property was too expensive to waste on the dead, and much of the rest of the Vulgamore Valley was being mined. The ground here is relatively easy to dig, fairly level, and as far as we know, devoid of valuable gems or minerals." She paused before a row of twelve simple stone markers, each bearing the name Shuttleworth. "People were also afraid of contagion. Epidemics were not unknown in mining communities."

"What kind of epidemics?" I asked.

"Dysentery, cholera, measles, malaria, diphtheria, smallpox . . ." Rose kept her eyes trained on the headstones as she reeled off the long list of diseases. "The scourges that spring up wherever malnourished people live in overcrowded conditions with poor sanitation. Influenza killed the entire Shuttleworth family, from the infant son to the grandmother. Their church had to bury them."

"The good old days," murmured Toby, gazing somberly at the Shuttleworths' graves.

"It wasn't Disney World," Rose acknowledged. She bent to lay a hand on the smallest headstone, then walked on. "Miners' lives were difficult and dangerous. Those who weren't killed by disease died in mining accidents or froze to death or drowned. Some drank themselves to death, some committed suicide. Others were shot or stabbed in drunken brawls. A few were hanged."

"Frontier justice at work?" I said.

"So-called frontier justice was swift and sure," Rose said sardonically, "but I'm not sure how often it was just. And, of course, silicosis took many miners' lives." She noted my puzzled expression and explained, "Silicosis is a form of pneumonia caused by breathing air filled with silica dust. Respirators didn't exist back then."

"Good grief," I said, pressing my hands to my chest. Rose's litany of woes seemed at odds with the earlier picture she'd painted of Bluebird. "How could they build an opera house in the midst of so much misery?"

"They needed the opera house—and the debating societies and the baseball teams—to take them away from the misery," said Rose. "Besides, their expectations were different from ours. They had no antibiotics, no advanced surgical techniques. To them, disease and death were an accepted part of life—dreadful, yes, but accepted."

"Not everyone died young, though." Toby had crouched down to examine the inscription on an unusually elaborate marker: a white marble plinth surmounted by a kneeling, weeping angel with folded wings. "Hannah Lavery lived to be eighty-five."

"Dear Hannah." Rose spoke with real animation for the first time since we'd passed through the entrance gate, as though she were speaking of a friend she'd known and loved. "Hannah Lavery was the daughter of a wealthy mine owner, an exceptional girl who became a truly remarkable woman. When Hannah saw suffering, she refused to look the other way. She spent her entire life working for the welfare of miners and their families. She died in Washington, D.C., still lobbying for humane labor laws, but she wished to be buried here, among the people whose struggles had first awakened her conscience."

"She never married," I observed.

"Victorian men of her class preferred passive women to rabble-rousers," said Rose. "But I find that crusaders in every age have difficulty finding suitable mates. It isn't easy to give one's heart to a man as well as a cause."

I ran my fingers along the angel's folded wings, then walked ahead of my companions, drawn by a monumental monument that stood silhouetted against a ponderosa pine at the end of the path.

The gleaming white marble obelisk towered over the phalanx of rough-cut red-granite headstones that surrounded it, and its inscription had been beautifully chiseled.

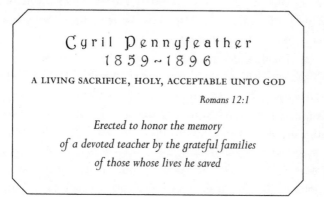

Cyril Pennyfeather
1859~1896

A LIVING SACRIFICE, HOLY, ACCEPTABLE UNTO GOD

Romans 12:1

Erected to honor the memory
of a devoted teacher by the grateful families
of those whose lives he saved

"Who was Cyril Pennyfeather?" I asked when Toby and Rose had caught up with me.

"He was a schoolmaster," Rose replied. "He came to the United States from England in 1880 and made his way to Bluebird in 1884. He and the men who lie buried near him died in the Lord Stuart mining disaster of 1896."

I blinked at her, looked back at the obelisk, and began silently to count the red-granite markers surrounding it.

"Twenty," I said finally. "Twenty men died in one accident—twenty-one, counting Cyril." I turned to Rose. "What happened?"

"A catastrophic cave-in," she answered. "No one knows what caused it. Some claimed that the mine manager had bought poor-quality wood to prop the shaft in which the cave-in occurred, but nothing was ever proved. The shaft was never excavated, and the mine closed shortly thereafter."

"What was a schoolteacher doing in a mine?" asked Toby.

"Many of his pupils or former pupils worked there," Rose told him. "When he heard about the cave-in, he went up to see if there was anything he could do to help. He led at least a dozen men to safety before he, too, was killed by falling rock." She nodded toward the inscription. "As you can see, the families of those he rescued raised money to pay for his memorial. He was much loved even before his death. After it . . ." Rose looked from me to Toby and back to me again. "After it, rumors of a curse began to circulate."

"Ah," I said as understanding dawned. "The Lord Stuart curse."

"Correct," said Rose. "I'm convinced that the Lord Stuart Mine closed because there was no more gold to be had from it, but others believe differently. When my husband and I first came to Bluebird, Rufe and Lou Zimmer took us up to the old mine site and told us about the disaster. Afterward, they brought us here, to show us the graves of those who'd died. They explained to us that the cave-in was the culmination of a series of fatal accidents that had plagued the Lord Stuart Mine almost from its inception. They held that the mine would have closed in 1896, even if the mother lode hadn't played out."

"Because of the curse?" I said.

Rose nodded. "Miners are superstitious, as men in hazardous occupations frequently are. If they came to believe in the curse, they might have been reluctant to work in the Lord Stuart."

"You can't run a mine without miners," I commented.

"I don't think the curse had anything to do with the mine closing," said Toby, shaking his head. "Don't you see? It was a cover-up. The mine owner closed the Lord Stuart to keep people from finding out about the substandard wood. A scandal like that wouldn't sit well with his investors."

"Maybe he invented the curse to keep inquisitive people away from the mine," I suggested, "and the accidents your grandfather told you about—the ones that happened in later years—reinforced the original lie."

"But why do they *still* believe in the curse?" Toby demanded. "The mine closed over a century ago. There's not a trace of it left aboveground. No one's ever been injured at the Aerie, much less died, but people *still* think it's risky to stay there."

"We still celebrate Gold Rush Days in Bluebird," Rose reminded him. "For some people, the past is always present. Your predecessor, for example, was deeply interested in the history of the Lord Stuart Mine."

"James Blackwell?" I said, suddenly alert.

"James came to the historical society toward the end of February," Rose said. "He wanted information about the mine. He already had reference books—Mrs. Auerbach collects them, apparently—so he didn't need to borrow ours, but I lent him newspaper clippings, photographs, town records, pamphlets, and other ephemera. He returned a few weeks later to ask for details about the 1896 disaster."

"Did you tell him about the curse?" I asked.

"I didn't have to," said Rose. "He'd already heard about it in town—yes, Toby, from the usual suspects. James wanted to know if the legend was based in fact. I told him exactly what I've told you and left him to draw his own conclusions."

"Did he seem disturbed by the information you gave him?" I asked.

"Not particularly." Rose shrugged. "But I have to confess that I didn't monitor his reactions very closely. I was busy at the time, developing the society's summer event and exhibition schedule." She glanced at her wristwatch. "I'm sorry to say it, but I have to get back to the parsonage. Maggie Flaxton is dropping by at four o'clock to discuss my role in Gold Rush Days. I don't want to keep her waiting."

"No, you don't," said Toby, shuddering. "Rub Maggie the wrong way and you'll find yourself cleaning up after the burros in the petting zoo. Let's go."

"Wait," said Rose. "I think we have enough time to make one more stop before we leave. Toby, you can lead the way."

⌒

Toby's grandparents had been buried beneath a large red-granite boulder, the kind the twins had clambered over on every one of our hikes. A square patch on one side of the boulder had been smoothed, polished, and etched with his grandparents' names and dates, as well as a simple outline of the mountain range that contained Mount Shroeder's distinctive profile.

"We climbed Mount Shroeder when I was ten years old," Toby recalled. "It was Granddad's favorite one-day climb. He loved the view of the valley from the summit."

"He passed his love on to you," I said. "It's a wonderful inheritance."

Toby squatted down to brush dead leaves from the grave. "I wonder why he didn't tell me about the disaster when I asked about the curse?"

"Being a man of science, I expect he refused to connect the two," I said.

"Yeah." Toby stretched out his hand to touch the boulder. "Because there is no connection, right, Granddad?"

We made sure the gate was firmly chained and padlocked before we left, then started back down the dirt road toward town. After spending so much time in the cemetery's cool shade, it was good to feel the sun's warmth on my skin again.

"Rose," I said, "did Mrs. Auerbach ever ask you about the curse?"

"I've never met Mrs. Auerbach," said Rose. "She wasn't a church-goer and she didn't spend much time in town. She kept herself very much to herself when she and the children were at the Aerie. I imagine Bluebird's attractions pale in comparison to the Aerie's. I've been given to understand that it's a marvelous place."

"Given to understand?" I repeated, surprised. "Do you mean you've never been to the Aerie?"

"Never." She gave me a sidelong glance and a half-guilty smile.

"To be honest, I'm hoping to wangle an invitation from you. I've always wanted to see what it's like inside. Apart from that, I'd like to pick up the material James Blackwell borrowed from the society."

"He never returned the papers he borrowed?" I said.

"He left so suddenly that it probably slipped his mind," said Rose.

"I'll bet it's in the library," I told her. "I'll look for it this evening. If I can't find it, you can help me look for it tomorrow, when you come to lunch. Will one-thirty work for you?"

"I can come earlier, if it's more convenient," Rose offered. "Due to lack of funding, the society is closed Tuesdays, Thursdays, and Sundays."

"How about high noon, then?" I suggested.

"High noon will work perfectly," said Rose, and she walked with a bounce in her step all the way back to the parsonage.

Thirteen

*T*oby and I collected our bags and packages from the hall table and thanked Rose Blanding sincerely for sharing her time as well as her incredible wealth of knowledge with us. I had no trouble believing her when she said that it had been her pleasure. She was a born lecturer, and Toby and I had given her a splendid opportunity to hold forth on a subject that was close to her heart.

We left by the front stairs, but we didn't take the lake path back to town. Instead, we followed a rough track through the stand of pines that shielded the parsonage and the church from the two-lane highway leading into town. Toby explained that, although the alternate route was slightly longer and marginally less scenic than the lake path, taking it would greatly increase our chances of avoiding a run-in with Maggie Flaxton. I backed his decision wholeheartedly, having employed the same tactics frequently in Finch, to avoid a rampaging Peggy Taxman.

Before we left the shelter of the trees, I asked Toby to stop.

"Look," I said, "I didn't know that your grandparents had died so recently. If I'd known, I wouldn't have been so idiotically chirpy when we reached the cemetery. I'm really sorry if spending time there upset you."

"It's okay," said Toby. "It turned out to be pretty interesting. I guess Grandma and Granddad are part of the . . . the repository of history, now."

"They are," I said. "A hundred years from now people will find their headstone as fascinating as we found Cyril Pennyfeather's."

"Only if they have a tour guide like Mrs. Blanding," said Toby.

I was ready to move on, but Toby stayed put, gazing down at me with a faintly troubled expression on his face.

"What's up?" I asked.

"When we were in the cafe," he said slowly, "you told Carrie Vyne that James Blackwell was interested in local history. You knew it *before* Mrs. Blanding told us about his visits to the historical society. How did you find out?"

"Brett Whitcombe," I replied. "He told me that James used to pester him with questions about what Bluebird was like in the olden days. He also told me that James was investigating some 'tomfool stories'—Brett's words, not mine. I think James went to Brett Whitcombe as well as Rose Blanding, looking for information about the Lord Stuart curse."

"Right." Toby pushed his hat back on his head. "The thing is, James left some stuff behind in his apartment—the apartment I'm using now. I would have shipped it to him, but I don't know where to send it."

"No forwarding address," I said, nodding. "Is it the material he borrowed from the historical society?"

"No," said Toby. "It's not books or papers, and I'm sure it belongs to him, not to the historical society—he left the receipts behind, too. I thought he was using it for . . ." His voice trailed off and his gaze wandered to a point somewhere over my right shoulder. "But after hearing Mrs. Blanding, I'm not so sure."

"Not so sure about what?" I asked.

Toby's eyes came back into focus. "I could be wrong. I'll show you when we get back. I'd like to know what you think."

My cell phone rang, frightening a camp-robber bird that had flown over to see if we had any crumbs to share. It flew off, twittering irritably, and I took the call. It was from Annelise, who wanted to know if she and the twins could have dinner at the ranch.

"They're having a cookout," she explained. "Will and Rob are dying to try buffalo burgers."

"What about you?" I asked.

"Belle Whitcombe took me out to see the buffalo calves today," said Annelise. "I'm planning to have a salad for dinner."

"A farmer's daughter turned vegetarian?" I said, feigning surprise. "Those calves must be cute."

"They're *adorable,*" she said. "We'll be back by seven, half past at the latest."

"Have fun," I told her. I put the cell phone back into my pocket and turned to Toby, announcing, "We're on our own for dinner. Annelise and the boys are eating theirs at the ranch."

"We can pick something up at the cafe," he suggested.

"Good idea," I said. "I wanted to go back into town anyway. I need to hit the grocery to pick up a few things for lunch tomorrow, and I'd also like to find a gift for Bill." I held up the bag from Dandy Don's. "Strange as it may seem, my husband isn't into stuffed animals, flower seeds, or earrings."

Toby laughed and we turned our steps once more toward Stafford Avenue. Fortunately, Maggie Flaxton was too busy browbeating a hapless neighbor into participating in Gold Rush Days to notice our presence in her store, so our shopping there went off without a hitch. I then spent twenty minutes meandering in and out of shops, rejecting one tacky souvenir after another, before Toby came up with his brilliant idea.

"How about a geode?" he proposed.

"Fantastic," I gushed. "What's a geode?"

"It's a round, hollow rock," Toby explained. "It doesn't look like much on the outside, but the inside's lined with crystals. When you break a geode in half, it looks like a twinkly cave inside. They're really pretty, but not in a girlish way. Granddad used one in his office as a paperweight."

"A man can never have too many paperweights," I said. "Where do we find geodes?"

"Mystic Crystals," Toby said promptly. "Also known as the rock shop." He began to walk rapidly toward the top of Stafford Avenue. "I hope it's still open. Amanda keeps her own hours."

"Amanda?" I said interestedly, scrambling to keep up with him. "The local loony-tune?"

Toby snorted disparagingly. "Amanda Barrow is Bluebird's resident hippie. She runs a commune in the geodesic dome with her cat, Angelique, and an ever-changing cast of crazies who think the dome sits on a vortex."

"Wouldn't it twirl around?" I said. "Like Dorothy's house in *The Wizard of Oz?*"

"It's not that kind of vortex," said Toby. "According to Amanda, it's a focal point for the mystical energies of the universe. According to me, it's a focal point for people who smoke too much wacky-weed—organically grown wacky-weed, of course."

"Do I detect a faint note of skepticism in your voice?" I asked, suppressing a smile.

"You detect a deafening roar of skepticism in my voice," Toby returned. "Don't get me wrong, I like Amanda well enough, but you never know what belief system she'll subscribe to next. Granddad used to say that she belonged to the goddess-of-the-month club. Grandma called her the queen of hocus-pocus."

"I'll bet she has some interesting theories about the Lord Stuart curse," I said, grinning.

"I'm sure we'll hear all about them," said Toby, "so brace yourself."

"I'm braced," I told him.

I probably could have found Mystic Crystals without Toby's assistance, but I wouldn't have known it was a rock shop. Amanda Barrow ran her business from a small Victorian house that stood between Eric's Mountain Bikes and the Mile High Pies pizza parlor.

The house had been painted an eye-catching shade of hot pink that clashed resoundingly with the fluorescent orange and lime-green sandwich board sitting next to the front door.

The sandwich board advertised a well-rounded menu of metaphysical services—palm reading, tarot-card reading, aura reading, rune casting, crystal-ball gazing, psychic healing, dream analysis, and past-life retrieval—along with aromatherapy, medicinal herbs, meditation aids, and yoga classes. A long-haired white cat lounged in the shop's prominent bay window beneath a dangling display of spinning prisms, wind chimes, dream catchers, and multifaceted crystals.

"Angelique," said Toby, nodding at the white cat.

"I didn't think it was Amanda," I said dryly.

"Couldn't be," Toby joked. "Amanda's a redhead."

I felt as though I'd stepped into the vortex.

"Whoa, hold on, stop . . ." I seized Toby's arm to keep him from entering the shop. "Are you telling me that Amanda Barrow has *red hair*?"

"Yeah," said Toby. "She's got freckles, too. So?"

I put a hand to my head in an attempt to stop the whirling, but the pressure only seemed to magnify the image spinning in my mind of Miranda Morrow, Finch's red-haired, freckle-faced witch, who lived with a black cat named Seraphina.

"Are you okay, Lori?" Toby asked.

"Yes," I managed. "Just a little dizzy."

"I shouldn't have walked so fast," he said contritely. "I always forget that Stafford Avenue goes uphill."

"I'll be fine in a minute," I said.

"Take your time," he urged me. "There's no hurry. The shop's still open."

I closed my eyes, breathed slowly and steadily, and forced myself to concentrate on the myriad of differences between Finch's Miranda Morrow and Bluebird's Amanda Barrow. Miranda conducted her business over the telephone and via the Internet, not in person. She lived in a modest stone cottage, not a geodesic dome, and she didn't have a garish sign on her front gate advertising her profession. The only time I'd seen her read palms was at the Harvest Festival, when she'd played the role of a gypsy fortune-teller in order to raise money for the St. George's Church roof repair fund. No one in Finch—not even Peggy Taxman—had *ever* referred to Miranda Morrow as a loony-tune.

"Okay," I said, when I'd regained a modicum of mental stability. "All better. Take me to the geodes."

"This way," said Toby.

He opened the front door and we stepped into a high-ceilinged, rectangular room filled with the cloying, sickly sweet fragrance of sandalwood. A handful of joss sticks burned in a brass holder next to the cash register on the rear counter. The smoke trailing up from the joss sticks was the only sign of life in the shop, apart from Angelique, who took one look at us, gave an unearthly yowl, and streaked through a bead curtain behind the counter.

"I'll be right with you!" a woman's voice called from beyond the bead curtain.

"Amanda," Toby murmured. "She really shouldn't leave incense burning unattended. If Angelique knocked it over, the place would go up like a tinderbox."

"She shouldn't be burning incense at all," I murmured back. "It's an insult to the pure mountain air."

The room was divided into two distinct spaces. To our right, bathed in the sunlight pouring though the bay window, freestanding glass shelves held candles, stone pyramids, bottles of aromatic oils, packets of incense, brass incense holders, onyx Buddhas, chunks of quartz crystal, strings of stone beads, and baskets of polished rocks. Necklaces, earrings, and bracelets hung from a Peg-Board behind the counter, and a wooden bookcase against the far wall was filled with books on a wide range of metaphysical topics. CDs featuring New Age music complemented the book display.

To our left, shielded from direct daylight by a gauze curtain, sat four wooden chairs, a round wooden table covered with a circle of star-spangled black velvet, and a tall dark-purple cupboard in which, I imagined, Amanda Barrow stored the tools of her trade: crystal ball, tarot cards, rune stones, possibly a Ouija board and some dousing wands as well. The walls on either side of the purple cupboard were decorated with posters illustrating acupuncture points, meridian lines, and the constellations.

Toby ignored the left side of the shop and went directly to a glass shelf displaying a selection of geodes that had already been split in half. They were exactly as he'd described them: dull and boring on the outside, but alive with twinkly amethyst crystalline formations on the inside. I picked one up and carried it to the bay window to look at it in the sunlight.

"It's like the Big Rock Candy Mountain," I said, smiling delightedly. "Bill will love it. He's one of those guys who has everything, but he doesn't have anything like *this*. Thanks, Toby. It was a great idea. I think I'll get one for my father-in-law as well. It'll add a certain something to his law office in Boston."

The bead curtain rattled and I looked over my shoulder as a short, stout, middle-aged woman emerged from the back room. She had to be in her late fifties, but she dressed as if she were still in her teens, wearing a low-cut, embroidered peasant blouse; a flouncy, ankle-length muslin skirt; clunky leather work boots; an apple-seed necklace; and a pair of huge hoop earrings accented with feathers. Her face, chest, and arms were plastered with freckles, and her henna-enhanced red hair fell almost to her waist.

"Hi, Amanda," said Toby.

"Hello, Toby," said Amanda, coming out from behind the counter. "You'll have to forgive Angelique. I don't know what's gotten into her. She's in the back room, hiding under the sink. I tried to get her to come out, but—" Amanda broke off abruptly as she caught sight of me. She gasped, her green eyes opened wide, the color drained from her face, and she raised a trembling finger to point at me.

"Death!" she cried. "You bring *death* with you!"

Fourteen

*A*manda's arm fell and she tottered as though her knees were about to buckle. Toby sighed impatiently, but he thrust the box of Calico Cookies into my hands and hurried over to guide the wobbling woman to a chair at the velvet-covered table. I stood in shocked silence for a moment, then returned the geode to its place on the glass shelves and crept quietly past the gauze curtain to stand a few feet away from Amanda and Toby.

The red-haired mistress of Mystic Crystals sat hunched over the table with her eyes squeezed tightly shut, massaging her temples and talking to herself.

"Yes, yes, I understand now," she muttered. "Angelique saw him, tried to warn me, to prepare me. . . . I should have listened, but how was I to know? Death comes to us unbidden, when we least expect it. Even those of us who see beyond can be taken unawares. . . ."

Toby rolled his eyes expressively, as though to reassure me that Amanda's histrionics were par for the course, then bent over her and asked, "Amanda? Can I get you a drink of water or anything?"

"Water, yes, water," Amanda whispered. "Water to cleanse, to clarify, to purify, to—"

"I'll get it," I said quickly.

I placed the cookies and my bag of souvenirs on an empty chair and headed for the back room. I didn't relish the prospect of facing a yowling Angelique again, but I didn't want to be left alone with Amanda Barrow, either. If she passed out, I doubted that I'd be strong enough to keep her from hitting the floor.

The back room turned out to be a small and remarkably tidy kitchen. After a hasty search, I found a clean glass in a cupboard and approached the sink. I did so with some trepidation, expecting at any moment to feel a set of sharp claws sink into my calf, but Angelique had evidently gotten over whatever had startled her. She leapt onto the draining board and sat there, watching interestedly, while I filled the glass with water. I stroked her fluffy back, then brought the glass to Toby to pass to Amanda. I wasn't sure she'd take it from my hand.

Instead of drinking the water, Amanda dipped her fingertips into it, pressed them to her eyelids, her forehead, and her breast, dipped them again, and flicked little splashes into the air, to the north, south, east, and west. Finally, she opened her eyes, threw her hennaed hair back over her shoulders, and turned slowly toward me. Her green eyes searched the empty space around me avidly before coming to rest on my face.

"He has gone," she announced. "His energy has traveled to another sphere. He didn't like being seen by me or by Angelique. He prefers to move undetected through the physical world."

"Who?" I asked.

"The male spirit who accompanies you," she replied. "Couldn't you sense his presence?"

I felt a prickling sensation on the back of my neck, as if a chill breeze had blown through the room. I knew of only one male spirit who would frighten cats and freak out psychics, and I didn't want him hovering within a hundred miles of me.

"Describe him," I said warily.

Amanda closed her eyes, spread her palms on the table, and breathed deeply through her nostrils. "Light hair. A slight build. The glint of spectacles. No." She frowned in concentration, then corrected herself. "Pince-nez. On a chain."

Tension drained from me. Whoever Amanda was describing, it wasn't Abaddon.

"I'm afraid I don't know what you're talking about," I said.

"He has not yet made himself known to you, though I sense . . ." Amanda peered at me intently, almost hungrily, as if she suspected that I, unlike most people who walked into her shop, had some experience in her chosen field of expertise. "Have you ever been in touch with the other side?"

"The other side of what?" I asked.

"Eternity," she whispered dramatically.

"I don't *think* so." I pursed my lips and frowned slightly. "No, probably not. I'm sure I would have noticed."

Toby sniggered and Amanda waited for me to go on, but I had nothing more to add. I wasn't about to tell the queen of hocus-pocus that I'd been in touch with "the other side" nearly every day for the past seven years. Aunt Dimity was a dear friend, not a psychic phenomenon. I didn't want her name bandied about by a bunch of aging hippies holding seances in the geodesic dome.

Amanda waved a freckled hand toward an empty chair. "Come. Sit with me. Tell me about your dreams."

"Sorry," I said, refusing the invitation. "I never remember my dreams."

It was a bald-faced lie, but my nightmare was strictly off limits, and no power on earth would compel me to speak of long, languorous dreams starring heroic, blue-eyed cocker spaniels while Toby Cooper was within earshot. He was a bright boy. He wouldn't need Amanda's help to interpret the symbolism.

"Perhaps the sphere will guide our sight," she suggested.

"Actually, we just came in to buy a geode," I told her.

"You may *think* you came into my shop for a mundane purpose," Amanda said, smiling complacently. "But I believe a greater power guided your steps. Shall we consult the orb?"

"Oh, why not?" I said carelessly.

I unbuckled my pack, added it to the pile on the chair, and took a seat at the table. After a brief hesitation, during which he no doubt struggled manfully to keep from voicing his opinion on orb consultations, Toby followed suit.

Amanda rose and removed from the cupboard a round object

covered with a fringed, jacquard-silk cloth. She placed the object in the center of the table, resumed her seat, and swept the cloth aside to reveal a large and quite beautiful crystal ball on a little wooden stand. As she bent over the crystal ball, she bracketed her face with her hands, as if to block everything else from view.

Toby sat back in his chair with his arms folded, looking askance at the proceedings, but I leaned forward, propping my elbows on the table and resting my chin in my cupped hands. If Amanda had seen Abaddon's unholy ghost dogging my footsteps, I would have been nervous. As it was, I felt calm, relaxed, and ready for a bit of fun.

"I see a long journey," Amanda intoned. "You have come from afar."

I almost laughed out loud at her pathetic attempt to impress me. Anyone linked to Bluebird's highly efficient grapevine could have learned that I lived in England.

"You will meet a short, dark stranger," she went on.

"Isn't it supposed to be a *tall,* dark stranger?" Toby muttered.

Amanda continued to peer intently into the crystal ball, as though Toby's words were beneath her notice.

"Those you love most will surprise you," she said.

Again, I had to restrain the urge to laugh. There was nothing remotely mystical in Amanda's mumbo jumbo. I had every reason to believe that she, like everyone else in Bluebird, knew all about my five-year-old sons. It didn't take psychic powers to predict that little boys would at some point surprise their mother. Will and Rob surprised me every day. It's what five-year-olds *do.*

"Death came to claim you," Amanda murmured, "but you escaped his grasp."

I sat upright and the laughter died within me. Amanda might be throwing darts blindly, but even blind throws struck the target from time to time. This one had hit a bit too close to home.

"He will come for you again," she continued. "You risk all by sleeping beneath the eagle's wings. The killing curse will not leave you unscathed."

"That's enough." Toby pushed his chair back and got to his feet. "I knew you'd get around to the curse sooner or later, Amanda, but I didn't think you'd give it such a sick twist. You're supposed to use your alleged gifts to do good, but I don't see anything good in scaring people. Did James Blackwell come here, too? Did you try to scare him?"

Amanda looked up from the crystal ball. "All of my consultations are private and confidential."

"How convenient," Toby scoffed. "It means you don't have to defend yourself when you're wrong."

"I describe only what the orb reveals to me," Amanda said serenely.

"*And* what you hear in the cafe, *and* what you make up," Toby snapped.

"The inner eye does not lie," said Amanda.

"I hate to interrupt such a rousing debate," I said, with forced nonchalance, "but the closest I've been to death lately is a stroll around the cemetery with Rose Blanding—although I may die of starvation if I don't have dinner soon. Lunch was a long time ago and we've done quite a bit of walking since then." I stood. "Thanks for your time, Amanda. If you don't mind, I'd like to buy two geodes and get back to the Aerie. I really like sleeping beneath the eagle's wings. Should I, er, cross your palm with silver here or at the cash register?"

"Neither," she said, as unfazed by my reaction as she'd been by Toby's. "Take the geodes as my gift. To commune with your spirit has been payment enough."

"You're very kind," I said, avoiding her gaze.

Toby and I were back on Stafford Avenue in less than ten minutes. I'd seldom been happier to breathe smoke-free air, but Toby looked angry enough to spit fire.

"I'm sorry about that," he said. "Amanda's always seemed harmless to me, but I guess she couldn't resist making the most of the curse."

"The *killing* curse," I corrected him. "It has a certain ring to it, don't you think?"

"I think," Toby said grimly, "that Amanda had better clean up her act or she's going to go out of business. Tourists don't enjoy being frightened. *You* weren't frightened, were you?"

"No," I said. "Personally, I think there are enough real horrors in the world. I don't have to go looking for them in crystal balls."

Toby gave me a searching, sidelong glance, as if to convince himself that Amanda's unsettling pronouncements hadn't upset me. My neutral expression must have reassured him because he relaxed and changed the subject.

"I'm glad you remembered dinner," he said. "I'm starving."

"Me, too," I said.

If I'd been completely honest with Toby, I would have admitted that I'd used dinner as an excuse to get away from Amanda Barrow and her orb. Amanda might rely on educated guesswork for most of her predictions, but she saw some things much too clearly for my liking.

Death *had* come for me, and I *had* escaped his grasp. Was he lying in wait for me at the Aerie, to complete the job he'd left undone in Scotland? Would I be the killing curse's next victim?

As we entered Caroline's Cafe, I felt a sudden rush of empathy for James Blackwell, lying alone in his bed, wondering what would happen next.

Fifteen

oby and I decided to have dinner at the cafe, to save ourselves the trouble of cleaning up afterward. We returned to the Lord Stuart Trail at half past five, stuffed to the gills with Carrie Vyne's excellent fried chicken, mashed potatoes, and three-bean salad. As we started up the trail I saw something I hadn't seen before in Colorado.

"Do my eyes deceive me?" I said, squinting at the sky. "Are those . . . clouds?"

Toby followed my gaze and nodded. "Looks like a cold front's moving in. We may have a rainy night."

I nodded, secretly reassured. I hadn't dealt very well with thunderstorms since I'd been shot—every lightning bolt ignited flashbacks of Abaddon's creepy, pale face hovering over me on the storm-wracked cliffs in Scotland—but I could handle a rainy night.

"What thoughtful weather you have here," I commented. "No rain until we're done hiking—or trail riding or cooking out."

"It's not always so considerate," said Toby. "Which is why—"

"We always bring our rain gear," I finished for him.

A brisk wind was swooping through the treetops by the time we reached the Aerie, and the temperature had dropped by at least fifteen degrees. I was very glad we'd departed from the cafe when we did. If we'd stayed a half hour longer, I would have seriously regretted wearing shorts.

I left Toby to fill the cookie jar with Calico Cookies while I put Annelise's aspen-leaf earrings on her dresser and propped the pair of fuzzy buffalo against the twins' pillows in the playroom tent. When I reached the master suite, I glanced thoughtfully at the blue journal, but decided to postpone my chat with Aunt Dimity until after Annelise and the boys had returned from the ranch. I knew that our conversation would be a long one—it had been a remarkably eventful day—and I didn't want to be interrupted in the middle of it.

After changing into a pair of soft jeans and a long-sleeved cashmere sweater, and swapping my hiking boots for the blissfully supple moccasins I'd bought at Dandy Don's, I brought the geodes back to the dining room and placed them on the table, where everyone would be able to see them.

While I'd been distributing largesse, Toby had changed into clean jeans, sneakers, and an old gray-plaid flannel shirt. I returned to the great room to find him kneeling before the hearth, laying a fire.

"No fire pit tonight," he said. "It's too windy."

"I wasn't planning on it anyway," I said, crossing to lend him a hand. "It'll be baths and bed for Will and Rob when they get back, and I doubt that Annelise will want to stay up late." I passed logs to him from the bin until the pile was ready for lighting, then stood back. "The geodes will look fantastic by firelight, won't they?"

"Yes," Toby said, but he spoke as if he had other things on his mind. He closed the fire screen, straightened, and turned to me. He studied my face for a moment, then said, "Lori, tell me the truth. After everything we've heard today, does the Aerie seem different to you?"

"No." I smiled up at him and raised my hand as if I were taking an oath. "Scout's honor, Toby, the Aerie feels just as welcoming now as it did when I first set foot in it. Even if I did believe in curses, I couldn't believe that this place has ever been anything but loved."

"I really could strangle Amanda," he said darkly.

"Let's forget about Amanda," I told him. "Weren't you going to show me the stuff James Blackwell left behind? You may as well do it now, while we have the place to ourselves."

"Okay," said Toby. "Come with me."

I followed him through the passageway at the end of the kitchen and up two flights of stairs to the caretaker's apartment. Since I was scrupulously respectful of Toby's privacy, I would never have invaded his space without his permission, but once I was there, I couldn't help taking a look around.

The caretaker's apartment turned out to be a small, self-contained unit with a kitchenette, a living/dining room, a bathroom, a bedroom, and a private deck. The rooms were comfortably if not extravagantly furnished and clearly intended to be used by one person. Toby had personalized his somewhat spartan living quarters by lining the windowsills with chunks of quartz crystal he'd collected during our hikes, but apart from that, the rooms were as immaculate and impersonal as a hotel suite.

I was a bit taken aback by the apartment's cleanliness—Toby was, after all, a college student—until I remembered that Toby had spent nearly all of his waking hours at the Aerie with us. If the rooms looked unlived-in, I reasoned, it was because he hadn't really lived in them yet.

Toby must have noticed my inquisitive glances because he grinned and said, "It's humble, but it's home. Come through to the bedroom."

The bedroom seemed to be the only room Toby used on a regular basis. The bedclothes on the single bed were rumpled, his hat hung from a bedpost, and his hiking boots sat next to the dresser in a circle of dirt and dust from the trail. Pine cones, rocks, and feathers littered the top of the dresser, and the nightstand was piled with books. When Toby opened the closet door, I caught a glimpse of flannel shirts on hangers and blue jeans on built-in shelves. His red jacket hung from a hook inside the door.

"Have a seat," he said.

Since there was nowhere else to sit, I sat on the bed. I was beginning to wonder why he'd brought me to the bedroom when, grunting with the effort, he dragged a large, open wooden crate out of the closet and pushed it to the side of the bed. Small though the apartment was, it would have taken a lot more effort to drag the crate all the way to the living room.

"Well?" he said, standing over the crate. "What do you think?"

The crate was filled with dirty, scratched, and dented tools: several pointy-ended hammers, a crowbar, a shovel, a sledgehammer, and a pickax along with a coil of nylon climbing rope, a battery-operated lantern, and a hard hat with a built-in headlamp.

"It looks like the kind of stuff a miner would use," I said.

Toby nodded. "When I found it, my first thought was that James had taken up prospecting as a hobby. A lot of people spend their free time smashing rocks for fun."

"And your second thought?" I inquired.

Instead of answering right away, Toby took several slips of paper from the drawer in the nightstand. He handed them to me, and I saw that they were credit card receipts from a hardware store in Denver, where James M. Blackwell had purchased everything he'd left in the wooden crate.

"See the dates?" Toby said. "He bought the crowbar and the lantern in mid-April and the rest of the stuff a couple of weeks later."

I shuffled through the receipts, then handed them back to Toby, saying, "Okay, I'm with you so far."

Toby put the receipts on the pile of books on the nightstand and sat beside me on the bed.

"I may be way off base," he began, "but the way I see it is, James went to the historical society in late February to ask for information about the Lord Stuart Mine. He went back in March to find out more about the mining disaster. In mid-April he bought a crowbar and a lantern. A couple of weeks later he bought a sledgehammer, a pickax, a shovel—tools he could use to . . ." Toby's voice trailed off, as if he couldn't bring himself to speak his thoughts aloud.

I pulled the crowbar onto my lap for a closer inspection. It was nicked and abraded, as if it had been used for some heavy-duty prying. As I ran my hand over the deep, gritty scratches, I recalled what

Toby had told me while we sat before the fire on my first night at the Aerie: *Mr. Auerbach had a team of engineers seal the entrance to the Lord Stuart Mine. It's tight as a drum. . . .*

I put the crowbar back into the crate and turned to Toby. "Do you think James was trying to break into the Lord Stuart Mine?"

"He'd be crazy to try," said Toby. "It's dangerous down there."

"*Could* he break into the mine?" I asked.

"Not by the main entrance," Toby answered. "But he could have tried to reach it by a secondary tunnel. I told you before, the mountains around here are riddled with mine shafts."

"You're right," I said, brushing the grit from my hand. "He'd have to be crazy to try a stunt like that."

"Crazy or . . . greedy." Toby chewed his lower lip worriedly, then went on. "You heard Mrs. Blanding. Men came from as far away as northern India to look for gold in the Vulgamore Valley. James had a gold mine on his doorstep. All he had to do to find his fortune was to break into it."

"But the Lord Stuart Mine was played out," I reminded him.

"What if it wasn't?" Toby swung around to face me. "What if the Lord Stuart Mine closed *before* it was played out, to cover up the truth about the cave-in? James had done a lot of research. He could have decided that it was worth risking his neck to find out if there was still some gold left down there."

"And if there was?" My eyes widened as I realized where Toby's argument was headed. "Are you saying that James quit his job because he'd filled his pockets with gold?"

"If he had, he wouldn't mention it to Mr. Auerbach," said Toby, "because the gold would rightfully belong to the Auerbach family." He leaned forward, his elbows on his knees, his hands tightly clasped together. "I hate to accuse a man I've never met of theft, but it would explain an awful lot: why he was so interested in the mine, why he bought the tools, why he left so suddenly without giving notice and without leaving a forwarding address . . ."

"But he was a nice guy," I protested. "Carrie Vyne, Brett Whitcombe, Rose Blanding—they all thought James was a good guy, and good guys don't steal from their employers."

"Gold fever does strange things to people," Toby observed sagely.

"He was an amateur historian, not a miner," I insisted.

Toby thrust a hand toward the crate. "What was an amateur historian doing with these tools?"

I pondered the question for a moment, then replied, "He was investigating history. Do you remember what Rose Blanding told us? James wanted to know if the Lord Stuart curse had some basis in fact."

"Not the curse again," said Toby, groaning.

"The curse is a part of the Aerie's history, whether you want it to be or not," I said sternly. "If James went into the mine, I think it was because he wanted to know what really happened down there. He wanted to establish the facts about the disaster in order to . . ." I glanced hesitantly at Toby, then took a deep breath and plunged ahead. "In order to *exorcise* the Aerie. He wanted to free it from the curse. He wanted to prove that the mine had collapsed for perfectly reasonable reasons, not because someone had cast an evil spell on it."

"You're not telling me that *James* believed in the curse, are you?" Toby said scornfully.

"It doesn't matter whether he believed in it or not," I said. "Enough people *did* believe in it to make him want to prove them wrong."

"Then why did he leave so suddenly?" Toby asked.

"Because *we* were coming," I said, struck by a blazing flash of insight. "He hadn't found the proof he needed, but he was afraid that Annelise or I or maybe even the twins would find out what he was doing. He knew that Danny Auerbach would be furious with him for reopening the mine—Danny doesn't want his kids falling down an abandoned shaft, right?—so he took off before Danny could fire him."

"I don't buy it," Toby said flatly. "Your scenario doesn't ring true to me. James would have to be a structural engineer *and* an archae-ologist to figure out what caused the cave-in. He couldn't just stroll in there and say, 'Aha! Weak braces!'"

"He's an intelligent man," I argued. "Maybe he found some books in the library that—"

"Books?" Toby interrupted. "If books taught James anything, it would be that he'd need years and years of special training to exca-vate the site and determine what went wrong. Sorry, Lori, but your explanation doesn't make sense."

"I like it better than yours," I said, eyeing him grumpily.

"I like it better than mine, too," said Toby. "But I think my ex-planation is closer to the truth. James found gold in the Lord Stuart Mine, stole it, and took off before anyone could catch him."

We lapsed into a somewhat prickly silence that lasted until my cell phone rang. I answered it, but the signal was so broken up that Annelise had to repeat her message several times before I could make out what she was saying.

". . . bad storm. . . . hail . . . high winds in the pass . . . stay the night?"

"Yes!" I shouted back. "Stay there! Don't even *try* to come back! I'll see you tomorrow!"

". . . tomorrow!" Annelise hollered and hung up.

"Wow," I said, looking down at the cell phone. "It sounds as if they're getting hit hard at the Brockman. Brett Whitcombe wants Annelise and the boys to spend the night there because of high winds in the pass. It's hard to believe they're only one valley away from us."

"The front's moving in from the west," Toby explained. "If the storm's hit the Brockman, it'll be here within the hour."

"You told me it would be a rainy night," I said, eyeing him re-proachfully. "You didn't say anything about a thunderstorm."

"A rainy night in the Rockies usually involves a thunderstorm," he said. "You'll love it, Lori. The lightning's fantastic and the thunder makes the floors shake."

Toby's peppy words made me feel sick to my stomach because I knew how I'd react to a thunderstorm that shook the floors. I could already feel my hands growing clammy. Experience had taught me that the only way to keep myself from curling into a pathetic, shivering ball during a really bad storm was to distract myself, to bury myself in a project so absorbing that the lightning would fade into the background.

"Thanks for showing James's stuff to me," I said. "Try to remember that we don't really know why he bought it. For all we know, he may have been hunting for geodes."

"Sure," said Toby, sounding thoroughly unconvinced.

I got up from the bed. "Get some rest, Toby. It's been a long day."

"Where are you going?" he asked.

"To the library," I replied, "to look for the stuff James borrowed from Rose Blanding."

"I'll come, too," he said, jumping to his feet.

"You will not," I said, pushing him down again. I hated to pull rank on him, but I didn't want him to see me lose it if the lightning *didn't* fade into the background. "You've got the night off. Listen to music, watch a movie, read a book, enjoy yourself. I *order* you to relax."

Toby looked down at his hands and asked in a subdued voice, "You're not angry with me, are you?"

"Why would I be angry with you?" I asked, nonplussed.

"Because I disagree with you about James," he said.

"Oh, for pity's sake, Toby," I said, laughing. "If I got angry with everyone who disagreed with me, I'd never *stop* being angry. I just want you to have some time to yourself for a change. You must be sick to death of looking after us."

"That's my job," he said.

"Not tonight it isn't," I declared.

"All right, I'll read a book or something," he said dully. He leaned forward to lift the lantern from the wooden crate. "You'd better take this with you. I've checked the batteries. It works. The emergency generator will kick in if the storm knocks the power out, but it takes a few minutes to get going. If you need me—"

"I now know *exactly* where to find you," I said, taking the lantern from him. "Good night."

I let myself out of Toby's apartment and made my way back to the great room. Roiling black clouds had filled the sky beyond the window wall, and cracks of thunder reverberated from the mountainsides, as if warning me to get away from the enormous plateglass window before the lightning arrived. I darted into the library, turned on the lights, closed the draperies, and put the lantern on the banker's desk. I hit the lantern's on switch just to be on the safe side. I didn't want to be plunged into darkness if the power went out, even for a few minutes.

I'd visited the library several times since we'd arrived at the Aerie, so the room was familiar to me. Custom-made bookshelves lined three of its walls. The banker's desk rested before the fourth, beneath the window I'd so hastily covered. A mahogany map case stood beside the desk, and four oversized armchairs, each with its own reading lamp and cozy afghan, provided comfortable places to curl up with a book.

I sank into the nearest armchair and allowed my gaze to travel back and forth across Florence Auerbach's collection of books. When a sudden onslaught of rain peppered the window, I ordered myself to ignore the sound and concentrate instead on Danny Auerbach's perplexing wife.

I hadn't been able to tell Toby about Florence Auerbach's curious behavior because I'd promised Bill I'd keep it to myself. I hadn't told Toby that Florence had for some unknown reason interrupted her family's Christmas holiday at the Aerie, that she refused to set foot in it again, or that she'd ordered her husband to sell the Aerie without explaining *why* she wanted it sold, but I knew that even if I'd told Toby all of those things, I wouldn't have been able to convince him that she'd turned against the Aerie because of the curse. Toby didn't want to hear about the curse.

James Blackwell, I argued silently, might have been more open-minded than Toby. James had been living and working at the Aerie at Christmastime. He'd witnessed the family's precipitate departure. As the days ticked by with no sign of their return, he must have asked himself why they'd abandoned a place they'd once used so often. He could have concluded that their flight had something to do with the curse he'd heard about in town. It was clear to me, if not to Toby, that James had decided to mount an investigation of his own.

Since James liked to read, it was logical to assume that he'd combed through the books in Mrs. Auerbach's library for information on the curse, but he hadn't confined himself to books. He'd gone to the ranch, to speak with Brett Whitcombe, and to the historical society, to look for newspaper clippings, photographs, anything that might tell him more about the curse. He'd also purchased the tools he'd needed to take a firsthand look inside the mine—the place where it had all begun.

The more I thought about it, the more convinced I became that James had gone into the mine for a very specific reason: to prove to the Auerbachs that their fears were groundless. Granted, he wasn't a structural engineer or an archaeologist, but he could have come across something in the library that told him what kind of proof to look for and where to look for it.

I had no intention of following James's footsteps into the mine, but I could try to reconstruct the thought process that had led him there. I wanted to prove to Toby that he was wrong about James Blackwell. I wanted to convince Toby that James had gone into the mine to investigate the true cause of the mining disaster, not to steal from his employers.

Hail was hammering the window when my eyes finally came to

rest on the lowest shelf of the bookshelves to my left, where a gray archival box marked BLUEBIRD HISTORICAL SOCIETY had until now sat unnoticed in the shadows.

"Right," I said, getting to my feet. "We start there."

I pulled the box from the shelf and placed it on the desk, beside the lantern. As I removed the box's lid, several things happened at once. An earsplitting crack of thunder rattled the window, the power went out, and I saw by the lantern's stark white glare Abaddon's evil eyes staring up at me.

Sixteen

"Lori? Lori, wake up! Talk to me, Lori."

I opened my eyes. I was lying flat on my back on the rug in the library. Swirling sheets of rain were still battering the window, but the lights had come back on. Toby was kneeling beside me, clasping my right hand in both of his, looking very young and very terrified.

"Hi, there," he said, with a heroic attempt at a smile.

I peered up at him woozily. "W-what happened?"

"I don't know," he said. "I heard you scream and came running."

"I screamed?" I said, frowning.

"Oh, yeah." Toby nodded earnestly. "I heard it all the way upstairs, with my door closed."

"But why would I—" A muted flash of lightning lit the draperies, and the memory slammed into me like a tidal wave. I clutched Toby's hand convulsively and whispered, "It's him, *him*!"

Toby's eyes widened in alarm and he glanced over his shoulder. "Is someone here? Did someone *attack* you?"

"Yes . . . no . . . not here . . . in Scotland . . . his face, I saw his *face*." I closed my eyes again and shuddered.

"Scotland?" Toby put the back of his hand to my forehead, as if he thought I might have a fever. "Are you feeling dizzy, Lori? You may be dehydrated. I've told you a thousand times to drink plenty of—"

"I'm not *dehydrated*," I said crossly. I brushed his hand aside and pushed myself into a sitting position. *"I saw his face."*

"*Whose* face?" Toby asked.

I groaned, slumped forward, and covered my own face with my hands.

"You're shivering, Lori. Let's get you up off the floor." Toby lifted me bodily and set me down in an armchair. He pulled the afghan from the back of the chair and draped it around my shoulders, then stood peering down at me anxiously. "Should I call your husband?"

"No!" I barked. "Absolutely not. I don't want you to call anyone. Not Bill, not Annelise, not *anyone*."

"Okay, okay, I won't." Toby scratched his head and looked around the room helplessly. "How about a cup of tea?"

I pulled the afghan closer and smiled wanly. "You sound just like my husband."

"Do you faint a lot at home?" he inquired.

"No, but I wake up screaming every morning." Tears began to blur my vision. "And Bill always makes me a cup of tea. He's so *kind*. Like you." I bowed my head. "I'm sorry, Toby. I ruined your night off."

"I didn't *want* a night off. What do you want me to *do*?" Toby's voice held a hint of desperation.

I dashed the tears from my eyes and pointed a trembling finger at the banker's desk, saying, "Bring the box to me."

Toby hesitated, then lifted the gray archival box from the desk and placed it carefully on my lap. I gripped the arms of the chair, took a shuddering breath, and lowered my gaze slowly to the old, sepia-toned photograph I'd last seen by the light of James Blackwell's lantern.

The man in the photograph stood ramrod straight against a backdrop of busy Victorian wallpaper, with one hand clutching the lapel of his ill-fitting suit coat, the other resting on the back of a dainty, velvet-covered chair. He had a thin, pale face; a halo of curly, black hair; and dark, piercing eyes—*crazy* eyes, eyes as black and fathomless as the pits of hell.

"Abaddon," I breathed.

"Aba who?" said Toby.

I couldn't tear my eyes away from the man's pale face. "Do you know who he is?"

Toby leaned over my shoulder to peer at the photograph, then picked it up and turned it over. "I have no idea, and there's nothing written on the back. Since the picture came from the historical society, my guess is that he came to Bluebird to strike it rich. A lot of men had portrait photographs taken in those days, to show the folks back home how successful they were, even if they weren't." He dragged an armchair close to mine, slid the box from my lap onto his, and began pulling out photo after photo. "See? There are lots more just like it."

He seemed relieved to have something to do, even if he didn't understand why he was doing it. He showed me one sepia-toned photograph after another, formal portraits of nameless men wearing suits that were too tight or too baggy or too short or too long for them. As their frowning, intent faces passed before me in rapid succession, I wondered if any of them had struck it rich, or if they'd all died the mean deaths Rose Blanding had described in the cemetery.

A guttural rumble of thunder rolled from one end of the valley to the other and I shrank back in the chair. Toby must have noticed my reaction because he waved a photograph under my nose like smelling salts.

"Look," he said, with determined cheerfulness. "I've found a picture with a label. It's Emerson Auerbach. He must be Mr. Auerbach's great-great-great-grandfather or something. Pretty interesting, huh?"

Emerson Auerbach had clearly struck it rich. He was vastly proportioned and meticulously attired. He wore a top hat, a pinkie ring, and a monocle, and a multitude of fobs hung from the watch chain that spanned his elegant, outsized waistcoat. He held his many chins high and regarded the camera with a look that seemed to say, "I am a man to be reckoned with."

"And here's a group shot taken at the Lord Stuart Mine," said Toby, pushing a larger photograph into my hands.

I peered down at the picture and for a moment forgot the storm. Twenty-one men in shirtsleeves sat on a parched and rock-strewn hillside, facing the camera. They were thinner, scruffier, and much dirtier than Emerson Auerbach. The hats they wore were shapeless, their shirts had no collars, and their fingernails were caked with grime, but they exuded an almost palpable air of cockiness. They, too, I thought, were men to be reckoned with. I bent low over the photograph to examine each individual face, then caught my breath and sat back with a start.

"It's him," I said, trying not to panic. "The man in the first picture."

"Where?" said Toby.

I pointed to the back row. "He has a beard and he's wearing a hat, but the eyes . . . the eyes are the same."

Toby took the photograph from me, studied the figure at the back of the group, and nodded. "It's the same guy, all right. He must have showered, shaved, and dressed in his Sunday best when he had the portrait taken. I wouldn't have recognized him if you hadn't." He shifted the archival box from his lap to the floor and held the photo out to me. "Does he remind you of someone, Lori? Someone in England? Like Brett Whitcombe did when you first saw him at the ranch?"

"The man Brett reminds me of is as close to a saint as I'll ever meet," I told him. "The man in the photograph reminds me of . . . death."

"I *knew* it," Toby said, under his breath. He stood abruptly and began pacing the room, muttering angrily, "I *knew* Amanda had messed with your head. I could see it in your face when she talked about death coming to claim you. I swear, I'm going to strangle that woman the next time I—"

"But Amanda was right," I interrupted. "Death came to get me, and I got away from him."

"What?" Toby stopped pacing and swung around to face me. "When? Where? *Tonight?*"

"Not tonight. It happened seven weeks ago." I sighed heavily. I didn't want to tell Toby about the shooting, but I didn't want Amanda Barrow to shoulder the blame—or to take credit—for my strange behavior, either. Apart from that, I was heartily ashamed of myself for lying to someone as open and honest as Toby. If anyone had earned the right to hear the truth, he had. I motioned him to his chair and said, "Please. Sit down."

Toby resumed his seat, and I looked fixedly at the floor. I didn't want to see the mingled horror and pity that would soon fill his eyes. I'd seen it too many times before.

"I didn't hurt my shoulder falling off a horse," I began. "I was shot. By a lunatic. In Scotland. During a thunderstorm."

"Ah," Toby said softly.

"The bullet nicked an artery. I almost bled to death." I heard a sharp intake of breath and pressed on. "The man who shot me called himself Abaddon. He wanted to kill Will and Rob, too, but I stopped him. His face . . ." I glanced down at the gray archival box, then quickly averted my gaze. "His face was as pale as milk. He had wild black hair, and his eyes didn't seem to have any whites. They were as black as pitch, without any spark of emotion, like tunnels to hell."

"Jesus," Toby said in a hushed voice. "What happened to him?"

"He was struck by lightning," I said, "and he fell hundreds of feet into the sea. He couldn't have survived, but his body was never recovered. I know it's absurd, but there's a part of me that thinks he's still out there somewhere." I swallowed hard and forced myself to go on. "I have trouble with storms. I have trouble with nightmares—or I did until I came here. I haven't dreamed about Abaddon once since I got here. I thought I'd made some progress on the road to recovery, but then I saw the man in the photograph and . . . back to square one."

"Why didn't you tell me?" Toby asked.

"I'm sorry I lied to you, but I don't like to talk about it," I said gruffly. "I don't want people who don't know me to think I'm weak."

"Weak?" Toby gave a short, incredulous laugh. "You took a bullet to save your children. You nearly bled to death for them. You're one of the bravest people I've ever met."

"Brave people aren't afraid of thunderstorms," I said.

"Wounded people are afraid of all kinds of things," he countered swiftly. "But wounds heal. You won't always be afraid of thunderstorms. But you'll always be brave."

I wiped away a tear that had trickled down my cheek and glanced at him. "I don't feel very brave at the moment. I feel like a quivering puddle of pudding."

"This, from the woman who laughed in Dick Major's face?" Toby tossed his head disdainfully and shoved the group photograph under my nose. "Look at the man who scared you, Lori. *Look at him.*"

I stared down at the man in the back row.

"He's not the man who shot you," said Toby.

"No, he isn't," I said, and with a faint sense of shock I realized that the man didn't even look as much like Abaddon as I'd first thought. "His eyes still give me the creeps, but his face is rounder than Abaddon's, he's shorter, and he's not as thin."

"He's also been dead for over a hundred years," Toby pointed out, with his usual, unassailable, common sense. "The man who shot you is dead, too. He was struck by lightning. He fell off a cliff. He's not out there anywhere."

I tapped my temple. "Too bad he's still in here."

"He won't always be," said Toby.

I raised my eyes to meet his gaze. "Because wounds heal?"

"They do," he said. "Trust me, Lori. I know about healing. I'm the son and the grandson of doctors."

Another burst of lightning brightened the draperies, but instead of flinching, I gave a snort of mirthless laughter. "Do you know how many doctors I've seen since I was shot?"

"But *I'm* Dr. Toby," he said, pressing his palm to his chest. "And *I* know what's good for you." He got up, threw the photograph into the box, seized my hands, and pulled me to my feet. "You know what they say, Lori. When you fall off a horse—"

"But I *didn't* fall off a horse," I protested.

"Don't be pedantic." He picked up the afghan that had tumbled from my shoulders and wrapped it around me again, then put his arm firmly around my waist and steered me out of the library. "Come on. We're going to enjoy the greatest light show on earth."

We stood at the window wall for twenty minutes watching a display of lightning that would have had me crawling under the bed a week ago. Every time I twitched, Toby tightened his hold on me and let out a whoop and a holler.

"That was a great one! Did you see *that*? Way to go, Zeus!"

"Way to go, *Zeus*?" I echoed, amazed to hear myself giggling.

"Make up your own cheers," he chided, and raising a fist, bellowed, "Rock on, Jupiter!"

The tumultuous thunderstorm finally worked its way out of the Vulgamore Valley, leaving a calmer and much less showy rainstorm pattering in its wake.

"We need the rain," Toby said quietly "If you listen hard, you'll hear the trees sucking it up." He tilted his head toward me. "How're you doing?"

"I'm still trying to invent a good cheer," I said. "But I don't think I can beat 'Rock on, Jupiter!'"

Toby smiled tolerantly, but continued to look down at me.

"How am I doing?" I gazed at the rain-streaked window and inspected my mind for any new dents or scratches. "To tell you the truth, I'm surprisingly okay. I don't think I'll sleep with that photograph under my pillow, but I think I'll be able to sleep." I looked up at him. "You're awfully wise for a twenty-one-year old."

"Grandma used to say that I had an old head on my shoulders," said Toby.

"Your grandmother knew what she was talking about," I said. "Your treatment seems to be working."

"It never fails," he said.

"Do you have many patients?" I asked teasingly.

"Just the kids in my dorm. Compared to them, you're a model of mental stability." He paused, then added without a trace of facetiousness, "I'm so sorry you were hurt, Lori, and I'm so glad you're still around to talk about it." He gave me no chance to respond, but glanced at his watch and went on in more businesslike tones, "It's only ten o'clock, but I think I'll turn in."

"I'm sorry I spoiled your night off," I said remorsefully.

"I told you before, I didn't *want* a night off," he responded. "But I *do* want a good night's sleep. We have a big day ahead of us tomorrow."

"Do we?" I said blankly.

"Mrs. Blanding," he reminded me. "Lunch."

I clapped a hand to my forehead. "I'd completely forgotten about her."

"You've had one or two other things on your mind," said Toby.

"I suppose I have," I agreed, dropping the afghan on the sofa. "Do you think Mrs. Blanding will be able to identify the man in the photograph?"

"I think she'll be able to identify *all* of the men in *all* of the photographs," said Toby with a sigh. "And she won't leave until she's told us their life stories in excruciating detail, so if I were you, I'd grab at least eight hours of good, sound sleep."

"I'll do just that," I said, "thanks to you."

I caught his hand in mine, squeezed it gratefully, and made my way to the master suite, where I took a hot shower, slipped into a flannel nightgown, and lit a fire in the corner fireplace. I turned back the bedclothes as well, but although I was tired, I had no intention of climbing into bed.

I wasn't afraid of nightmares, curses, or lurking lightning bolts, but I was rather anxious to avoid the volley of sarcasm that would come my way if I postponed my chat with Aunt Dimity a moment longer.

Seventeen

After an evening rife with alarms and diversions, it was heavenly to curl up with Reginald before a crackling fire, with the blue journal in my lap. The familiarity of it all was infinitely comforting. If I closed my eyes, it was easy to pretend that we were at home in the cottage, sitting before a crackling fire in the study.

"Here we are," I murmured to Reginald, "my two old friends and me. No surprises, no shocks to the system, just a pleasant, peaceful conversation to round out the day." I chuckled wickedly as a fresh thought struck me. "I'll bet Amanda Barrow would go green with envy if she could see how easily I get in touch with 'the other side.'"

Reginald's black button eyes twinkled merrily in the firelight, as if he found the notion as amusing as I did. I touched the faded grape juice stain on his snout, tucked him into the crook of my arm, and opened the journal.

"Dimity?" I said. "Are you there?"

The curving lines of royal-blue ink spun across the page with a certain sense of urgency.

I'm most certainly here, and I wish to be brought up to date on everything you've learned since our conversation last night. Is Bluebird's grapevine less or more efficient than Finch's? Is Dick Major a murderous madman or simply a cranky old fusspot? Have you gleaned any new information about James Blackwell or the Auerbach family? As you can tell, my dear, I'm agog to hear about your day.

"It's been *such* a strange one, Dimity," I said, with feeling. "I mean, I should have known *he'd* show up because everyone else has—not just Kit Smith and Nell Harris, but Peggy Taxman, Christine and Dick Peacock, Mr. Wetherhead, and Lilian Bunting—"

Lori?

"—not to mention Ruth and Louise Pym, but they were identical, tottering old men instead of identical, tottering old women—"

Lori!

"—and the Calico Cookies. You won't believe me when I tell you about Carrie Vyne's Calico Cookies because it's just too coincidental to be believed. They're *exactly* like Sally Pyne's Crazy Quilt Cookies, right down to the different nuts and things she puts in them every time, but thank heavens Carrie Vyne isn't one bit like Sally Pyne, except that they both run similar businesses and make wonderful pastries and simply *ooze* gossip, so I suppose they're sort of alike, but the main thing is, they don't *look* alike."

LORI!

I paused to take a breath, glanced down at the journal, and realized that Aunt Dimity had been trying for some time to gain my attention.

"Yes?" I said.

Good evening. When I expressed an interest in your day, I rather hoped I'd hear about it in a coherent fashion, but your account has so far been baffling rather than enlightening. You make it sound as though your neighbors in Finch have come to join you in Colorado, bringing with them a supply of your favorite biscuits. Although I don't for one moment doubt the sincerity of their affection for you, it seems to me highly unlikely that they would leave the village to languish in their collective absence for no reason other than to satisfy your sweet tooth. I must conclude, therefore, that I've misunderstood you. Would you please gather your thoughts and begin again?

"Sorry, Dimity," I said, abashed, "but as I said, it's been a strange day. I guess I got a little carried away."

There's no need to apologize. Just start from the beginning and move on from there. Slowly.

I silently reviewed the parade of familiar strangers that had passed before me in Caroline's Cafe, then carefully described them to Aunt Dimity, adding telling details I'd left out earlier.

"You already know about Dick Peacock's homemade wine," I said. "Well, Nick Altman is just as fat as Dick, and *he* makes undrinkable *beer*. And Greg Wilstead has a model train layout in his garage that sounds a lot like the one George Wetherhead has in his living room. And Maggie Flaxton is big, loud, and pushy, just like Peggy Taxman. The only person in Bluebird who doesn't remind me of someone in Finch is Dick Major, for which I am profoundly grateful, because although Dick *isn't* a murderous madman, he *is* a jerk who likes to intimidate people, and we don't need someone like that in Finch."

Did he succeed in intimidating you?

"Certainly not," I said. "To tell you the truth, he came as something of a relief— a fresh face in a cornucopia of clones. Honestly, Dimity, I'm expecting to run into *me* pretty soon."

Would it be so strange if you did? Bluebird and Finch are small towns, and small towns tend to be populated with stock characters: the bossy organizer, the plump publican, the vicar's wife, the train enthusiast, and so forth. You, my dear, are the amiable foreigner. I wouldn't be at all surprised if you discovered someone in Bluebird who closely resembles yourself.

"I'd need a medic to revive me if I came face-to-face with myself," I said flatly. "It was bad enough when I came face-to-face with Abaddon."

I beg your pardon?

"Okay, it wasn't Abaddon," I admitted sheepishly. "But before I get ahead of myself again, let me tell you about the Lord Stuart mining disaster, the Lord Stuart curse, the set of tools James Blackwell left behind, and the box of photographs he borrowed from the Bluebird Historical Society."

I recounted everything I'd learned at the cafe, at the parsonage, in the cemetery, in the caretaker's apartment, in the Aerie's library, and afterward at the window wall in the great room, watching lightning with Toby by my side; then I waited in silence while Dimity digested the information. After some time, the old-fashioned copperplate began to curl across the page again, but the topic Dimity chose to address first surprised me a little.

What a remarkable young man Toby Cooper is turning out to be. He picked you up from the floor in more ways than one tonight.

I nodded. "When he told us at the airport that he could fix things, I didn't think he meant broken minds. But he has a gift for healing. I don't think I'll ever be afraid of thunderstorms again."

Toby seems to be a true caretaker—in every sense of the word. How fortunate that he was nearby when you saw the dark-haired man in the sepia-toned photograph.

"The one who scared the bejabbers out of me," I said.

Indeed. It's possible, I suppose, that the man in the photograph reminded you of Abaddon because he's one of Abaddon's ancestors. After all, Abaddon was an Englishman and Englishmen helped to settle the American West. I think it more likely, however, that you exaggerated the resemblance because Abaddon has been so much on your mind of late.

"The lantern light and the storm may have influenced my eyesight," I conceded with a wry smile. "I was already on edge when I saw the photograph. After I'd calmed down a little, Toby had me take a closer look, and I realized that the man wasn't Abaddon's twin. He still gives me the willies, but he's not the creep who shot me on the cliffs."

From your account, I gather that the dark-haired man is featured in two photographs in the archival box—the individual portrait as well as the group portrait. Does the same hold true for the other men in the group photograph? Is each man in the group represented by an individual portrait?

"I don't know," I said. "I didn't compare the group shot to the other photographs in the box. Does it matter?"

It might. If the dark-haired man is the only individual singled out from the group, it may mean that James Blackwell took a particular interest in him. I wonder who he was? I hope you'll make a point of asking Mrs. Blanding about him when she joins you for lunch tomorrow.

"I intend to," I assured her. "I'll check out the other photographs, too, to see if they're of men in the group shot."

Excellent. As for the curse . . . I've detected no trace of it, yet I feel certain that something frightened Mrs. Auerbach.

"What else could it be but the curse?" I said. "Why else would she suddenly decide to sell a place she'd grown to love? And why would she refuse to explain her decision to her husband? She was probably afraid that he'd laugh at her for being scared of a silly superstition."

James Blackwell knew all about the silly superstition. He made it his business to learn as much about it as he could.

"And he didn't start looking into it until *after* Florence Auerbach had left the Aerie," I said. "Which suggests to me that her fear triggered his interest."

I agree. Still, we must ask ourselves: Did James enter the Lord Stuart Mine in order to investigate the curse or simply to line his pockets with ill-gotten gold? If he's a common thief, we can wash our hands of him. If, on the other hand, he was an honest man searching for the truth behind the curse, then why did he leave the Aerie so hastily?

"I've told you what I think," I said. "James went into the mine to investigate the curse, and he left the Aerie because he knew Danny Auerbach would fire him for reopening the mine. It might even be illegal to go into old mines. He might have been afraid that Danny would have him arrested."

James had no reason to believe that Danny Auerbach would discover his scheme. Danny hadn't visited the Aerie in six months, and he gave no indication of returning.

"But James knew that other witnesses were on the way," I reminded her. "I refer, of course, to me, Annelise, Will, and Rob."

Why would you worry James? He was forewarned of your arrival. He had enough time to conceal his excavation project and enough sense, one imagines, to steer you away from it while you were here.

"What if Annelise or I had stumbled across it accidentally?" I asked. "We might have given him away."

I doubt it. Neither one of you knows the first thing about mine entrances. If you'd seen one that had been reopened, James Blackwell could have told you that it was a colorful relic of the Old West, and you would have believed him. You would have avoided the hazard, certainly, but you wouldn't have reported it to Danny Auerbach. You would have assumed—or James could have told you—that Danny knew about it already. James Blackwell would have had nothing to fear from you or Annelise—or the twins, for that matter.

"All right," I said reasonably. "If James wasn't a thief, and if he wasn't afraid of being fired or arrested, then why *did* he take off in such a hurry?"

I believe he discovered something in the mine that seemed to confirm Mrs. Auerbach's worst fears.

"He found proof that the curse is *real?*" I frowned in confusion. "But you just said—"

I've detected no trace of a curse, but facts have never stopped people from believing in fantasies. James Blackwell had witnessed Mrs. Auerbach's sudden flight. He'd spent months on his own, immersing himself in local lore. When he finally descended into the darkness of the mine, his mind might have betrayed him. A strange shadow, a queer sound, an oddly shaped rock could have taken on a terrifying significance.

I glanced at the shivering shadows on the ceiling and understood at once what James might have gone through, alone in the mine's pitch-black depths. If I'd been in his shoes, it wouldn't have taken much to make me believe in every superstition known to man.

"He convinced himself that the Aerie was cursed," I said, "without finding any real proof."

I believe he did, but I wonder . . . Was he frightened by a mere trick of the light or by something more substantial?

"If you think I'm going down there to find out," I declared, "you've got another think coming."

I would never ask you to engage in such a dangerous undertaking. But you must admit that it's an intriguing question.

"It'll be a cold day in Panama before I risk my neck to answer an intriguing question," I said firmly.

Naturally.

"Bill would kill me if I even *thought* about poking around in a collapsed mine shaft," I insisted.

I don't want you to set so much as a toe in the old mine, Lori. As I said, there may be nothing down there but shadows and dust.

"And bats. I'm sure there are bats." I shuddered theatrically, then frowned. "If James Blackwell believed in the curse, he should have warned us. It wasn't very nice of him to leave us in the dark, so to speak. It's as bad as leaving us at the mercy of a murderous madman."

Before you condemn him, Lori, please try to remember that we're indulging in pure speculation.

"Our speculation is based on fact," I retorted. "We're not pulling ideas out of thin air. We're not making things up as we go along, like Amanda Barrow."

Amanda Barrow? I don't believe you mentioned her.

"Didn't I?" I clucked my tongue at my oversight. "Amanda would be crushed if she knew I'd forgotten her, but it's hard to remember everyone in a sea of doppelgangers."

Not another one, surely.

"Yes, another one," I said, smiling. "Amanda Barrow is Bluebird's version of Miranda Morrow, but Amanda's more flamboyantly psychic than Miranda, and she uses more props."

What do you expect? She's an American.

"Are you implying that Americans lack subtlety?" I asked, feigning indignation.

As a rule, yes, but there are, of course, exceptions to every rule.

"You're supposed to add, 'and I count you among the exceptions, Lori dear,'" I hinted.

But I don't count you among the exceptions, Lori dear. As you've just demonstrated, subtlety is not your strong suit.

"Ah, well," I said, shrugging, "I can't be good at everything."

Tell me more about Amanda Barrow. I adore flamboyant psychics. They have such vivid imaginations.

"Like me," I said without rancor.

I've never known anyone quite like you, Lori. What props does Amanda Barrow use?

"You name it," I said. "She specializes in palmistry, tarot-card reading, rune casting, crystal-ball gazing, past-life retrieval, and dream interpretation, but I don't think she'd turn down a chance to read tea leaves if one came her way. Oh, and let's not forget about her inner eye. You should have seen the act she put on when I walked into her shop. She went all wobbly and mystical because, according to her, I was"—I raised my arm in a melodramatic gesture—"accompanied by a spirit from the great beyond."

That would be me, I'm afraid.

I glanced down at the journal, did a double take that nearly sent Reginald flying, and lowered my arm very slowly.

The last sentence hadn't been written by Aunt Dimity. The handwriting was more flowery than hers, and the ink was bottle green instead of royal blue. I closed my eyes, hoping that fatigue had produced a fleeting hallucination, but when I opened them again, the sentence was still there.

"Who . . . who are you?" I managed.

An excellent question. Who are you and what are you doing in my journal?

Cyril Pennyfeather, at your service. I'm frightfully sorry to intrude on your private conversation, but there's something I simply must tell you!

Eighteen

*A*s I gaped, dumbfounded, at the page, Amanda's words came back to me with stunning clarity.

"Light hair?" I said unsteadily. "A slight build? Pince-nez on a chain?"

Again, that would be me. I fit your excellent description in life, and under the right set of circumstances it applies to me still.

"Are you the . . . the male spirit who accompanies me?" I asked, my voice cracking like a teenaged boy's.

Only when decency allows, I assure you. I may have many faults, but I am not a voyeur, Mrs. Shepherd.

I giggled weakly and fastened on the one thing my shocked brain could handle.

"Please, call me Lori," I said. "May I, er, introduce Miss Dimity Westwood?"

I'm delighted to make your acquaintance, Miss Westwood. And may I tender my compliments on the wonderful means of communication you have devised? It's so much more civilized than disembodied voices.

"Disembodied voices?" I said faintly and looked around the room, half expecting an invisible army to start whispering on cue. My befuddlement was such that the reappearance of Aunt Dimity's old-fashioned copperplate seemed like a welcome return to normalcy.

Cyril Pennyfeather? The name seems familiar. Are you the schoolmaster who led the miners to safety after the Lord Stuart mining disaster?

Indeed, madam, I am he.

Forgive me if my next question is an indelicate one, Mr. Pennyfeather, but would I be correct in saying that you died in 1896?

You would be entirely correct, my dear lady. I have been dead for well over a century.

"Reginald," I muttered, "forget what I said about no shocks to the system."

Aunt Dimity carried on as if I hadn't spoken. *Are you by any chance English, Mr. Pennyfeather?*

I am. I was born and raised in Bibury, in the county of Gloucestershire, the third son of a vicar who could scarcely afford to send his first two to university. Without a university degree, I had little hope of advancement in England, so I made my way to America and eventually to the American frontier, where the educational standards were less rigid. I was twenty-five years old when I opened my school in the boomtown of Bluebird, Colorado, and I taught there until my untimely death ten years later. They were the happiest ten years of my life.

It must have been a fascinating experience to live in an American boomtown, Mr. Pennyfeather.

It was, Miss Westwood. To witness firsthand a young, dynamic country growing by leaps and bounds, unfettered by outmoded social constraints

The handwriting stopped when I cleared my throat, and I had the eerie sensation that Cyril Pennyfeather was standing mutely beside the hearth, regarding me attentively through his gleaming pince-nez.

"I'm sorry to interrupt, Mr. Pennyfeather," I said, "but how long have you been, er, accompanying me?"

I've looked in on you from time to time since the first night you arrived at the Aerie, though I assure you that your privacy

"Yes, yes, I understand about my privacy," I cut in. "What I want to know is, was Amanda Barrow telling the truth this afternoon? Did she see you with me when I walked into her shop?"

I'm afraid so. Her cat saw me as well. I don't know why the cat made such a fuss. I was quite fond of cats when I was alive, and they were fond of me. Be that as it may, when I became aware of the commotion I'd created, I immediately made myself as inconspicuous as possible. I'm a shy soul, really. I dislike being the center of attention.

"If Amanda Barrow and her cat can see you, why can't I?" I demanded, feeling distinctly shortchanged.

It does seem unfair, doesn't it? I can, alas, offer you no conclusive answer, although I suspect it may have something to do with genetics. I'm sure you have gifts Miss Barrow lacks.

"I certainly have better dress sense, but that's beside the point," I said. "You've been hanging out with me for nearly a week, Mr. Pennyfeather. Why haven't I been able to sense your presence?"

More to the point, Mr. Pennyfeather, why haven't I sensed your presence?

You have both sensed my presence, dear ladies. You simply didn't recognize what you were sensing.

"Sorry?" I said uncomprehendingly.

I'm afraid you're going to have offer a more detailed explanation, Mr. Pennyfeather.

I will do so gladly. When you arrived at the Aerie, Lori, your nerves were standing on end, and you, Miss Westwood, were too anxious about Lori to be conscious of anything else. Your mutual distress touched my heart, so to speak. I decided, therefore, to exert a . . . calming influence . . . on Lori. I'm rather good at that sort of thing, you know. Virtually unflappable, in fact. I was always able to calm a frantic pupil.

"Good grief," I said softly. "You made my nightmare go away."

It would be more accurate to say that I created an atmosphere of tranquility and security in which you found it easier to sleep, and sleep, saith the Bard, is the balm of hurt minds, great nature's second course, chief nourisher in life's feast. Macbeth, Act two, Scene two. But I digress.

I'm afraid you do, Mr. Pennyfeather.

I beg your pardon. To sum up: Once Lori found respite in rest, you, too, relaxed, Miss Westwood, but by then you'd grown so accustomed to my presence that it failed to catch your attention.

In other words, Mr. Pennyfeather, you flew in under my radar.

Radar, Miss Westwood? What is radar?

Forgive me, Mr. Pennyfeather. The word wasn't coined until 1941, but never mind. Suffice it to say that you've taken me quite by surprise.

"Me, too," I put in. "Although I did see your obelisk in the cemetery."

My obelisk is rather handsome, isn't it?

"It's lovely," I said and since I'd only mentioned it in passing to Aunt Dimity, I went on to describe it in more detail. "It's at least ten feet tall, made of polished white marble, with a beautiful inscription carved into it, a quotation from the Bible, something about a living sacrifice——"

Holy, acceptable unto God. They chose Romans Chapter twelve, Verse one, Miss Westwood.

How very humbling, Mr. Pennyfeather.

Indeed. More humbling still was the second inscription.

"It's below the Bible verse," I explained to Dimity. "It says that the obelisk was erected by the families of the men Mr. Pennyfeather saved, to honor his memory. Mrs. Blanding told Toby and me that the families took up a collection to pay for it."

They must have gone without bread to raise such a sum. I'm more deeply touched than I can say. I had no idea that they'd gone to so much trouble on my behalf.

"You didn't?" I said, frowning in confusion. "Haven't you seen the obelisk before?"

I'd never seen it until today. No one from the Aerie has ever gone to the cemetery. Therefore, I could not go.

"Why would you need someone to take you there?" I asked. "I hate to state the obvious, Mr. Pennyfeather, but it's *your* grave."

You are under a slight misapprehension, Lori. The obelisk does not mark my grave.

"It doesn't?" I said, feeling more perplexed than ever.

I'm afraid not. I wasn't interred in the cemetery after my death because there was nothing to inter. My body, you see, was never recovered from the mine.

I instinctively lifted my feet and glanced uneasily at the floor. "We're living on top of your *grave?*"

Not directly, no, but we're not far from it. After the dust had settled, they managed to retrieve every corpse but mine. Mine was in a rather tricky location, you see. To remove it would have caused another cave-in, so they left it where it was.

"I'm so sorry," I said.

As am I, Mr. Pennyfeather. Truly sorry. I'm perfectly content to remain as I am, but I sense that you are not.

It's true. I wish to move on. If I'd received a proper burial, I might have proceeded to the next stop in my journey. Instead, I'm stranded in a way station between this world and the next. I cannot leave the mine site on my own, and I can accompany only those people who, like you, Lori, have a sympathetic and tolerant nature.

"I know a few people who would be surprised to hear me described as sympathetic and tolerant," I commented dryly.

You didn't shriek when you saw my handwriting. You didn't slam the book down and run from the room. Your acquaintance with Miss Westwood has broadened your mind in a very special way.

"I guess I do have gifts Amanda Barrow lacks," I said, lifting my chin proudly.

If you didn't, I would not have been able to visit the cemetery with you. I'm grateful to you for allowing me to go there, Lori. I've long wished to pay my respects to Hannah.

"Hannah Lavery?" The name hadn't come up in my conversation with Aunt Dimity, so I continued, "Hannah Lavery was the daughter of a rich mine owner. She became a social activist, a reformer who worked to improve the lives of miners and their families. Toby and I saw her grave at the cemetery. Rose Blanding called her a rabble-rouser."

Were you referring to Hannah Lavery, Mr. Pennyfeather, or to another Hannah?

In my eyes, there was no other Hannah. Hannah Lavery made my work possible, Miss Westwood. I taught grown men and women as well as children, you see. The mine owners frowned on educated workers—it's harder to cheat a man who can read—but Hannah defied them. She supported my school with her own funds. My doors would not have stayed open if not for Hannah.

"You were both rabble-rousers," I observed, smiling.

We were also engaged to be married. But the call went out that the mine had collapsed, and I went up to lend a hand. I had to, you understand. My pupils needed me. I helped extricate a handful of men, but too many died. I wish I could have done more, before the second cave-in caught me.

I'm sure you did everything you could, Mr. Pennyfeather.

I pictured the angel weeping over Hannah Lavery's grave and remembered Rose Blanding's comments about Victorian men preferring passive women, and how difficult it was for a crusader to give her heart to a man as well as a cause. I knew now that in one particular case, Rose had gotten it wrong. Cyril had loved his crusader, and she'd given her heart to him. Only a tragic twist of fate had kept them apart.

"I don't know if you noticed," I said quietly, "but Hannah Lavery never married."

I noticed. Foolish girl.

The flames in the fireplace quivered, as though Cyril had released a melancholy sigh. I sighed, too, at the thought of what might have been, but Aunt Dimity was more interested in history than in heartache.

Why did the Lord Stuart Mine close so soon after the disaster, Mr. Pennyfeather? Was it because the miners believed the mine to be unlucky? Or was it because the owners were afraid of the scandal that would ensue if their use of inferior wood was discovered?

I sincerely doubt that fear of any kind influenced the decision to close the Lord Stuart, Miss Westwood. In those days, scandals didn't matter to investors as long as there was money to be made. And although the miners were a superstitious lot, they also had families to feed. They couldn't afford to leave their jobs simply because the mine they worked in happened to be accident-prone. The only reason a mine ever closed was that there was no more gold to be had from it.

"So the mine *was* played out," I said happily. "James Blackwell couldn't have been a thief because there's no gold left to steal. He *must* have been investigating the curse."

At last, we come to the curse.

What can you tell us about the curse, Mr. Pennyfeather?

Quite a lot, actually, but I'm not sure where to begin.

"From the beginning," I said, to save Dimity the bother of writing it.

Very well. I will begin, then, by telling you that prospectors came from all walks of life, but very few came from well-to-do families. It was not uncommon, therefore, for a rich vein of gold to be discovered by a man who could not afford to exploit it properly. If he could, he found investors to provide him with capital. If he couldn't find investors, he had little choice but to sell his claim to the highest bidder. Just such a situation arose in the Vulgamore Valley in the year 1864. The prospector was a poor Polish immigrant named Ludovic Magerowski, and the highest bidder was a prosperous businessman called Emerson Auerbach.

"I saw Emerson Auerbach's photograph in the library," I said. "He looked like a high bidder."

Emerson Auerbach was extremely wealthy. He bought Ludovic's claim to the Lord Stuart Mine for five thousand dollars. It must have seemed like a vast sum to Ludovic, but it was a pittance compared to the mine's actual worth. By 1890, the Lord Stuart had yielded two hundred million dollars in gold.

"Wow," I said, impressed. "That's a spanking return on an investment."

Did Mr. Magerowski realize what he'd done, Mr. Pennyfeather?

Eventually. He returned to Bluebird some twenty years later, with a wife and young child, having tried unsuccessfully to strike it rich elsewhere.

I gave a low whistle. "It must have killed him to see someone else reaping such outrageous profits from a mine he'd sold for chump change."

It angered him, certainly. He initiated a lawsuit, claiming that Emerson Auerbach had swindled him, but the lawsuit was dismissed for lack of evidence. He took his complaint to the newspapers, but they ignored him, as did everyone else in Bluebird. They'd grown accustomed to hearing a prospector cry foul after a claim he'd sold fairly and squarely had yielded a fortune. No one but Ludovic believed that Emerson Auerbach had done anything wrong. Apart from that, no one liked Ludovic.

"Why not?" I asked.

He was a blustery, self-aggrandizing fellow. He claimed to have an English benefactor—the famous Lord Stuart, in whose honor he'd named the mine—but when I asked him why an English nobleman would deign to sponsor an impoverished Polish immigrant in a venture as risky as prospecting, he had no answer. Since he had no money, either, I concluded that the famous Lord Stuart was a figment of his imagination.

What happened to Mr. Magerowski after the lawsuit failed?

Strangely enough, he went to work in the Lord Stuart Mine. I can only assume that the mine manager felt sorry for his wife and child, because Ludovic had gone quite mad by then. I remember seeing him just before I died.

I gasped. "He was *there*?"

Yes, Lori, Ludovic was there on the day of the disaster. When I saw him, he had a look of insane triumph in his eyes.

"His eyes," I whispered, as the hairs on the back of my neck rose. More loudly, I asked, "Did he have dark curly hair? And a beard? And intense dark eyes?"

Yes. He grew the beard after he came to work in the mine.

"I think I've seen his photograph, too," I said. "He reminded me of someone, a homicidal maniac I, um, ran into once."

I don't know if Ludovic was a homicidal maniac, Lori, but I do know that he put a curse on the mine. He raised his lamp, looked directly at me, pointed to the bloodstained rocks, and growled, "No accident. I did it. I damned it all to hell. If I can't have it, let the devil take it." He gave an unearthly howl of laughter, then sprinted to freedom. A moment later, the shaft's roof collapsed, and I was buried inextricably beneath a ton of debris.

"What an evil-minded little man he must have been," I said heatedly. "Your final moments of life were stressful enough, Mr. Pennyfeather. Ludovic had no right to make them worse with his ranting."

You said earlier that you had something to tell us, Mr. Pennyfeather. Did you wish to warn us about the curse?

Why should I wish to warn you about something so trivial?

Do you believe it to be trivial?

Naturally. I know that Ludovic cursed the mine——I heard him do it——but I do not believe that a lunatic's ravings can affect affairs in the tangible world. No mere mortal has such power.

"Then why was the Lord Stuart so prone to accidents?" I asked. "And why were so many people hurt at the site after the mine was shut down?"

One needn't turn to the metaphysical realm to explain mining accidents, Lori. Mining is a hazardous occupation in and of itself, an occupation rendered even more hazardous by managers who cut corners when purchasing building materials, which the Lord Stuart's manager most certainly did.

If you knew the mine was unsafe, Mr. Pennyfeather, why didn't you bring it to someone's attention?

I did. Hannah and I wrote to congressmen, senators, and newspapers, decrying the perilous state of the Lord Stuart Mine, but no one listened. Profits, as I mentioned earlier, were worth more than men's lives.

"Hannah Lavery kept fighting the good fight right up to the day she died," I said.

Of course she did. She was indefatigable. There was a pause, as though Cyril was taking a moment to collect himself, then the flowery handwriting continued. *As for the accidents that occurred after the mine closed, they, too, happened for entirely mundane reasons. Indeed, when I remember the foolhardy risks taken by those who explored the site, it seems incredible to me that so few were killed or injured. I would also point out that no accidents have occurred since the site was cleared.*

"I agree with everything you've said," I said stoutly. "I've never believed that anything was wrong with the Aerie."

If you don't wish to warn us about the curse, Mr. Pennyfeather, why have you made yourself known to us?

I'm afraid I have news that you may find a bit disturbing.

"Well?" I said eagerly. "What is it?"

Very well, then. Prepare yourselves for a shock. The Lord Stuart Mine has been reopened!

"Oh," I said, unable to disguise my disappointment. "I know that it's been reopened, Mr. Pennyfeather. Toby figured it out."

You don't seem disturbed by the knowledge.

"That's probably because I'm not," I admitted. "I'll keep the twins away from the danger zone and let Danny Auerbach—the present owner—know about it. The Lord Stuart is really his problem, not mine."

I suppose it is. Forgive me for alarming you unnecessarily. My big news seems to be old news.

A sense of anticlimax lingered in the air, but only for a moment. It had suddenly dawned on me that Cyril Pennyfeather might be able to answer a question I'd been asking almost from the moment I'd arrived in Colorado.

Why had Florence Auerbach and James Blackwell abandoned the Aerie? I no longer believed that they'd been chased off by a bully, but while I still held out hopes for the curse as the root cause, Cyril's unanticipated appearance suggested another explanation for their flight. Had they run as if they'd seen a ghost because . . . they'd seen a ghost?

"Mr. Pennyfeather," I said, "have you tried to contact other people who've stayed at the Aerie?"

I have not. It would be a most imprudent thing to do. Not everyone would welcome me as warmly as you have, Lori. Most people would react like Miss Barrow's cat if I revealed myself to them in any way.

I accepted his answer philosophically. After all, I still had the curse to fall back on.

"Well, it's their loss," I declared. "I think you're a perfect gentleman."

Thank you, Lori. I've always felt that there's no need to forget one's manners simply because one has lost one's life.

In the interest of good manners, Mr. Pennyfeather, I must point out that we are keeping Lori up rather later than we should. Have you noticed the time, my dear?

I swung around to face the clock on the bedside table and realized to my dismay that it was nearly half past eleven.

"Whoops," I said. "I've enjoyed meeting you, Mr. Pennyfeather, but you'll have to excuse me. If I know Annelise—and I do—she and the twins will be back from the ranch bright and early tomorrow morning, and I don't want to be groggy when they get here."

I understand completely, Lori. Would you care to stay a while longer, Miss Westwood? I was rather hoping you'd explain radar to me.

It would be my pleasure, Mr. Pennyfeather, though I'll have to explain a great many other things first.

I smiled as I watched both sets of handwriting fade from the page. Neither Cyril Pennyfeather nor Aunt Dimity needed the journal to continue their conversation. I had a feeling that they'd communicate more easily without it, which was just as well—Cyril had a lot of catching up to do.

I left the blue journal on the chair, damped the fire, and took Reginald to bed with me. My mind should have been spinning like a top, but as my head hit the pillow I felt nothing but a great sense of relief. My private demon seemed to be in full retreat, I had Cyril's reassurance that the Aerie was untainted by evil, and I would never, for as long as I lived, have to break the news to Toby that the queen of hocus-pocus—and her cat—had been telling the truth.

Nineteen

F awoke refreshed and well rested at eight o'clock the following morning, threw on shorts, a T-shirt, sneakers, and a lightweight cardigan, and met Toby in the kitchen for breakfast. It was yet another picture-perfect Colorado day. The air was crisp, the sky bluer than blue, and leftover raindrops hung like diamonds from the branches of every tree.

I stayed in the kitchen after breakfast to assemble the lasagna I intended to serve for lunch. I planned to throw together an artichoke salad later, while the lasagna was baking, but I asked Toby to run into town to pick up a fresh loaf of crusty bread to serve with the meal—I was unwilling to foist my first attempt at high-altitude bread-baking on an unsuspecting guest.

I'd just put a pitcher of sun tea out to brew on the breakfast deck when Bill called. I flopped onto a cushioned lounge chair and propped my feet on the railing while I told him everything that had happened since we'd last spoken. It was a joy to be able to speak freely about Cyril Pennyfeather to a tangible human being, but Bill, bless his heart, was far more impressed by my ability to weather the thunderstorm than he was by my encounter with the great beyond.

"Why should I be astonished by Cyril?" he asked, when I teased him about his nonchalant reaction. "I was sure that someone like him would show up sooner or later. Dimity can't be the only one of her kind in the world, or in between worlds, or wherever she is."

"Amanda Barrow would know the proper term," I said, laughing. "Think I should ask her?"

"Only if you want her to camp out on your doorstep with her crystal ball for the remainder of your vacation," Bill said sardonically.

I wrinkled my nose. "Nah. Doesn't sound appealing. I guess I'll keep the news about Cyril between you and me."

"It's too bad you can't share it with Florence Auerbach," said Bill. "If she had Cyril's guarantee that the Aerie isn't cursed, she might change her mind about selling it."

"I can't see myself trying to explain Cyril to a complete stranger," I said, shaking my head. "I'll just have to find another way of convincing Florence."

"Are you sure this curse business isn't bothering you?" Bill asked suspiciously.

"Do I sound bothered?" I asked back.

"You sound great," Bill admitted.

"I sound even better in person," I said, sighing. "I wish we were talking face-to-face."

"You may get your wish sooner than you expect," said Bill.

I carefully removed my feet from the deck railing and sat forward in the lounge chair. "What do you mean?"

"I mean that I have to fly to Boston next week to confer with Father about a few clients," he replied. "If all goes well, I should be in Colorado in ten days."

"Oh, *Bill* . . ." I grinned so hard I nearly strained my face. "That's *brilliant*. Will and Rob will do backflips when they see you, but be warned—they'll run you ragged, showing you the sights."

"Don't tell them I'm coming," Bill cautioned. "I don't want them to be disappointed if I'm delayed."

"I won't say a word. It'll be a big surprise." I perked up even more as another happy thought occurred to me. "Just think, Bill, I'll actually have a chance to prove to you that the Bluebird doppelgangers aren't a product of my homesick imagination."

"I look forward to meeting every one of them," said Bill. "With the possible exception of Maggie Flaxton."

With an especially cheery good-bye, he rang off. I sat for a moment, savoring my good fortune, then went to the laundry room, where I sang cowboy songs at the top of my lungs while I folded the clean laundry. Toby returned a short time later with a loaf of Carrie Vyne's Italian bread and a box full of her exquisite lemon tarts.

"The twins and I can dig into the Calico Cookies after lunch," he informed me. "But I thought the ladies might prefer a more sophisticated dessert."

"You are a pearl beyond price," I told him, beaming.

"I'm not bad," he agreed complacently.

Brett Whitcombe brought Annelise and the twins back to the Aerie at half past nine. The three prodigals had already eaten breakfast at the ranch, so they went straight to their rooms to change into fresh clothes. Annelise emerged first, wearing beige shorts, a short-sleeved cotton blouse, the aspen-leaf earrings, and a big smile.

Will and Rob were distracted by the stuffed-toy buffalo I'd left in their tent, but I eventually managed to get them into clean shorts and T-shirts. They thought the geodes were the coolest things they'd ever seen, apart from the *real* baby buffalo they'd seen at the ranch, but after examining the sparkling crystals and telling me all about their day in the saddle and their stormy night in the bunkhouse, they were ready to tackle the next adventure.

"We're going fishing," Will announced.

"Excellent," said Toby. "We'll go up to Willie Brown Creek, see if we can hook a few rainbows."

"We don't want *rainbows*," Rob objected. "We want *fish*."

"Rainbows *are* fish," said Toby. "Come on, I'll tell you all about rainbow trout while we pick out some poles."

When Toby and the twins had left the great room, Annelise beckoned to me to join her at the breakfast bar. I could tell by her expression that something was troubling her, so I quickly took a seat beside her.

"I wanted to have a word with you before I went off again with the boys," she began.

I nodded, wondering what was wrong.

"I put the idea of fishing into the boys' heads," she went on.

"It's a great idea," I said. "They love to fish."

"Yes," said Annelise, "but I put the idea of fishing into their heads because I think they should have a few days off from the ranch."

"Problems?" I said quietly.

"As a matter of fact——" She broke off as the menfolk returned to the great room, bristling with fishing poles. "Never mind. I'll tell you later."

"I'll come with you. You can tell me on the way." I got up, intending to change into my hiking boots, but I'd moved no more than a few steps away from Annelise when the doorbell rang. I stopped short and looked toward the foyer in surprise. "Who on earth can *that* be?"

"Don't ask me," said Annelise, shrugging. "I didn't even know we had a doorbell."

"It can't be Mrs. Blanding," I said, glancing at my watch. "It's only ten o'clock. She's not supposed to be here until noon."

"Maybe she decided to come early," Annelise suggested.

"Two hours early?" I said doubtfully.

Toby strode across the great room to peer through the window wall. "There's a pickup parked out front, but I don't recognize it."

The doorbell rang again.

Toby turned toward me and squared his shoulders protectively. "Do you want me to answer it?"

I looked from the twins, who were dancing impatiently from foot to foot, to Annelise, who was clearly anxious to get going before Will or Rob started casting for trout in the kitchen sink, and reluctantly shook my head.

"No, you guys run along," I said. "I know how to get to the creek. I'll catch up with you later."

Toby glanced once more at the mystery truck, then led the others to the mudroom behind the kitchen. The mudroom door opened onto the trail that would take them to Willie Brown Creek, so when I heard the door open and close, I knew they were on their way.

The doorbell rang again, and I felt a surge of annoyance with the ringer for interrupting my conversation with Annelise. If there'd been problems at the ranch, I wanted to hear about them, not waste time with a casual caller. As I hastened into the foyer and flung the front door open, I was already devising ways to get rid of the man I found standing on the doorstep.

He was short and stocky, with short, dark hair, green eyes, and a face so deeply tanned it looked like leather. His faded black T-shirt fit snugly across his muscular shoulders, but hung loosely over the waistband of his faded jeans, and his work boots were dusty and well broken in. He looked as though he might be in his early thirties.

"May I help you?" I said crisply.

" 'Morning," he said. His voice was deep and resonant, and he spoke with a western twang. "My name is James Blackwell."

The man's lips kept moving, but a faint buzzing in my ears obscured his words.

"James Blackwell?" I squeaked, grasping the door jamb for support.

"Yes, ma'am," he said. "As I was just saying, I used to work for Mr. Auerbach. I have a paycheck and a letter from him, and my driver's license, too, if you want proof of who I am."

"James Blackwell?" I repeated, dazed with disbelief. "The caretaker?"

"Yes, ma'am," said James. "I've come to pick up a few things I left here. I'll be out of your hair in a minute."

"Oh no, you won't," I said, snapping out of my daze. I seized his wrist determinedly and pulled him into the foyer. "I have about a thousand questions to ask you, James Blackwell, and you're not going anywhere until you've answered them."

"But ma'am——" he began.

"Resistance is futile," I declared, tugging him toward the great room. "I'm the mother of twin boys."

"Yes, ma'am," he said, and came along docilely.

As soon as the great room door was closed behind us, I introduced myself and offered James a cup of tea, which he declined.

"I wouldn't say no to a cup of coffee, though," he added.

"You'd say no to my coffee," I said flatly. "I don't make it very often and when I do, it looks like mud. God alone knows what it tastes like."

"No problem," he said. "I'll make it."

I could tell by the way James moved around the kitchen that he'd been there many times before. He knew where to find the coffee and the coffeemaker, and he selected a large blue mug from the cabinet as if it was the one he always used. He certainly didn't seem nervous or fearful. From what I could see, he was completely at ease in the Aerie.

I sat at the breakfast bar and watched him mutely, glad to have a chance to recover from the shock of meeting a man I'd never expected to meet. By the time we'd settled on the sofa before the hearth, I'd calmed down enough to feel a twinge of guilt for lunging at him and dragging him into the Aerie against his will.

"I suppose you're wondering why I greeted you so . . . unceremoniously," I ventured.

"Not really." James took a sip of coffee and cradled the blue mug in his large hands. "A man can't just vanish like I did without leaving a trail of questions behind him. I expect you want to know why I quit my job."

"I have no right to interrogate you," I admitted, "but yes, I would *really* like to know why you quit your job, and so would everyone else within a fifty-mile radius of the Aerie."

"I expect word'll get out quick enough once I tell you, so I may as well get it over with." James smiled briefly, then pursed his lips and sighed. "The first thing you have to understand, Lori, is that I'm a married man. The second thing is that I was laid off from my job last September. I was still out of work at the end of November, when my wife told me she was pregnant with our first child."

"I'm so sorry," I said, adding swiftly, "Not about the baby, of course, but about your losing your job."

"Thanks." James took another sip of coffee. "The caretaker's job sounded like it was custom made for me. I work construction, so I can fix almost anything, and I'm right at home in the high country. The only catch was, Mr. Auerbach didn't want to hire a married man."

I recalled the single bed in the caretaker's apartment and nodded.

"I'd heard from a friend that Mr. Auerbach paid top dollar, and with a baby on the way, I needed the money," said James. "So I lied. I told him I was single. And I got the job."

"Didn't your wife mind being separated from you?" I asked.

"Sure, but when I told Janice—that's my wife—how much I'd be making, she went along with it," said James. "Besides, we live in Denver, so I wasn't too far away. I went to see her whenever I could think of an excuse to drive into the city. It wasn't an ideal situation, but we both thought it would pay off in the long run."

"Did Mr. Auerbach find out about Janice?" I asked. "Is that why you left?"

"No, that's not why I left." James put the blue mug on the coffee table and swung around on the sofa to face me. "I got a call from Janice last week—three days before you were due to arrive at the Aerie. She'd gone into labor. The baby's not due until August, Lori. Since you're a mother, you can imagine the state my wife was in."

"She must have been scared," I said.

"She was," James acknowledged. "As for me, I panicked. I threw my stuff in a bag, left a short message on Mr. Auerbach's answering machine, and hightailed it out of here. I met up with Janice at the hospital in Denver."

"Is she all right?" I asked solicitously.

"They managed to stop the contractions," he said, "but she'll have to stay in bed until the baby comes. So I can't work here any-more. I can't work at all. I have to stay at home with my wife."

"How are you paying your bills?" I asked worriedly, then held a hand up to forestall his answer. "Forgive me, James. It's none of my business."

"No offense taken," he said easily. "Janice and me'll be fine. As I said, Mr. Auerbach pays top dollar. I earned enough here in seven months to get us through till I can go back to work. And next time I'll find a job closer to home."

"I'm glad to hear it," I said, smiling. "I'm glad about Janice and the baby, too."

"Thanks," said James, reaching for his coffee.

"You'll probably laugh at me," I said, "but I was convinced that you'd left the Aerie because you thought it was cursed."

Instead of laughing, James compressed his lips into a thin line and looked faintly disgusted.

"I wouldn't let a curse run *me* out of the Aerie," he said. "Mrs. Auerbach did, though. Stupid woman. She shouldn't have listened to Tammy."

"Tammy?" I said inquiringly.

"Tammy Auerbach," James explained.

"The teenaged daughter?" I guessed, glancing in the direction of Annelise's room.

"That's right," said James. "Tammy didn't like being cooped up with her little brothers—what fifteen-year-old girl does?—so she started hanging out with a crowd of crazies in Bluebird."

"Amanda Barrow's crowd of crazies?" I said, intrigued.

James nodded. "Tammy Auerbach thought every word that came out of that fool woman's mouth was the gospel truth, so when Amanda told her about the curse, she took it to heart."

"So *Tammy* Auerbach believed in the curse," I said, half to myself.

"Tammy Auerbach would've believed that cows laid eggs if

Amanda Barrow said it was so." James's face darkened. "When I got wind of what was going on, I went into town to tell Amanda to lay off the kid, but the damage had already been done. Tammy was having trouble sleeping, and Mrs. Auerbach started acting all weird. She had me check the plumbing and the floorboards in the family suite."

"Why?" I asked.

"No idea," answered James. "Everything was fine in the family suite, and I told her so, but next thing I knew, she upped stakes and took off out of here."

"She left some clothes and other things behind," I said. "Why didn't you ship it to her?"

"She didn't tell me to," said James, "so I thought she'd be coming back. She didn't, though. I haven't seen or heard from the Auerbachs since Christmas. Rumor has it that they're thinking of selling the Aerie."

I suppressed the urge to confirm or deny the rumor and said instead, "You must have wondered about the curse."

"I did," said James. "I don't believe in it any more than I believe pigs can fly, but once I'd seen with my own eyes how it could affect people, I got interested in finding out more about it. With the Auerbachs gone and nobody else coming, there wasn't much else to do. I spent a fair amount of time in Bluebird, asking folk about the curse. One guy in town took a sort of ghoulish interest in the subject, so I spent a lot of time listening to him."

"Was it Dick Major?" I ventured. "I heard that he was harassing you."

"Dick *thought* he was harassing me," said James, "but I was pumping him for information. When I finished with the folk in Bluebird, I drove out to the ranch to find out if Brett Whitcombe knew anything. Brett's a good guy, but he didn't want to talk about the curse, so I went to the historical society to find out more. I struck pay dirt there. Have you met Mrs. Blanding, the pastor's wife?"

"I have," I said.

"She can talk the hind leg off a bull elk once she gets going," said James, shaking his head, "but she knows her stuff. She loaned me all kinds of old photographs and newspaper clippings. They're in a box in the library. I'm planning to return it to the parsonage on my way back to Denver."

"There's no need," I said. "Mrs. Blanding is coming here for lunch today. She'll take the box with her when she leaves. I'll explain why you didn't return it. I'm sure she'll understand."

"Thanks. Give her my thanks, too, will you?" James finished his coffee and took the mug to the dishwasher.

I followed him into the kitchen. His mention of the gray archival box had reminded me of another box—the wooden crate Toby had discovered in the caretaker's apartment—and another question. I wanted to know what James had done with the tools he'd left in the crate. Had he used them to steal gold from his employer? Or had he used them to find out what had caused the Lord Stuart Mine to collapse? After a brief inner debate, I decided to tackle the issue head-on.

"James," I said, leaning on the breakfast bar, "while you were investigating the curse, did you try to break into the Lord Stuart Mine?"

James turned toward me, grinning sheepishly. "I guess you found my tools, huh? Well, yes, I did open the big steel door Mr. Auerbach put on the mine entrance. As I said, with no family and no guests to cater to, there wasn't much else to do. I'd learned an awful lot about the Lord Stuart and here I was, living right on top of it, so I figured, why not take a look-see?"

"Did you find gold?" I asked, leaning forward.

James gave me a quizzical look, then cocked his head toward the forest beyond the breakfast deck. "Come with me and I'll show you what I found."

One part of me watched in startled dismay while the rest of me responded like a cat to curiosity's call.

"Lead on," I said.

Twenty

We didn't have far to go, which was fortunate since I was wearing sneakers instead of my trusty hiking boots. The entrance to the Lord Stuart Mine was no more than fifty feet from the back wall of the third guest suite, but it was so well hidden by trees, shrubs, and boulders that I would never have spotted it if James hadn't pushed branches aside and led me to it.

A square arch some ten feet tall and eight feet wide had been carved into the side of the mountain. Within the arch, Danny Auerbach's team of engineers had installed a steel door painted in a swirly camouflage pattern. The door's left edge had been bent outward in uneven scallops, and it had no handle, only a heavy-duty hasp from which hung the broken remains of a once imposing padlock.

"I smashed the lock with the sledgehammer," said James. "I would have replaced it with a new one if I hadn't left in such a hurry."

I nearly swooned at the thought of what might have happened if the twins had discovered the metal door with the broken lock.

"Don't worry," I said unevenly. "I'll replace it."

"You don't have to," James told me. "I managed to pry the door open with the crow bar, but after that . . ."

He stepped forward, slipped his hands into two of the larger scallops, and heaved with all his might, but he could only pull the steel door open a foot or two before it came up against a boulder. He then stood back and gestured for me to take a look inside.

I stepped over a low shrub, ducked under a branch, and crept up to peer timorously into the Lord Stuart Mine. I expected to see a yawning, bat-and-rat-infested hellhole. I saw instead a slightly chipped concrete wall that completely blocked the entrance.

"But . . . but . . ." I sputtered. "Where's the *mine*?"

"Somewhere behind the concrete plug." James tapped the wall with his knuckles. "I thought I might break through it with the pickax, but I gave up pretty quick. The angle makes it hard to take a good swing, and only Mr. Auerbach knows how thick the plug is. He made damned sure his sons couldn't get into the mine, so I don't think you'll have to worry about your twins."

I pressed my palms against the cool concrete and nodded. "Since Rob and Will are only five years old and not *quite* as strong as you are, James, I'd have to agree." I withdrew my hands and heaved a little sigh. "I have to confess that I'm a tiny bit disappointed. I was kind of hoping to see a glint of gold in the darkness."

"If any gold's left inside the Lord Stuart, it's out of our reach," said James. "But you should watch yourself, Lori. Gold fever's a nasty bug. You don't want to get bit by it."

I moved out of his way, he pushed the door shut, and we walked back to the great room in the Aerie. Since it was already eleven o'clock, I made a detour to the kitchen to put the lasagna in the oven, then helped James carry the wooden crate to his truck. After we'd loaded the crate, James closed the tailgate and turned to survey the Aerie.

"I liked it here," he said. "One day Janice and me and the kid are going to have a cabin in the mountains. It won't be as fancy as this one, but it'll be ours."

"With scenery like this, you don't need fancy," I said, sweeping a hand through the air to indicate the lake, the forest, the snowcapped peaks, and the dazzling blue sky. "Are you sure you can't stay for lunch? There's plenty of food and you're more than welcome. I know for a fact that your replacement, Toby Cooper, would love to meet you."

"Thanks, but I'd better be going," said James. "I left Janice with one of her girlfriends, but she gets fretful if I'm gone too long."

"You're a lucky man," I said, clapping him on the shoulder. "You have so much to look forward to. Give Janice my best."

"I'll do that, Lori." James climbed into the cab of his truck, started the engine, and drove down the steep lane toward the dirt road that would take him back to the highway.

It wasn't until the truck was out of sight that I remembered the lantern I'd left in the library. I felt a stab of guilt for forgetting to give it to James, but there was nothing I could do about it, so I went inside to make the artichoke salad and set the dining room table for lunch.

While I puttered from one task to another, I reran the past hour in my mind, rehearsing the revelations I planned to share with Bill, Aunt Dimity, Toby, and Rose Blanding. I was fairly certain that I could rely on Rose to share my news with every living soul in and around Bluebird.

The fishermen returned from Willie Brown Creek at half past eleven, crowing over the trout they'd caught and thrown back. Rob and Will were wet, muddy, and in dire need of baths, so I had no chance to speak privately with Annelise or to inform Toby of James Blackwell's unexpected visit. While Toby put the salad and the bread on the table, filled water glasses, and added ice to the sun tea, Annelise and I whisked the boys first into the bathtub, then into their room to dress them in clean, dry clothes.

I ran back to the kitchen to check on the lasagna, and Annelise brought the boys and their buffalo into the great room to play quietly—and cleanly—while we waited for the doorbell to ring. At precisely twelve o'clock, it did.

Rose Blanding stared avidly around her as I ushered her into the great room and introduced her to Annelise, Will, and Rob.

"How lucky you are to have such a lovely place to stay," she said to the boys.

"We slept in a *bunk bed* at the ranch," Rob informed her airily.

"And we saw *two* snakes," said Will.

"But they weren't rattlers," said Rob, with a wistful sigh.

The twins continued to extoll the ranch's virtues while we ate, but Rose seemed to be preoccupied with the Aerie's. She appeared to listen attentively to the boys' chatter, but her eyes roved around the room as if she were memorizing every detail of her surroundings. I was confident that a minute description of the Aerie's interior would find its way onto the local grapevine before sunset.

After we'd finished the meal, I left Rose to wander at will while Toby and I cleared the table and Annelise took the boys outside to hunt for fossils. Rose seemed captivated by the objects displayed in the rustic cabinet. She was still peering at them when I joined her.

"The twins took naps when we first got here," I told her. "But they don't seem to need them anymore."

"They're acclimatized," Rose observed knowledgeably. "It's amazing how quickly children adjust to the altitude." She favored me with an inquisitive, sidelong look. "Did I see James Blackwell's truck pass by the parsonage this morning?"

"James Blackwell!" Toby exclaimed from the kitchen. He threw down a dish towel and hurried over to where Rose and I were standing. "Did *he* ring the bell this morning? Did you get a chance to speak with him, Lori? Did you find out if he"—he glanced at Rose and finished cautiously—"did what I thought he did?"

"Let's all have a seat," I said. "James's visit was extremely informative. I have a lot to tell both of you."

Toby perched on the hearth ledge while Rose and I made ourselves comfortable on the sofa. They listened raptly while I told them a slightly abbreviated version of James Blackwell's story. I enjoyed shooting a significant look at Toby when I described James's unsuccessful assault on the Lord Stuart Mine. I had no intention of discussing Toby's unworthy suspicions in front of Rose, but I relished the prospect of forcing him to admit—after Rose had gone—that he'd been wrong to accuse his predecessor of theft.

Rose was shocked to learn that Amanda Barrow had played such a pivotal role in the Auerbachs' departure, but Toby wasn't even mildly surprised.

"Amanda tried to pull the same stunt yesterday," he informed Rose indignantly. "She tried to use the curse to scare Lori."

"But it's nonsense," Rose protested. "The curse is utter nonsense."

"So is everything else Amanda does," said Toby, "but it doesn't stop people from believing in her."

Rose's gray eyes narrowed. "I'll have to have a little talk with Amanda. I don't mind it when she practices her profession on adults, but when it comes to frightening an impressionable teenaged girl . . ." She gazed fiercely into the middle distance, then cleared her throat and turned a much gentler visage toward me. "I'm sorry for the Auerbachs, of course, but they'll be all right. People with money always are. James, on the other hand, may find himself struggling to make ends meet once the baby arrives. I'm worried about him."

"I am, too," I admitted. "What if he can't find a job after the baby's born? Danny Auerbach won't hire him back."

"Leave it to me," said Rose. "I'll think of something. James was well liked in Bluebird. I may be able to find a way to bring him back—with his family, of course."

"That'd be great," I said. "He loves it up here."

Rose folded her hands in her lap. "You certainly had an interesting morning, Lori. Thank you so much for telling me about James. The lasagna was delicious, by the way. And your sons are adorable, so big for their age and so articulate."

Rose added a few more compliments before it dawned on me that she was waiting to be taken on the promised tour.

"Would you like to see the rest of the Aerie?" I asked.

"I would," she replied instantly.

I took Rose Blanding from one end of the Aerie to the other, leaving out only the caretaker's apartment and cleverly making the library our last stop. I wanted her full attention when I asked her about the photographs in the gray archival box.

Rose's face lit up when we entered the library. She walked straight to the shelves to look over the books and uttered soft cries of delight when she found ones she knew to be rare or out of print.

"I realize that envy is a sin," she said, sighing deeply, "but I can't help being envious of Mrs. Auerbach. Her collection is truly priceless."

"Here's your box, Mrs. Blanding," said Toby, drawing her over to the banker's desk. "Lori and I were looking through it last night. We wondered if you could identify any of the men in the pictures."

"I can identify *all* of them," Rose assured us, opening the box.

My eyes met Toby's over Rose's bowed head, but we looked away quickly, suppressing smiles.

"James Blackwell was interested in the Lord Stuart mining disaster," said Rose, "so I gave him contemporary accounts of it: articles from the local newspaper, photocopies of relevant correspondence, and so on."

"Toby and I are interested in the photographs," I reiterated, to keep Rose from going off on a tangent.

"The group portrait is the key," she explained. She lifted the large photograph out of the box and showed it to Toby and me. "Every man in the photograph, but one, died in the disaster."

"Oh, my gosh," I said, peering down at the proud faces of the doomed men. "I should have guessed. Twenty red granite headstones in the cemetery, twenty-one miners in the photograph."

"I included an individual portrait of each man in the group portrait." Rose passed the group portrait to Toby and raised a handful of photographs from the box, fanning them out like playing cards. "I also included a portrait of Cyril Pennyfeather, whose obelisk we saw in the cemetery." She plucked one photograph from the rest and handed it to me, then put the others back into the box.

A wave of affection tinged with sorrow swept over me me as I took in Cyril's narrow chest and shoulders, his wavy blond hair, and the pince-nez perched on the bridge of his rather prominent nose. He was dressed in a serviceable tweed suit and held an open book in one long-fingered hand, as if he'd looked up from his reading to have his picture taken. He stood at a slight angle to the camera, before a backdrop that included a classical bust on a truncated Doric column. If I hadn't already known he was a schoolmaster, I would have guessed it.

"He has such intelligent eyes," I murmured.

"He was, by all accounts, a highly intelligent man," Rose said. "He could speak French, German, Latin, and Greek, and he knew most of Shakespeare's works by heart."

"Macbeth," I murmured, returning the photograph to the box. "Act two, Scene two."

Toby was still examining the group portrait. He handed it back to Rose and asked, "Which one of the men survived?"

A shiver traveled up my spine as Rose pointed unerringly to the wild-eyed, bearded man in the back row.

"He brought water to the other miners," she said. "He was refilling his can when the mine collapsed and so escaped unharmed. His name was Ludovic Magerowski."

"I *knew* it!" I cried, as Cyril Pennyfeather's words came rushing back to me. "I *knew* he was crazy."

"How did you know?" Rose asked in mild surprise.

I blinked at her, then said quickly, "His eyes. He has crazy eyes."

"You do judge men by their eyes, Lori," Rose commented, looking amused. She turned back to the photograph. "But you were right about Cyril Pennyfeather, and you're right again about Ludovic. He was deranged. That's why they wouldn't allow him to handle tools or to have anything to do with explosives. No one trusted Ludo to do anything but deliver water."

Rose went on to describe Ludovic Magerowski's life. Her account tallied with the one Cyril Pennyfeather had written in Aunt Dimity's blue journal, but Rose had one enormous advantage over Cyril—she knew what had happened after the disaster.

"Rumors flew," she said. "The most popular one was that Ludo had sabotaged the mine to exact revenge from Emerson Auerbach for cheating him out of a fortune." She rifled through the box and came up with a frail newspaper clipping encased in a protective clear plastic envelope. "As you can see, Ludo didn't help matters. He gave an interview to the Bluebird *Herald* in which he claimed to have special powers."

"Like Amanda's?" Toby hazarded.

"Just like Amanda's," Rose confirmed. "Ludo announced that he had, indeed, sabotaged the mine, but that he'd done so with mind power alone. In other words, he'd *willed* the mine to collapse."

"That must have gone over big in Bluebird," I said sarcastically.

"They couldn't arrest him for the illegal use of willpower," Toby pointed out. "What happened to him, Mrs. Blanding? Did the townspeople take the law into their own hands?"

"I'm sure they would have, if they could have gotten to him in time," said Rose. "Fortunately—or unfortunately, depending on your point of view—the *Herald*'s editor arranged for Ludo to be spirited away to an asylum near Denver before the interview appeared in the newspaper. I suppose he didn't want Ludo's blood on his hands."

"What happened to Ludo's wife?" I asked.

"She had relatives in Ohio, but she chose to stay on in Bluebird. I imagine it was easier for her to stay here, where the story was already known, than to confess the awful truth about her husband to her family. There was a great stigma attached to mental illness in those days." Rose sighed as she returned the group portrait and the newspaper clipping to the archival box. "A year to the day after the mining disaster, her body was found floating facedown in Bluebird

Creek. The coroner ruled her death accidental, but I suspect that he was being kind. Suicide would have barred her from being buried in the cemetery."

"And the child?" I asked.

"He was sent to an orphanage. As for Ludo, he was never seen in Bluebird again. He died two months after he entered the asylum." Rose replaced the lid on the box. "It's been said before, but it bears repeating: Gold fever is sometimes a fatal illness."

Toby and I stared down at the archival box in somber silence, but our thoughts were interrupted by the doorbell.

"Three times in one day?" I said, astonished. "I'm going to have to hire a social secretary."

Toby must have been hoping for a return appearance by James Blackwell because he ran to answer the door before I could make a start toward it. A moment later we heard him bellow angrily, "What are *you* doing here?"

Rose and I exchanged alarmed glances and hastened into the great room, arriving just in time to see Amanda Barrow, in full gypsy regalia, sweep in from the foyer with Toby hot on her heels.

"I did not come here of my own volition," she declared. "I was *summoned*!"

Twenty-one

"*F*didn't summon you," said Toby, eyeing Amanda contemptuously.

"Nor did I," I said.

"You misunderstand." The bangles on Amanda's wrists rattled as she spread her arms wide and gazed toward the ceiling. "I was summoned by no earthly power. I responded to a call beyond the reach of human hearing."

"Like a dog?" Toby said scathingly.

I didn't even try to disguise my hoot of laughter with a cough. I had no idea what had brought Amanda to the Aerie, but her timing couldn't have been worse. The baleful influence she'd exerted on young Tammy Auerbach was still fresh in my mind and although I couldn't bring myself to send her packing, I wasn't inclined to give her a warm welcome.

Toby, on the other hand, looked as though he might take a swing at her, so I hurried over to place myself between them.

"Amanda," I said, "what can I do for you?"

"You can do nothing for me," she said, lowering her arms. "But *I* can do something for *you*."

"Thanks, but we've already washed the dishes," said Toby, in tones of withering scorn.

Amanda spared him one disdainful look, then focused her attention on me. "I do not, of course, refer to a mundane chore."

"Pity," said Toby. "The mudroom could use a good scrub."

"Good afternoon, Amanda," Rose said, crossing to join our merry group.

"It is afternoon, Rose, but whether it be good or bad I cannot yet tell." Amanda sidled past me and began to prowl around the great room with her eyes half closed and her arms stretched at full length in front of her.

"If you want to see the Aerie, we can schedule a tour," I said.

"I do not wish to see the Aerie," said Amanda.

"Then what in heaven's name *are* you doing?" Rose demanded. "Playing blindman's buff?"

"I am allowing myself to be guided," Amanda replied, continuing her circuit of the room. "I sense your hostility, Rose, but you and I are not so very different."

"Aren't we?" Rose said skeptically.

"We both believe that the supernatural plays a role in everyday life." Amanda paused to wave her palms over the rustic cabinet, then moved on. "We believe in a power greater than ourselves. We believe in revelations, prophecies, and the continuation of the spirit after death."

"I *don't* believe in using fear to intimidate innocent children," Rose said tartly.

"Yes, you do," Amanda countered evenly. "You believe in hellfire and eternal damnation, and you use those beliefs to intimidate children in every Sunday school class you teach."

"I beg your pardon," Rose began heatedly, but I decided to redirect the conversation before things got out of hand. I didn't want the pastor's wife to take a swing at Amanda, either.

"Sorry," I said firmly, "but my guests aren't allowed to discuss religion or politics under my roof, even when I'm only borrowing the roof. Since you're an uninvited guest, Amanda, the rule applies doubly to you."

"But I *was* invited," Amanda insisted, moving her hands in a circular motion over the dining room table. "I was summoned soon after you left me yesterday. Your unwillingness to accept the orb's insights made me hesitant to respond to the call, but ultimately it became irresistible. Ahhhh . . ." She let out a hair-raising moan and glided toward the foyer as if an invisible force had seized her by the wrists and pulled her there.

"Good," said Toby, standing aside. "The exit's to your right."

But Amanda didn't turn toward the front door. Before anyone could stop her, she plunged through the foyer, up the stairs, and into the family suite corridor. Rose and Toby stood rooted to the spot, as if they couldn't believe what they'd just seen, but I tore after Amanda, half afraid that the invisible force would take her straight to Aunt Dimity's blue journal. I didn't want the inner eye that had "seen" Cyril Pennyfeather to get anywhere near the journal's pages.

"Get back here, Amanda!" Toby roared, finding his voice.

I heard scurrying footsteps behind me and knew that he was on his way, with Rose Blanding bringing up the rear. I would have knocked Amanda down with a flying tackle if she'd attempted to enter the master suite, but she didn't. She allowed herself to be dragged along until she reached the boys' room, where she stopped so suddenly that I had to hop sideways to avoid running into her.

"Here," she whispered loudly. "The vibrations emanate from *here.*"

Rose collided with Toby, who collided with me, and before we could sort ourselves out, Amanda was off and running again, with her bangles rattling, through the boys' bedroom and on into the playroom. By the time we caught up with her, she was standing stock-still in front of the freestanding tent. Her stillness was so absolute, her concentration so razor-sharp, that instead of ordering her to leave the room, as I'd intended, I found myself hushing Rose and Toby and motioning for them to keep back.

"The curse lingers in the very fabric of the building," Amanda intoned.

She raised her arms slowly, lowered them inch by inch until her palms faced the floor of the tent, then snatched them back, as if they'd been scalded. I jumped, Rose clucked her tongue irritably, and Toby scowled.

Amanda inhaled deeply, then closed her eyes and addressed the ceiling. "Dark things abide here."

"I'll have you know that my *sons* sleep here," I said, bristling.

"I see darkness, I see flames, I see a hate-filled heart seeking to destroy." Amanda pivoted on her heels, raised a hand to point at me, and cried, "A full moon rises tonight. Heed my warning! Escape while there's still time!"

My companions' furious gasps made me hope that Amanda would heed her own warning, but she didn't move.

"Amanda Barrow," Rose said awfully, sparks of hellfire dancing in her eyes. "I've never in all my life seen such a revolting display of cheap theatrics. Your circus act may impress fifteen-year-old girls and inebriated acolytes, but I can assure you that it does not impress us."

"Actually, I thought she did it pretty well," I murmured, but Toby talked right over me.

"Listen up, Amanda," he said coldly. "If you ever mention the curse to either one of Lori's sons, I'll throw your crystal ball *and* your rune stones *and* your entire stock of tarot cards into Lake Matula." He raised his arms and wheeled around slowly until his palms were facing the corridor. "Hey, look, Amanda, you've been summoned again! A voice beyond the reach of human hearing is telling me it's time for you to leave."

"I will go," said Amanda, drawing herself up with great dignity. "I have done my best. I can do no more."

"I'll walk you to the front door," said Toby and followed Amanda out of the playroom like a prison guard escorting a fractious inmate.

"Well, *really* . . ." Rose released an indignant breath, then turned to me. "I feel as though I should apologize, Lori, though I don't know why I should. We've always exercised tolerance toward Amanda and her band of followers, but it looks as though she needs to be reined in. It's completely unacceptable for her to march into a private home and carry on in such an appalling manner. She'll be disrupting church services next."

"No, she won't," I said soothingly, hoping to head off a witch hunt. "She won't invade the church or the parsonage or any other house in Bluebird. Don't you see, Rose? The Aerie holds a special attraction for Amanda because of the so-called curse. She simply can't resist performing on such a ready-made stage."

"What if she drops by while your sons are here?" asked Rose.

"Maybe I'll let her conduct an exorcism," I said with an easy-going shrug. "It'd be worth it to get her out of my hair."

"You're more generous than I am," said Rose. "The *nerve* of the woman . . ."

"Let's not let her spoil the day." I nodded toward the corridor. "Why don't we cool our tempers with a couple of tall glasses of iced tea?"

"I'd love to, but I can't," said Rose, looking at her watch. "I have to attend a Gold Rush Days committee meeting in less than an hour. Besides, I don't want to overstay my welcome. I'll just collect my box and be on my way."

We met Toby in the foyer, where he was keeping an eagle eye on Amanda's car as it disappeared down the twisting drive. After she'd gone, he fetched the archival box from the library and stowed it in the trunk of Rose's car. Annelise and the twins joined us as we waved good-bye to Rose.

Neither Will nor Rob had discovered any fossils, but they'd found enough rusty nails, railroad spikes, and leftover bits of mining machinery to make me thankful that their tetanus shots were up to date. They lovingly arranged their finds on the hearth ledge in the great room, then asked if they could go to town with Toby, who'd volunteered to pick up dinner at the cafe. Toby didn't believe that anyone on vacation should have to cook two big meals in one day, and I agreed with him, but before giving the twins the go-ahead, I took Toby aside.

"I need to speak with Annelise," I said quietly. "Can you handle both of the boys on your own?"

"Sure," said Toby. "They're great kids. I won't have any trouble with them at all."

"I hope not," I said and gave my sons the thumbs-up.

Toby and the twins headed for the van while Annelise and I settled down on the breakfast deck with glasses of iced tea, to discuss her reasons for keeping the boys away from the Brockman Ranch. I was a bit apprehensive about what I would hear. Annelise didn't usually consult with me or Bill about the twins unless she needed serious backup, which she very seldom did. Will and Rob really were great kids.

"Okay," I said, gripping my glass with both hands. "What happened at the ranch?"

"Two things," said Annelise. "First, we had a little language problem while we were on the trail ride."

I smiled with relief, though I was frankly surprised that she'd felt the need to bring such a trivial complaint to my attention.

"The boys can't help using English words and phrases," I said reasonably. "They've grown up with them. Besides, you were there to translate."

"I didn't have to translate," said Annelise. "The Americans on the trail ride understood Will perfectly when he called the little boy ahead of him a 'son of a bitch.'"

My jaw dropped and iced tea sloshed onto the table. *"What?"*

Annelise nodded. "They understood Rob, too, when he used the word that rhymes with 'duck.'"

"He . . . *what?*" I sputtered, spilling more tea.

"I don't have to spell it out for you, do I?" Annelise shook her head bemusedly. "They weren't even angry. The words just popped out of their mouths as if they used them every day. Heaven knows what the other adults on the ride thought about their upbringing."

"My sons have had an *excellent* upbringing," I said, shaking drops of iced tea from my hands. "You know very well that we don't use that kind of language at home. They must have picked it up from someone at the ranch."

"I'm sure they did," said Annelise. "Two of the guest children are foul-mouthed little beasts, and their parents are just as bad, if not worse."

"Did you have a talk with Rob and Will about good manners and polite language?" I asked.

"Naturally," said Annelise. "That's when we ran into the second problem. When I asked Will and Rob where they'd heard those words, they told me they'd heard them *here*, at the *Aerie*. Now, you and I don't use that kind of language, and I don't think Toby Cooper does, either."

"Toby would never swear in front of children," I agreed.

"Will and Rob assured me that they didn't learn the words from Toby," said Annelise, "but they can't say who they *did* learn them from. They insist that they heard them in their *tent*, in the *playroom*, during the *night*. They must be lying, Lori, and to tell you the truth, the lying troubles me more than the smutty language." She paused. "Lori? Are you listening?"

I nodded vaguely as I stared into the middle distance at an image only I could see—the image of Amanda Barrow's hands recoiling from the playroom tent as if they'd been scalded.

"Those you love most will surprise you," I said under my breath.

"Sorry?" said Annelise.

"Nothing." I cleared my throat and stood. "I'm sure you handled the situation perfectly, Annelise. I don't think we should make a big deal out of it, but I'll . . . I'll call Bill to see what he thinks." I drummed my damp fingers on the teak table. "Yes. I'll call him right now. I'll be in the master suite, and I don't want to be disturbed."

"All right," said Annelise. "Give him my best."

"Who?" I said blankly.

"Bill," said Annelise, eyeing me curiously. "Give Bill my best."

"Oh yes," I said. "I'll do that."

I left the breakfast deck and crossed the great room at a rapid pace, breaking into a run as soon as I reached the foyer. I dashed up the stairs, through the corridor, and into the master suite, where I snatched the blue journal from the white armchair and opened it without bothering to sit.

"Dimity," I said urgently. "I need to talk to you. You, too, Mr. Pennyfeather, if you're around. Something really weird is going on."

Twenty-two

*A*unt Dimity's familiar handwriting was the first to appear on the page, followed closely by Cyril Pennyfeather's flowery script.

What seems to be the problem, my dear?

May I help in any way?

"Are both of you one hundred per cent *sure* that the Aerie isn't cursed?" I asked.

I think I can speak for both Mr. Pennyfeather and myself when I state categorically that the Aerie is curse-free. What's troubling you, Lori?

"Amanda Barrow." I lowered myself into the white armchair and stared pensively at the ashes in the grate.

The psychic? Aunt Dimity clarified.

The hysterical psychic? Cyril added.

"She may have been hysterical, but she gave me a pretty accurate description of you, Mr. Pennyfeather," I reminded him. "After you took off, she looked into her crystal ball and started telling me things. I thought it was a big joke at the time, but I'm not so sure anymore."

What sort of things did she tell you?

"She said I'd come from afar," I began, "and she was right—I came to Colorado all the way from England."

She could have heard of your journey from any number of sources.

"That's what I thought," I said. "But she also predicted that I'd meet a short, dark stranger."

Shouldn't it be a tall, dark stranger?

I glanced down at Cyril's polite inquiry and remembered that Toby had muttered the same thing as Amanda had peered into her orb, but I was too distressed to crack a smile.

"Amanda predicted that I'd meet a *short,* dark stranger," I said, "and she was right again. James Blackwell showed up at the Aerie this morning. He's short, dark-haired, and deeply tanned, and until today he was definitely a stranger."

James Blackwell, the missing caretaker, returned to the Aerie this morning?

"Yes, but let's stick with Amanda for the moment," I said, refusing to be distracted. "She also said that Death had come to claim me, but I'd escaped his grasp."

How clever of her. After Abaddon attacked you, you came as close to dying as anyone can come, but you rallied and recovered. Have you mentioned the incident to anyone who could have passed the news along to Amanda?

"Annelise knows about the shooting, of course," I said, "but she'd never breathe a word about it to anyone here. Toby knows about it, too, but I didn't tell him about it until last night, *after* Amanda had said her piece."

I see. What other interesting tidbits did Amanda Barrow share with you?

"She told me that those I loved would surprise me," I said, "and guess what? She was right *again.* Bill surprised the heck out of me this morning when he told me that he'd be arriving at the Aerie next week."

Why were you surprised? It's exactly the sort of thing Bill would do.

"True," I allowed, "but he wasn't the only loved one who surprised me today. Annelise just finished telling me that Will and Rob not only used smutty language at the ranch yesterday, but lied to her when she asked them where they'd learned it."

Will and Rob don't use smutty language or tell lies.

"I know," I said emphatically. "That's why I was surprised."

To summarize: Amanda Barrow was correct about Mr. Pennyfeather, your long journey, your meeting with James Blackwell, your close encounter with death, and the twins' surprising naughtiness. Perhaps she does have a gift after all, over and above her ability to accurately describe ethereal escorts.

"If she does," I said, "then something's seriously out of whack because, unlike you and Mr. Pennyfeather, Amanda thinks the Aerie's cursed. She convinced Tammy, the Auerbachs' teenaged daughter, that the Aerie is cursed, and she came here today to inform me of the same thing."

Amanda Barrow is mistaken.

No one can be right all the time.

"Amanda's batting average is pretty spectacular so far," I said anxiously.

True. What, exactly, did she tell you about the curse?

"She seemed to sense something underneath the tent in the playroom," I said. "There's nothing under the tent but floorboards, but Florence Auerbach was so concerned about the floorboards in the family suite that she asked James Blackwell to take a look at them. Why is everyone taking such a keen interest in floorboards?"

Floorboards make noises, Lori, especially when a new building is settling onto its foundations.

"The Aerie was built only two years ago," I said. "It must still be settling."

A new building's normal noises can seem quite eerie, especially if they're heard in the dead of night by a listener who is predisposed to hear eerie sounds.

"So if Tammy Auerbach heard a floorboard creak or a door squeak, she'd think it was a manifestation of the curse," I said.

The poor child must have been a nervous wreck. Florence Auerbach probably asked James Blackwell to check the family suite's floorboards in order to convince Tammy that nothing was wrong with them.

"But Tammy was too far gone by then," I said, nodding. "James Blackwell told me that Tammy was so jittery she was losing sleep—"

The balm of hurt minds.

"That's right, Mr. Pennyfeather," I said. "And without her nightly dose of balm, Tammy got more and more jumpy, just like I did."

I suspect that Florence Auerbach took her daughter away from the Aerie for much the same reason Bill sent you away from the cottage.

"She didn't want Tammy to have a nervous breakdown," I said.

"But Tammy was so afraid of the curse that she refused to return to the Aerie, so Mrs. Auerbach decided to sell it."

If Tammy told Amanda about the strange sounds she'd heard at the Aerie, Amanda would naturally make a fuss over the floorboards. Their curious creaks and moans would lend credence to her claim that the Aerie is cursed.

"But Amanda went to the playroom when she came here today," I said. "Why didn't she go to Tammy's room?"

I imagine she chose a room at random. As long as it was in the family suite, it would serve her purpose, which was to give a convincing performance.

"I suppose so," I said reluctantly.

You still sound troubled, my dear.

"I am," I admitted. "According to Amanda, the curse is in the fabric of the building. I can't help remembering that Danny Auerbach recycled lumber from the old mine buildings when he constructed the Aerie. What if the curse is still . . . clinging to the old wood in the floorboards under the tent?"

There is no curse, Lori. There is only a woman who needs to convince others of its existence. Amanda Barrow is a local. She's known about the recycled lumber ever since the Aerie was built. If I were her, I'd use that knowledge to give my false claims the ring of truth.

Aunt Dimity's argument made good sense, but I was still worried.

"Will and Rob told Annelise that they learned their smutty vocabulary in the playroom tent," I said. "When Amanda came here, she made a beeline for the tent. She may be blowing smoke about the curse, but what if she actually sensed something sinister in the playroom? You mentioned disembodied voices when we spoke the other night, Mr. Pennyfeather. What if a foul-mouthed spirit is hanging around the tent at night, teaching my sons to swear?"

Miss Westwood and I are the only spirits currently in residence at the Aerie, Lori, and we are not in the habit of using rude language.

"Can you be sure there's no one else?" I persisted. "Maybe a demon flew in under your radar."

Ah yes, I know about radar now, thanks to Miss Westwood's excellent explanation, and I can assure you that no demon has flown under ours. A demon's signal, so to speak, is quite distinctive. I would be instantly aware of it, as would Miss Westwood.

"My sons don't lie, Mr. Pennyfeather," I said stubbornly. "And you admitted only a moment ago that Amanda might have real gifts, Dimity."

So I did, but she also appears to crave attention almost as much as she enjoys upsetting people. I repeat: There is no curse. Since Mr. Pennyfeather and I seem unable to reassure you on that score, however hard we try, might I suggest an experiment?

"Go ahead," I said.

Sleep in the playroom tonight, Lori. I strongly doubt that you'll hear a demonic chorus serenading you with obscenities, but I'm certain that a night spent with your ear pressed to the floorboards will convince you that Mr. Pennyfeather and I are more reliable than Amanda Barrow when it comes to the detection of curses and evil spirits.

"I'll do it," I said. "I'll spend the night in the playroom. It's not that I doubt you, Dimity—"

I understand, Lori. You're protecting your sons. It's what mothers do. I wouldn't have it any other way.

Nor would I.

"Thanks," I said. "I'll let you know if anything happens."

If a demon happens, you won't have to let us know.

I smiled wryly as the two sets of handwriting faded from the page, then closed the journal and put it on the bedside table, next to Reginald.

"Do you think I'm being silly, Reg?" I asked my pink rabbit.

Reginald was understandably noncommittal. The notion of spending a night on a cold, hard floor when I had a warm, soft bed at my disposal was already beginning to strike *me* as silly.

"Nevertheless, I can't afford to take chances where Will and Rob are concerned," I said staunchly, then bent low to whisper in his ear, "But don't tell Toby or Annelise what I'm planning to do, okay? They'll think I've gone off the deep end."

Reginald's black eyes gleamed supportively. I touched the faded grape juice stain on his snout and cocked an ear toward the corridor, listening for the thunder of little feet that would signal the twins' return from Bluebird. When I heard nothing, I left the master suite and returned to the playroom.

I gazed speculatively at the freestanding tent for a moment, then grabbed hold of it with both hands and slid it to one side. I was so afraid that my sons had spent the past week sleeping on a blood-stained, curse-ridden, demon-haunted remnant of the Lord Stuart mining disaster that it took every bit of courage I had to look at the spot where the tent had been.

It was indistinguishable from every other patch of floorboard in the playroom. I got down on my knees and rapped the floor with my knuckles. It sounded reassuringly solid. I pushed on the floorboards, stomped on them, and hopped up and down on them, but they didn't emit so much as a squeak. I was beginning to wish that James Blackwell had left his pickax behind instead of his lantern when I heard telltale noises coming not from the floor, but from the foyer.

Toby and the twins had returned. I stomped on the floor one more time, then gave up and went to join the others in the great room.

Toby had decided that Caroline's Cafe wasn't the only local eatery that deserved our patronage, so we dined on pizzas from Mile High Pies and peach ice cream from Sweet Jenny's Emporium. The ice cream eliminated any possibility of s'mores at the fire pit, but I eased the twins' disappointment by announcing that they would spend the night in the great room.

Will and Rob were enthralled by the idea of mounting an expedition to another part of the Aerie and ran off after dinner to help Toby move the tent from the playroom to their new camping spot.

Annelise, by contrast, was . . . Annelise. After considering the vast number of things the boys could break, dismantle, and/or wedge their heads into in the great room, she elected to sleep on the sofa, where she could keep a close eye on their nocturnal activities. Since it would be easier to sneak into the playroom after lights-out if I had the family suite all to myself, I put up token resistance, then happily allowed her to have her way.

I pushed furniture aside to make room for the tent, Toby set it up in the space I'd created, and the twins furnished it with foam pads, sleeping bags, headlamps, and fuzzy buffalo. After Annelise had made up the sofa and I'd popped the boys into their jammies, Toby said good night and retired to his apartment.

Will and Rob were so tired that it didn't take long to get them settled in their tent. I kissed them good night, thanked Annelise for taking the night shift, turned out the lights, and went into the foyer, where I stood listening at the double doors. When the boys' drowsy whispers died down, I tiptoed to the master suite, changed into blue jeans and a thick woolen sweater, gathered up a pillow, a blanket, and my headlamp, and carried them to the playroom.

The full moon shining through the tree branches outside the picture window cast an intricate pattern of shadows across the room. I felt a twinge of guilt as I thought of Annelise trying to sleep in the bright moonlight streaming through the great room's window wall, but after a few moments on the floor, I would have gladly traded places with her. It didn't take long for me to realize that it was impossible to sleep comfortably on a floor while fully dressed, though I doubted that a pair of silk pajamas would have made any difference.

I was on the verge of retreating to my cozy bed when a queer sound brought my heart into my throat. I couldn't tell whether it was the creak of a door or the tenor in a demonic chorus, but it seemed to come from the corridor. I sat up, turned my headlamp on, and nearly jumped out of my skin when a shadowy figure loomed over me in the darkness.

"I knew I'd find you here," said Toby. "Is it time for me to throw you in the lake?"

Twenty-three

"What are you talking about?" I demanded, pressing a hand over my galloping heart.

"Keep your voice down or you'll wake Annelise," said Toby.

"What are you talking about?" I whispered.

Toby switched on James Blackwell's lantern, set it on the floor, and sat next to it. "You gave me your permission to throw you in the lake if you showed the slightest sign of being obsessed by the curse."

I scowled at him. "I'm not obsessed by the curse."

"Uh-huh," Toby said disbelievingly. "Amanda's act this afternoon had no effect on you whatsoever. You changed everyone's sleeping arrangements simply because you thought it would be fun to sleep in here instead of in the master suite. I admire your spirit of adventure."

"I didn't change the sleeping arrangements because of Amanda's act." I lied without hesitation. I did not intend to tell Toby, of all people, that I was on the lookout for a lurking demon. "If you must know, Will and Rob used some pretty ripe language at the ranch yesterday."

"I know," said Toby. "While we were waiting for the pizza they reviewed all the words they mustn't say."

"Audibly?" I said, wincing.

Toby grinned. "Don't worry, I shushed them before they got too far down the list."

"How long was the list?" I asked, horrified.

"Not very long," said Toby. "But what does their cursing have to do with the curse?"

"Nothing," I said. "I'm not here because of the curse. I'm here because Will and Rob heard those smutty words while they were sleeping in the tent. I'm convinced that they're telling the truth, so I want to find out what's going on and put a stop to it."

"Okay," Toby said, drawing the word out to twice its normal length. "You want to find out how the twins learned to swear in the middle of the night while they were all by themselves. Shouldn't you be searching for a hidden tape recorder left behind by the Auerbach boys?"

"Gosh," I said, brightening. "I hadn't thought of that."

"You don't have a very high opinion of the Auerbach boys," Toby said dryly.

"I've never met the Auerbach boys," I said. "For all I know they could be potty-mouthed pranksters. They could have rigged a tape recorder to come on when the clock strikes midnight. The twins wouldn't know it was weird. They'd think it was just another fantastic feature of the Aerie."

Toby stared at me wordlessly for a few moments, then got to his feet and picked up the lantern.

"Where are you going?" I asked.

"To get a couple of lawn chairs," he replied. "It's only ten o'clock. If we're going to be here past midnight, we might as well be comfortable."

"You don't have to stay," I said, though I hoped he would, not only because I enjoyed his company, but because I'd be less tempted to abandon my vigil if he shared it with me.

Fortunately, Toby had already made up his mind to keep me company.

"If you think I'm going to miss the Auerbach boys' nightly tutorial on swearing," he said, "then you're not the model of mental stability I thought you were." He chuckled softly to himself as he left the room.

He returned a short time later with two folding chaise longues, which he set up side by side on the spot where the tent had stood. I offered him half of my blanket as we stretched out on the chaise longues, but he refused, so I covered myself with it and leaned back with a contented sigh. The chair was a great improvement over the floor.

We doused the lights to save the batteries and endured five grueling minutes of utter silence before one of us couldn't stand it anymore. Much to my surprise, it wasn't me.

"You know," Toby said softly. "It's possible that Will and Rob could have heard a *live* voice in their tent."

"Whose?" I asked. "The smut fairy's?"

"No," said Toby. "A real, live human being's."

I snorted derisively. "Are you suggesting that some pervert crept into the Aerie in the dead of night in order to teach my sons how to swear?"

"He wouldn't have to enter the Aerie," said Toby. "Did I ever tell you about the mine shaft underneath the Aerie?"

"There's a *mine shaft* underneath the Aerie? I said, sitting bolt upright.

"I've been trying to picture it in my mind," Toby murmured. "It's a horizontal shaft, and I'm pretty sure it runs beneath the family suite."

"We've been *sleeping* over a *mine shaft*?" I said, thunderstruck.

"Relax, Lori," said Toby. "It's a small shaft and it's been underpinned, so it's perfectly stable."

"How do you know so much about it?" I asked.

"I've been in it," he replied.

I switched on my headlamp, swung my legs to the floor, and sat sideways on the chaise longue. "I thought your grandfather ordered you not to go into the mines."

"He did," said Toby, "but I went into them anyway."

"Toby," I said, scandalized.

"What else was I supposed to do?" said Toby. "I was already the city kid, the kid from back east. You think I wanted to be the goody-

goody as well? Forget it. By the time I was thirteen, I'd explored every abandoned mine on this side of the valley." He glanced heavenward. "Sorry, Granddad, but a kid's gotta do what a kid's gotta do."

"It's a miracle you lived long enough to go to college," I said, shaking my head.

"Anyway," he went on, "if someone was in the shaft, the boys could have heard a voice coming up through the floor."

"But how would anyone get into the shaft?" I asked. "I've seen the Lord Stuart's main entrance, and it's blocked good and proper."

Toby tilted his head to one side. "I can think of at least three other ways, if they haven't caved in."

"But——" I broke off suddenly and stared at the floorboards between our chairs. "Did you hear that?"

Toby nodded, swung his legs over the side of his chair, and seemed to hold his breath as he, too, stared at the floor.

A faint thumping noise sounded beneath our feet, followed by a few indistinct words uttered by a muffled voice.

"Somebody's down there," I whispered.

"I don't think it's the smut fairy," Toby whispered back. "I'll bet you anything it's one of the crazies from Amanda's commune."

"Why would . . . ?" My voice trailed off as the answer to my question exploded in my head. It didn't take a huge amount of brain power to figure out exactly why someone from the commune would prowl beneath the Aerie, frightening Tammy Auerbach and unwittingly entertaining my fearless sons.

"That conniving *cow*," I whispered furiously. "She's been sending her acolytes into the mine shaft to make spooky noises so we'd buy into her story about the curse. She's been *manufacturing* the curse."

Toby's jaw set in a grim line. "They're trespassing on private property. I'd love to catch them at it."

"Me, too," I said fervently.

He raised an eyebrow. "Well, then?"

"Well, then, what?" I said.

"Let's go." He pointed at the floor. "Let's go down there and get them."

"Are you out of your *mind*?" I squeaked. "No, no, no, and absolutely not-in-a-million-years *no*."

"Fine," Toby shrugged. "I just thought you might want to get back at Amanda for teaching your sons to swear. I thought you'd want to punish her for scaring Tammy Auerbach. I thought you'd want to get even with her for trying to dupe you. But if you want to let her off the hook . . ."

I didn't consider myself an abnormally vengeful person, but Toby's words were having their desired effect. I could feel myself weakening.

"I know which tunnel we could use to ambush them," he murmured tantalizingly. "If we do it right, we'll give them as big a scare as they gave Tammy."

"If we do it wrong, we'll kill ourselves," I countered.

"We won't do it wrong," Toby insisted. "Trust me, Lori. I know my way around the shafts."

"Okay." I took a deep breath and let it out in a rush. "Let's go."

Toby stood and pulled me to my feet. "We'll leave through the master suite, to avoid disturbing Annelise."

"Good," I said as we headed for the corridor, "because I have to change my shoes. I'm not going into any mine shaft wearing sneakers."

Toby fidgeted impatiently while I pulled on my hiking boots, then led the way onto my deck. We climbed over the railing, jumped, and hit the ground running, though we slowed to a fast walk when Toby ducked into the trees and onto a trail downhill from the Aerie.

The moon was so bright that we didn't need the lantern or my headlamp to find our way, and in less than ten minutes we were standing before a sagging wire fence strung across a rough-edged hole in the mountainside. Toby pulled the fence aside easily and waited for me to join him in the mouth of the mine shaft. I stepped past the fence, then hesitated.

"Toby?" I said. "How cold do you think it is in Panama?"

"Huh?" he said.

"Never mind," I said and plunged in after him.

Twenty-four

The tunnel wasn't nearly as horrible as I'd expected it to be. The floor was surprisingly uncluttered by debris, there was ample headroom, and the rough-hewn walls were far enough apart for Toby and me to walk side by side. Better still, the wooden supports didn't look as though they were on the brink of giving way, I didn't hear or see a single rat, and the bats had apparently gone out for supper.

Granted, the thought of getting lost and wandering blindly from pillar to post until our lights failed made me want to howl with fear, but Toby seemed to know what he was doing. We passed several openings leading to other shafts, including a rubble-filled one that made me think of Cyril Pennyfeather. I was still contemplating Cyril's sad fate—and praying silently that we wouldn't meet with the same one—when Toby skidded to a halt before an opening that looked different from the others.

"Well, well," he said quietly. "Amanda *has* been industrious."

"What do you mean?" I asked.

"She's carved a new tunnel," he answered, shining his light into a shaft that was much smaller and more roughly hewn than ours. "I've never seen this one before."

"How could she dig a tunnel without anyone knowing about it?" I said doubtfully. "Where would she put the dirt and rocks?"

"They have a big garden up at the dome," said Toby. "They could have dumped the diggings there. And if the tunnel mouth is near the dome, they'd have no trouble keeping it secret. The townspeople leave the commune pretty much alone." He peered into the tunnel again and frowned. "Still, it seems like an awful lot of trouble to go to just to scare the Auerbachs."

"Oh my," I said softly, struck by a revelation that should have come to me much sooner. "It might be worth the trouble if it helps Amanda buy the Aerie at a bargain price."

"What are you talking about?" said Toby. "Mr. Auerbach would never sell the Aerie."

"It's been on the market for the past six months," I informed him. "No one's put in an offer, so Danny's lowered the price twice already. Bill told me about it in confidence, so I couldn't tell you."

Toby's stunned expression quickly gave way to one of outrage. "If Amanda Barrow conned Mr. Auerbach into selling—"

"Of course she did," I broke in excitedly. "Amanda wants to expand her empire by buying the Aerie. She targeted Tammy and dug the tunnel in order to scare the Auerbachs into selling it. She must think *I'm* interested in buying it now that the price has come down. That's why she tried to scare *me*."

"What did you call her?" Toby said darkly. "A conniving cow? Not strong enough, Lori. I'm thinking of a few choice phrases from the twins' list."

I waved a hand toward the new tunnel. "Let's not ambush her gang under the Aerie. Let's confront their ringleader, face-to-face, at the dome."

"I'm in," Toby growled.

He stiffened suddenly, then pressed a finger to his lips, reached over to turn off my headlamp, and switched off the lantern. The darkness was absolute, but the silence was broken by a faint clanking noise and the distant shuffle of footsteps farther down the shaft in which we were standing. Toby's voice came out of the darkness so softly that I could scarcely hear him.

"Give me the headlamp," he said.

I slipped it off and passed it to him. A moment later a dim red glow shone in the darkness. Toby had wrapped the headlamp in a red bandana. It would provide enough light to guide us without giving us away.

"Useful," I breathed, pointing to the red bandana.

Toby grinned, handed the unlit lantern to me, and nodded for me to follow him into the freshly carved tunnel. It descended at a fairly steep angle, but my hiking boots kept me from slipping. Toby had to bend low to keep from hitting his head on the jagged roof, but the awkward position didn't hinder his speed. He'd clearly lost none of the skills he'd honed in childhood, while disobeying his grandfather.

After a few hundred yards, my thighs began to ache with each jolting, downward step and by the time the tunnel leveled out, my knees were pleading with me to stop torturing them, but I was too distracted by then to listen to them. A faint splash of light had appeared far down the tunnel.

Toby glanced over his shoulder to make sure I was still with him, then increased his speed, racing toward the splash of light as if he wanted to reach it before it went out. I jogged gamely in his wake, wondering what Bill would say when I told him where I'd spent the night. The words *stupid, harebrained,* and *suicidally irresponsible* came immediately to mind.

We'd almost reached the source of the mysterious glow when Toby slowed to a walk, slipped the bandana from the headlamp, and let its beam play over a solid wall of rock directly ahead of us. The dead end was illuminated from above by light leaking past the edges of what appeared to be a fairly large trapdoor. The top rung of a wooden ladder had been nailed to the wooden rim surrounding the trapdoor, and its legs were planted firmly in two slots cut into the tunnel's floor.

Toby didn't hesitate. He shoved the bandana and the headlamp into his pocket, climbed the ladder, and pushed the trapdoor open. I had to close my eyes against the harsh glare that flooded the tunnel, and when I opened them again, Toby had vanished. I scrambled up the ladder after him, hauled myself through the opening where the trapdoor had been, and found Toby standing a few steps away, looking utterly perplexed.

I was just as confused as he was. I'd expected to find myself in Amanda's garden, surrounded by row upon row of organic wacky-weed, but there was nothing remotely organic about the tunnel's terminus, nor was there any sign of the geodesic dome.

We were standing in what appeared to be the living room of an oddly furnished house. Its oddness stemmed from the fact that, apart from a single bare lightbulb dangling from a ceiling fixture directly above the trapdoor, there were no furnishings. Instead, the room was filled from floor to ceiling with densely compacted piles of dirt and rubble. Swathes of cyclone fence nailed to sturdy posts held the piles in place and created a passageway that led from the trapdoor to a hallway off the living room.

"What in heaven's name . . . ?" I said, in a hushed voice.

"I don't know," said Toby. "Let's look around."

Toby closed the trapdoor, took the lantern from me, and held it high as we entered the hallway. The front door was to our left, but we turned right, to explore the rest of the house. The bathroom and the kitchen were spotless, but rubble filled the dining room and the largest of the two bedrooms at the back. A small, windowless storeroom behind the rubble-filled bedroom held tools similar to those James Blackwell had stored in the wooden crate at the Aerie, but these tools looked as if they'd been put to much harder use than James's.

We paused briefly in the storeroom, then retraced our steps to the second bedroom. It was, in its own way, the strangest room of all. The single bed in the corner had been so fastidiously made up that it would have passed muster in a Marine boot camp. The chest of drawers was aligned precisely with the desk opposite the bed, and both were neat as a pin. I found the room's excessive tidiness unsettling, but two other features made it seem downright weird: The window above the bed had been heavily coated with black paint, and the walls were papered over with maps.

Some of the maps were hand drawn, some were standard, government-issue topographic maps, and some were so old that they'd been sandwiched in clear sheets of plastic to keep them from falling apart. Toby crossed to the desk to examine the hand-drawn map that hung on the wall above it.

"Look," he said, tracing lines with his fingertip. "It shows the underground route between the new tunnel and the shaft underneath the Aerie."

"Does it tell you where we are at the moment?" I asked.

Before he could answer, a loud thud sounded in the living room.

I leaned close to Toby and whispered, "Someone's opened the trapdoor."

The first thud was followed by a second, as the trapdoor fell back into place. Toby quickly extinguished the lantern and stationed himself in front of me. I stared past his shoulder, spellbound, as the clump of heavy footsteps approached the bedroom. My nerves were strung so tight I could feel them twanging, and I nearly shrieked when a hand reached around the doorjamb to hit the light switch, but my reaction was tepid compared to Dick Major's.

He was dressed in coveralls, work boots, and a miner's helmet, and he carried a lantern similar to ours. His pink face contorted with rage when he saw us, and his pale blue eyes nearly popped out of their sockets. He let loose a string of expletives, as if to illustrate from whom my sons had learned them, and finished with the relatively mild, "What the *hell* are you doing in my house?"

"Hello, Dick," Toby said calmly. "We were just about to ask you the same thing."

"*You.*" I inched around Toby as comprehension dawned. "It wasn't Amanda. It was *you.*" I looked at the maps surrounding us and gave a satisfied nod, convinced that I'd finally seen the light. "Your house is on the edge of town, closest to the Aerie. You drove off your neighbors so they wouldn't spy on you, and you made yourself the most unpopular man in town so no one would ever visit you." I glanced at the blacked-out window. "Did you pile the diggings around the house when you ran out of room inside? Is that why you collected so much junk? Are the mattresses and old couches there to disguise the piles of rubble?"

Dick took a step toward me and balled his free hand into a fist. "You think you're pretty smart, don't you, little lady?"

"I do, as a matter of fact," I said defiantly and pointed a trembling finger at his face. "You're *pink*! Everyone else in Bluebird has a tan, but *you* don't, because *you* hardly ever see the sun. You dig at night and sleep during the day. That's why you never show up at Carrie Vyne's cafe until late afternoon. That's why your usual drink is strong black coffee."

Dick snarled, but I was on a roll and barely noticed.

"You're even built the right way," I said. "Look at your shoulders, look at your big hands. You don't get muscles like that *fishing*. You've been *digging*. You hacked a tunnel from your house to connect with the one leading to the Aerie because . . . because . . ." I fell silent, having run out of revelations.

"I know why you did it, Dick." Toby jerked his head toward the hand-drawn map above the desk. "You've been searching for gold, haven't you? You've been scavenging whatever's left down there. You've been stealing gold that doesn't belong to you."

Dick thumped his chest furiously, bellowing, "It *does* belong to me. It *all* belongs to me. My great-great-grandfather discovered the Lord Stuart Mine, and the Auerbachs *stole* it from him."

I staggered back a step and my mouth fell open. "You're Ludovic Magerowski's great-great-grandson?"

"The Auerbachs drove Ludovic *crazy*," Dick shouted, flecks of spittle flying from his lips. "They drove his wife to *suicide*. They put his son in an *orphanage*. My great-grandfather changed his last name to Major, but it didn't change our luck. Nothing's gone right for us since the Auerbachs stole the Lord Stuart."

"So you decided to balance the books?" said Toby. "You came here to take what's rightfully yours?"

"*Yes*. But I came too late." Dick's voice sank to a hoarse whisper, and his eyes became bleak. "There's no gold left. The Auerbachs took it all."

"If there's no gold left in the Lord Stuart," I said, "why did you go back down there tonight?"

"If I can't have gold, I'll have justice," Dick shouted, shaking his fist at me. "I know how to get it, too. I worked bomb disposal in the army." He bared his teeth in a savage grin. "I left a surprise package under the Aerie tonight, a little thank-you gift for the Auerbachs. It's set to go off at midnight. By then I'll be on my way to Denver."

For a heartbeat, Toby and I stood as if carved out of stone. Then Toby launched himself at Dick, punching him so hard that the big man collapsed in a heap.

I leapt over Dick's prone body, dashed up the hallway, and flew through the front door. I didn't stop to check my watch or to see if Toby was following. I charged up the dirt road and onto the Lord Stuart Trail with only one thought thundering in my head: I had to get my sons and Annelise out of the Aerie before Dick's "surprise package" exploded.

Moonlight silvered the trail and scattered it with shadows. Aspen leaves chattered overhead, but I could scarcely hear them above my gasping breaths. My lungs ached, my legs burned, and flashbulbs seemed to pop before my eyes, but I ran on, hurtling myself upward, past the wildflowers, past the ponderosa pines, past the fir tree I'd leaned against, giggling with Toby, one day ago.

When the Aerie came into view, I realized with a sickening jolt that the front door would be locked. I instantly changed course, flung myself over the railing and onto my deck, sprinted through the master suite, and raced down the corridor, shouting for everyone to get out. By the time I reached the great room, Annelise had roused the twins and pulled them from their sleeping bags, though they were still clutching their fuzzy buffalo.

"Out!" I shouted breathlessly. *"Get out!"*

Annelise scooped Rob into her arms, I darted forward to lift Will, and we fled the Aerie as if the hounds of hell were after us. We nearly crashed into Toby as he bounded across the clearing, but he swerved in the nick of time, took Will from me, and led us back down the Lord Stuart Trail. We'd just spilled out onto the dirt road when a deafening explosion rocked the ground beneath our feet. I stumbled, turned, and saw a fireball billow gracefully into the night sky .

"*Reginald,*" I whispered, stricken. "*Aunt Dimity.*"

Twenty-five

F could feel my heart breaking as the devouring flames leapt
skyward, taking with them my precious Reginald and the
blue leather-bound journal that had connected me for so
long to my dearest friend and wisest counselor, the remarkable,
unforgettable Aunt Dimity. Tears filled my eyes and spilled down
my cheeks. My breath came in rasping sobs, and when Toby
spoke, his voice seemed to come from a distant planet.

"Well," he panted, "thank God for that."

"Thank God for *what*?" I snapped, rounding on him.

"Dick's aim was bad," he said. "He missed the Aerie."

"He . . . he *missed*?" I stammered as a knee-weakening wave of
relief flooded through me.

Toby shrugged. "It's easy to get turned around in the tunnels if
you haven't grown up exploring them. I'd say he planted his bomb
about a half mile to the west of where he intended to plant it. If we
can get the fire under control, the Aerie should be okay."

"Bomb?" said Annelise, raising an eyebrow.

"I'll explain later," I told her.

A siren howled in Bluebird and a cacophony of voices echoed
over Lake Matula. The townspeople were awake. A truck from the
volunteer fire department roared past us as we limped along Lake
Street and Toby flagged down the local sheriff as he drove by.

"Hey there, Tobe," said the sheriff, running an eye over our little
band of refugees. "Any idea what caused the explosion?"

"Yeah." Toby jutted his chin toward Dick Major's house. "You'll
find him in the back bedroom. Lock him up, Jeff. I'll drop by the
jailhouse and explain everything once we find beds for these kids."

"Carrie Vyne's got an empty guest cabin," the sheriff suggested.

"Thanks, Jeff," said Toby. "Fire service on its way?"

"You bet," said the sheriff. "Got 'em coming in from as far away as Boulder."

"Can we ride in your police car?" Will asked, rubbing his cheek against his buffalo.

"With the siren?" Rob added hopefully.

"Maybe another time, boys," the sheriff said kindly. "Right now I've got some business to take care of."

He put two fingers to his brow in a casual salute, then pulled over to park in front of Dick Major's house. As we continued to trudge up Lake Street, I wondered what he'd make of the place once he stepped through the front door.

I also wondered what Amanda Barrow would do when she realized how accurately she'd predicted the night's tumultuous events. She'd told me in her shop that Death would come for me again, and he had. She'd told me I risked all by sleeping beneath the eagle's wings, and she'd been right. She'd stood before the playroom tent, warning of darkness, flames, and a hate-filled heart seeking to destroy, and in no time at all, I'd encountered the darkness of the mine shaft, the flames on the mountainside, and a man so filled with hatred that he was willing to kill innocent women and children in his insane bid for revenge.

What would Amanda do when she discovered she'd been right from start to finish? I wondered. As we walked up Stafford Avenue toward Caroline's Cafe, I shuddered to think of Amanda Barrow camping out on the Aerie's doorstep, babbling nonstop about the great beyond, and hoped with all my heart that I'd be back in England long before she realized how truly gifted she was.

Carrie Vyne was in the cafe, preparing food and drink for the swarm of firefighters who would soon descend on Bluebird. She welcomed us with open arms, took us to the vacant guest cabin, put sheets and blankets on the beds, lit a fire in the living-room fire-place, and brought sandwiches and a thermos of hot chocolate out to us from the cafe.

Carrie also brought bandages, antibiotic ointment, and arnica cream for Annelise's feet. My intrepid nanny hadn't bothered to don bedroom slippers when my frantic call to action had startled her from sleep. She'd been so intent on saving my sons' lives that she'd run all the way from the Aerie to Bluebird *barefoot*. I wanted to pin a great big shiny medal on her nightgown, but since medals were in short supply, I simply tended to her cuts and bruises and helped her hobble to her bed.

"You're a bona fide heroine," I said as I smoothed her blankets.

"It's all in a day's work," she replied, smiling.

I hugged her, turned out the light, and joined the boys and Toby, who'd gathered around the fireplace to drink hot chocolate. Despite the fact that they had bunk beds in their bedroom, Rob and Will fell asleep curled up in blankets on the floor while Toby and I watched a seemingly endless stream of emergency vehicles speed through the streets of Bluebird.

"I have to go back to the Aerie," I said quietly, after the boys had fallen asleep. "Tonight."

"The road will be blocked off," Toby warned.

"I don't need to take the road," I said. "Will you stay here with the twins?"

"I'll keep an eye on them," he promised. "I hadn't planned on getting any sleep tonight anyway."

It took me less than an hour to hike to the Aerie, tuck a few nec-essary and two irreplaceable items into my carry-on bag, and return to the guest cabin. Toby was still awake when I got back, so I put the carry-on bag in my bedroom and sat up with him through the night. We didn't say much, though he did compliment me on my record-breaking uphill dash.

"You carried Will in your arms all the way to the edge of the clearing, too," he reminded me. "You were too weak to lift him out of the van a week ago."

"It's amazing what you can do when your children are in danger," I told him. "You'll find out one day, when you're a father. You'll give your life for your kids, one way or another."

I touched a hand to the scar on my shoulder, then turned to watch the burning mountain.

Epilogue

*F*t took three days to put the fire out. By then it had burned a hundred acres, turning majestic trees into charred matchsticks, but thanks to the firefighters' skill and the recent heavy rain, it spread no farther and the Aerie was untouched. We moved back the day before Bill arrived, and although he could stay for only a week, the rest of us stayed there until the end of August, when Toby returned to college.

When news of the fire reached Danny Auerbach, he came to Bluebird to check on his property. While he was in town, I took him to Caroline's Cafe for lunch and a long talk, at the end of which he decided to have a still longer talk with his wife and daughter, take his beloved tree house off the market, and build a small cabin for James and Janice Blackwell and their child. He also decided to plug the mine entrance Toby and I had used, before his sons discovered it.

The Blackwells—with their healthy baby girl—moved into their cabin two months after Toby left. James resumed his caretaker's duties as if there'd been no interruption, and the Auerbachs are once again staying at the Aerie every chance they get.

Will and Rob spent much of the summer at the Brockman Ranch, though Toby coaxed them away every now and then to hike, fish, and hunt for fossils. When he offered to teach them how to pan for gold, however, I put my foot down. Gold fever was a nasty bug. I didn't want my sons to be bitten by it.

Maggie Flaxton bullied me into selling raffle tickets during Gold Rush Days, but Bill adamantly refused to participate in Nick Altman's beer-tasting contest. He wasn't as impressed as I was by Bluebird's doppelgangers, but he'd learned through hard experience to avoid anything that was both homemade and alcoholic.

I put an end to Amanda Barrow's visits to the Aerie by telling her straight out that I held long conversations every night with a magic book that talked back to me. She accused me of mocking her and never darkened my doorway again.

Dick Major followed in his infamous ancestor's footsteps when he entered a high-security prison for the criminally insane. Once there, he began to call himself Ludo Magerowski and to curse everyone who tried to help him. His house on Lake Street was demolished before the year was out and the rubble it contained was put to good use by the highway department.

Toby and I made one more foray into the Lord Stuart mine shafts that summer. On a hot and sunny day in early August, Toby used his local knowledge and a photocopy of Dick Major's hand-drawn map to help me find the cave-in that had killed Cyril Pennyfeather. I knelt at the spot to fill a plastic bag with handfuls of dust.

I took the dust to the cemetery the next day and sprinkled it on Hannah Lavery's grave. There must have been something of Cyril mixed in with it, because I never heard from him again.

"Do you miss Cyril?" I asked Dimity on our last night at the Aerie.

I do, but I'm not sorry he's gone. He fulfilled his purpose. It was time for him to move on.

"What purpose?" I asked.

I believe that Mr. Pennyfeather remained in the Aerie in order to save more lives, and he tried his best to do so. Do you remember? He warned us that someone had reopened the Lord Stuart Mine. We thought he was referring to James Blackwell at the time, but he was, in fact, speaking of Dick Major. If we hadn't jumped to the wrong conclusion, we would have heeded Mr. Pennyfeather's warning and thwarted Dick Major's plot.

"I never thought I'd live to see the day when you'd admit that you'd jumped to a conclusion," I said, grinning.

There's a first time for everything. And I am sincerely happy for Mr. Pennyfeather. Having fulfilled his purpose, he has continued his journey and rejoined the woman he loves. He's earned the right to rest in peace.

"Have you ever thought of continuing your own journey, Dimity?" I asked.

You're part of my journey, Lori. I don't mind putting the rest of it on hold. I have all of eternity at my disposal.

"Do you think I'll spend the rest of my life rescuing my children from homicidal maniacs?" I asked wistfully.

I imagine you'll have a few hours to spare for knitting socks and baking cookies. But if a situation arises that requires you to save your children's lives, you will. It's what mothers do. Besides, you've made progress—you came away from your latest feat of derring-do unscathed.

"Annelise didn't," I said. "Her feet are still sore. And Toby nearly broke his hand punching Dick Major, but he enjoyed it so much that I don't think he feels scathed."

Toby Cooper is a remarkable young man.

"I tried to thank him today, Dimity, but I just got all teary-eyed," I said. "He looked as embarrassed as if I'd spit up on his shoes."

I'm sure he was embarrassed because he, too, was choked up. You, Annelise, Will, and Rob have been his family for several months. He'll miss you.

"I've invited him to visit us in England," I said. "We may not have rattlesnakes, dust storms, or snow in July, but we have pretty good thunderstorms. I hope he comes."

As do I. You haven't mentioned your shoulder lately, my dear. Is it still troubling you?

"My shoulder is completely healed," I said. "If the scar wasn't there, you'd never known I'd been shot. I'm happy to report that I have my brain to myself again, too. Abaddon has finally moved out."

On the whole, your visit to America has been most satisfactory.

"No one in Finch will believe it," I said. "When they think of America, they think of vulgarity and violence. To be honest, I did, too, but I don't anymore. With the truly gigantic exception of Dick Major, everyone I've met has been cheerful, helpful, and kind."

Including Maggie Flaxton?

"I may not be Maggie's biggest fan," I said, laughing, "but women like her make the world go round."

They do indeed. Will you miss Bluebird?

"I'll miss the Rocky Mountains," I acknowledged. "I'll miss the blue sky and the crisp air and the snowcapped peaks. I'll miss the wildflowers and the aspens, the mule deer and the buffalo."

But will you miss Bluebird?

I leaned back in the white armchair and gazed into the fire. I thought of gossip and Calico Cookies and scones. I thought of a place rich in history and blessed with great natural beauty. I thought of good people doing their best to keep their small town alive, and as always, my thoughts came around again to Finch. Bill might not see the similarities, Annelise might ignore them, and Aunt Dimity might discount them, but I knew what home felt like when I found it.

"No, I won't miss Bluebird," I said, smiling. "After all, I'm not really leaving it behind."

Carrie Vyne's Calico Cookies

Preheat oven to 350 degrees F. Makes about 5 dozen cookies.

Ingredients
1 cup (2 sticks) butter
$\frac{1}{3}$ cup white sugar
$\frac{1}{3}$ cup brown sugar
2 eggs
2 teaspoons vanilla extract
1 teaspoon almond extract
1$\frac{1}{2}$ cups all-purpose flour
1 teaspoon baking soda
1 teaspoon cinnamon
$\frac{1}{2}$ teaspoon ginger
pinch of salt
2$\frac{1}{2}$ cups oatmeal
$\frac{1}{2}$ cup each: chocolate chips, dried cranberries, sliced almonds,
   toffee bits.
May also use raisins, butterscotch morsels, peanut butter pieces,
   or white chocolate chips.

Mix and match to your heart's content!

Cream butter with sugars. Add eggs, vanilla, and almond extracts.
Beat well. Add flour mixed with baking soda, cinnamon, ginger,
and salt. Fold in oatmeal and beat well. Fold in the nuts, chips, and
bits; mix well. Place teaspoon-sized rounds of dough on foil-lined
cookie sheets. Bake 7–8 minutes. Freezes well.